SOMETHING SPECIAL,
SOMETHING RARE

SOMETHING SPECIAL, SOMETHING RARE

OUTSTANDING SHORT STORIES BY AUSTRALIAN WOMEN

Black Inc.

Published by Black Inc.,
an imprint of Schwartz Publishing Pty Ltd
37–39 Langridge Street
Collingwood VIC 3066 Australia
email: enquiries@blackincbooks.com
www.blackincbooks.com

The National Library of Australia Cataloguing-in-Publication entry:

Something special, something rare: outstanding
short stories by Australian women / Various authors.

9781863957298 (paperback)
9781925203233 (ebook)

Short stories, Australian
Australian fiction – Women authors.

A823.01

Book design by Peter Long

CONTENTS

BUSHFIRE

KATE GRENVILLE

The radio said that Mindurra was in *no immediate danger*, but the television had a different message. There were pictures of walls of flame flickering and leaping up into trees. *Ringed by fire* was a phrase the journalists seemed to like. Against the ragged angry blaze, ant-like silhouetted figures scurried ineffectually, flapping wet bags and squirting water from backpacks.

No immediate danger. Louise repeated the words to herself. But Mindurra was such a little place, with hillsides of bush all around. It was easy to imagine a fire swallowing it down without missing a beat. As she walked down Homer Street towards the shops, brown smoke hid the contours of the hills over in the distance and smudged the sky. After a term at Mindurra Public School she had got used to seeing the hills, always there at the end of Homer Street. It was unsettling to have lost them now.

They were hoping for a change in the wind. A man from the Weather Bureau had come on and pointed at isobars with a ruler, but he had not committed himself on the matter of a change in the wind.

With the town in crisis, it had seemed the right thing for the new teacher to offer to help. But Valda in the school office had looked doubtful.

Got any First Aid, love? She had asked. Class B licence? Anything like that?

Valda did not want to be rude, but it seemed that the only place for a person without such skills was down in the Country Women's Association Hall, helping with the sandwiches.

Grand Street, Mindurra, did not normally generate a lot of traffic, but today as Louise turned the corner, there was quite a bottleneck: three cars and a lorry, and then one of the old red fire trucks from the Volunteer Bush-Fire Brigade. A man on the back, half-hidden among hoses and tanks, lifted a hand to her, but he took her by surprise and by the time she waved back, the truck had gone.

She thought it could be that Lloyd. The one who'd bought her a cup of tea at the Picnic Races.

Valda had more or less made him do it: she loved to match-make. Valda had already tried to set her up with her cousin from Gulargambone, and then with the man from the Pastures Protection Agency. Neither event had been a success.

Lloyd had agreed willingly enough, but she felt herself going stony. She had sat at the wobbly table in the Refreshments Tent, staring into her cup of powerful Ladies' Auxiliary tea, watching Lloyd stirring the sugar into his. Behind her, she could feel everyone skirting around them – Valda, and Mrs Mitchell the principal, and John the man from the garage. They were ostentatiously not watching. It was like grown-ups leaving children alone to *make friends*.

It never worked. She could have told them that. It didn't work with kids and it wasn't going to work any better with two wary frumps past their prime. *Frump:* that was how she thought of herself. She knew how she looked: too big, too plain, and with that uncompromising set to her mouth. This Lloyd was a frump, too, with his ears that stuck out, his big freckled face, his awkward smile, the way he kept fiddling with his spoon. They were two of a kind, but the wrong kind.

She'd always hated being paired off, hated the way people thought you'd be grateful. No one seemed to realise that a failed marriage wasn't like a broken plate. You didn't just go out and get another one.

Lloyd seemed no more comfortable than she was, but with the whole of Mindurra watching them sideways, they felt obliged to exchange some information about themselves. It turned out that Lloyd was something with the Water Board. He was here to check the reservoir.

As conversational material, Louise felt this was less than promising.

Oh, the Water Board, she said, and heard it as the other kind of *bored*, the one that they both seemed to be experiencing there and then. She hurried on before she could laugh.

Been with them for long?

It was only to be polite.

Few years, he mumbled, and it seemed as if that was going to be that, but he suddenly blurted out:

Take Mozart!

Pardon? She'd had to say.

Dead of typhoid at thirty. Just think – if they'd had decent water! Another six symphonies!

He was radiant at the thought of it.

Yes, she'd managed to say, feeling the startled look on her face, hearing it in her voice.

I wanted to write music, he said. But Dad thought I ought to go into something solid.

He cleared his throat unnecessarily, glanced at her. She was too much taken by surprise, could not rearrange the muscles of her face into a more welcoming expression in time.

So here I am.

He picked up the spoon and made a big show of putting sugar in his tea and stirring it, even though he'd already put two spoonfuls in before. Her mouth refused to make any of the encouraging sounds she wished to make.

And now he was blushing through his pale freckled skin.

Even his neck was blushing. And his ears. She had never seen such a blush. It was like ink spreading through water. She looked at where his shirt opened at the neck, where she could glimpse soft fair skin that the sun had never roughened. She caught herself wondering how far down the blush went.

Then he met her eye, and a funny thing happened: she felt herself blushing as well. It was ridiculous. There was nothing to blush about. She was angry with herself for blushing, and with this man, for watching her. He was not bold, but he was paying attention. She tried to take a sip of tea, to stop him looking, but the tea was scalding, and only added heat to her blush.

She had no reason to blush: it was just her skin doing it. It was as if her skin and his were having a conversation with each other, all by themselves.

*

Down in the Hall it was all sandwiches and hearsay. It was so hot up at the fire, they said, that you could fry an egg on the front of the truck. A fireball had jumped right across the highway, from the top of one tree to another. The paint had been burned off the number-one fire truck as neatly as with a blowtorch.

Mrs Cartwright, mother of Lee-Anne in second class, was mass-producing the sandwiches. It was easy to see she had done it before, for other fires, for floods, for any kind of disaster requiring sandwiches. Her hands moved quickly and deftly among the bread, the wrapping-paper, the beetroot and shredded lettuce. Her finished parcels were as smooth as little pillows.

Being the novice, Louise was given plain cheese to do. You would think you could not go wrong with plain cheese. But she forgot to put the wrapping paper under first, so the wrapping took twice as long. Or, when she cut them in half at the end, she cut through the paper as well. Her finished packages were lumpy, and unravelled as soon as you let go of them.

She imagined the fire-fighters, sitting on the running board of the fire truck eating the sandwiches. Lloyd would be there, perhaps picking shreds of sliced wrapping paper out of his. She did not think he was the sort to laugh at a failed sandwich, but someone else might.

A man with a soot-dark face, his eyes bloodshot, rushed in to pick up a load of food. He took a sandwich in each hand and spoke with a wild look in his eyes.

Not bloody burning, he was insisting. Bloody exploding!

His hands flew out, demonstrating, and a baked bean landed in Louise's bowl of cheese.

We lost two last time, Mrs Cartwright said, her face gone grim. The wind changed on them.

She laid out another couple of flaps of bread.

They said it looked like they'd tried to run. Dropped the backpacks and that. But you can't outrun a fire.

Louise had seen the fire trucks standing in their garage.

They were very shiny, with the words *Mindurra Volunteer Bush-Fire Brigade* in fancy letters on the doors, and some kind of coat-of-arms thing. They were picturesque, but now that she thought about it, she saw that they were picturesque because – to put it bluntly – they were old. They'd be a disaster. Stalling, boiling over, every trick in the book.

So what should you do? Louise asked. She'd learnt that city people were expected to ask the stupid question.

You find a little dip in the ground, Mrs Cartwright said, and get something over your head, a bag or whatever. It does go over real quick.

She glanced at Louise.

You'd be inclined to give running a go, but, wouldn't you?

It was easy to imagine how it would happen. There would be a few of you working in a line. You'd be flapping away with your wet bags and your little squirters, but the fire would suddenly come up at you from behind. Its size and power would make the idea of wet bags and squirters absurd. You would shout to each other and climb aboard the truck, but it would not start.

You would have just a few moments, after you saw it was hopeless and before the fire got you. There would be no time to think any great thoughts or to review the shortcomings of your behaviour. There would be no point in scribbling a note to anyone. In the moment before the breath was sucked out of your lungs, you might turn and hide your face in the person beside you. In that moment of extremity, it would not matter who it was.

The idea that a man who checked reservoirs for the Water Board might have once wanted to write music had seemed nothing more than ridiculous, that day in the Refreshments Tent. Now, watching her hands automatically buttering bread, she saw how interesting it was that his way of going into something solid had been to go into water.

At the time it had seemed merely silly. It occurred to her now that it could be a kind of heroism.

*

One of her ex-husbands had made a hobby of apocalypse. He'd done a chart in coloured pens, extrapolating forward from the fifteenth century, and had announced that another big war was due any time. He was ready. He kept a knapsack packed ready in the garage, with a compass and a knife and something he called iron rations. At the weekends he ran up and down hills, and practised lighting a fire with a magnifying glass and two dry leaves.

If the bomb drops, he had told her, and we get separated, I'll meet you at Gunnedah Post Office. It's far enough out to be safe.

Gunnedah Post Office, she had repeated, but doubtfully.

Don't forget.

She had not forgotten. But if a bomb dropped, she did not think she would go to Gunnedah Post Office. He would have made other plans now, with some other woman.

And he was not the man she would want to find, in the event of apocalypse.

She did not really know anything about the man who'd gone into water because it was solid. Lloyd. From the Water Board. That was all she knew about him: that, and the way he had of looking at you with a kind of intensity, as if wondering.

She hardly knew him, had only met him the once. She did not have any arrangement with him about the steps of Gunnedah Post Office. Or anywhere else. Why was there, all at once, an emptiness, thinking that it might be too late now to have any arrangement with him, of any kind, about anything at all?

She had got the hang of the sandwiches now. She was churning them out, fast, faster, as if racing the fires eating up the bush. He would not be burned alive. He would come back down

7

as he had gone up, perched in among the hoses, and she would be ready for him this time. He would wave, and she would be there, waving back. Then, perhaps, they could continue the conversation that their skins, so much wiser than they were themselves, had already begun.

THE MEANING OF LIFE

MANDY SAYER

Each week, in Darlinghurst, there are more people dying than being born. They die from drive-by shootings and accidental overdoses, bar brawls and binges, bikie contracts and suicidal leaps from art deco buildings. Occasionally, they're the victims of more common causes: bowel cancer, heart attack, but rarely old age. By the time she was twelve, Ginger knew this – and more – because her father was the undertaker at the local funeral home.

An only child, she'd grown up in the four-storey Victorian terrace amid the smells of cosmetic powders and embalming fluid. The family residence was on the top two floors, filled with furniture and carpets from the century before, when her grandparents had run the business. From the time she could remember, Ginger had witnessed an average two or three funerals a week in the large candlelit parlour, just to the right of the entry foyer. She'd seen extravagant ceremonies involving string quartets and flocks of doves, floral wreaths the size of doors, digital slideshows on wide plasma screens. More often than not, however, the services were small and modest: a closed cardboard coffin, a clutch of weeping friends, maybe two or three relatives arguing in a corner about who was going to pay for the cremation.

The funeral of her mother had been an entirely different affair. Filling up the first rows of seating were the wives of members of the Australian Association of Funeral Directors – mostly stiff-backed women with serious faces who considered themselves modern because they no longer felt obliged to wear black at a funeral. Instead, they paraded their progressiveness with grey twin-sets, brown tweed – one even had the temerity to don a yellow hat. There were also women from the Parents and Teachers Association at Ginger's school, all dressed in various shades of charcoal, and her mother's two younger brothers and surviving uncles.

Ginger had been seven at the time of her mother's death. Her father had explained to her that she'd been transformed into an angel by God and now lived on the gabled roof of their house, between the two chimneys. For a short time afterwards, when she was walking home from school, she would gaze up at the roof, squinting through the afternoon glare, trying to catch a glimpse of her mother's long fair hair, and her fluffy white angel wings silhouetted against the sky.

At the time, Ginger didn't fully understand the concept of death and assumed her mother would one day return to their home after God no longer required her services. She'd been told her mother had passed away *from a stroke*, which hardly seemed serious, let alone terminal. Some afternoons, she'd creep into her parents' bedroom and try on the silk dresses and high-waisted skirts left hanging in the closet. She'd dab on musky perfume and parade around the room in high heels, impersonating her mother at the butcher shop, pointing at imaginary cuts of steak and ordering legs of lamb.

After her mother's funeral, her father had been so grief-stricken he'd stayed down in the basement for weeks, unable to work and eating very little. Ginger had always been forbidden to enter the basement and, following the loss of her mother, the strict rule continued to be enforced. During that time it felt as if she'd lost both her parents and the rooms of her home seemed larger and more ominous.

A housekeeper was engaged by a concerned relative to look after Ginger, and to monitor the funeral home's telephones and email. Most of the time Mrs Kite simply told prospective clients that Mr Moss was on an overseas holiday and operations at the home had been temporarily suspended. Each afternoon, before dinner, Ginger would stand at the top of the basement steps and call down to her father, telling him the details of her day at school. As usual, he would not allow her any closer than the top landing of the staircase – and sometimes, when he didn't respond to her daily reports, she wondered if he was still down there at all.

When he did finally emerge from the basement, after a month or so, he was so thin and pale he looked positively cadaverous. Ginger had always been conscious of the fact that her father and mother (when she'd been alive) seemed to be so much older than the parents of her friends. At the school gate she'd noticed women with glossy hair and apple-smooth skin picking up their kids and chasing them towards parked four-wheel drives, while her own mother, her ash-blonde hair flecked with grey, her face deeply lined, leaned on the fence to ease her arthritis. Her father was tall and thin, with pewter-coloured hair, and a long solemn face that suggested he was in constant pain, though she had never once heard him complain of an ailment. Strangers meeting the family for the first time had often assumed that her mother and father were, in fact, her grandparents, which was a frequent source of social embarrassment. After having lived in the basement for weeks, her father was sporting a white beard, and thick strands of tobacco-coloured hair were sprouting from his nose.

Not previously a man of many words, the bearded father before her now babbled incessantly, about his childhood, his first love, the toxicity of formaldehyde, as if he'd suddenly forgotten she was merely a little girl who'd recently lost her mother and was too young to fully understand his ramblings. Gulping down mouthfuls of absinthe, he talked of his travels through Western Europe, his English parents, the first time he'd seen a sunset and a full moon on opposite horizons of the same sky. At night, by the open fire in the sitting room, he began to tell her wild tales of exploding crypts, stolen corpses and premature burials.

The story that haunted her the most was the one about a heavily pregnant woman in the nineteenth century, who, after having suffered a bout of scarlet fever, was pronounced dead by the local priest. Following the woman's burial, the attending nurse voiced her doubts about the possibility of the woman's death, and the shocked and panicking husband promptly had the body exhumed. Not only did they discover the corpse lying on her stomach, clutching a fistful of hair, they also found that, after she'd been buried, the woman had given birth to a baby girl, who was lying between her legs in a pool of dried blood and still attached to her mother by the umbilical cord.

Ginger was so rattled by the tale she began to suspect her own mother might have suffered a similar fate, that she was not in fact a winged angel hovering above their home, but a living woman trapped in a wooden box two metres beneath the earth. Why, at her funeral, only weeks before, she'd lain in her open coffin, smiling serenely, her cheeks aglow, as if she were only asleep and having a pleasant dream. And could her father have accidentally buried other people alive, without anyone realising his fatal mistakes? If a priest – a man of God – could make such a serious error, surely so could the old man before her.

One night, sitting at his feet, she grew teary and breathless and pressed her face into his lap. He rested his hand on her head and stroked her hair, asking over and over what was wrong with his little girl. She trembled and hiccupped and wiped her eyes, trying to find the words to describe her despair.

Finally, she voiced her fears: the premature burials, her visions of babies being born in deep graves, the possibility that her mother might still be alive beneath the buffalo grass in Waverly Cemetery.

It was then that she heard him swallow hard. He took her face in his hands and lifted it from his lap, so they faced one another directly and she could smell the chemical whiff of alcohol on his breath.

'Now,' he whispered, 'I've got something important to share with you. You must promise not to tell anyone. It will be our secret.'

*

The calls usually came at night, from hospitals, hostels and private homes. If the telephone didn't wake her, the creak of her bedroom door would, and by the time her father had bundled her up in her flannel dressing gown, she'd be rubbing crust from the corners of her eyes. It generally took two adults to lift and transport a corpse, but since her mother had died, her father preferred to work alone or, rather, he preferred to work in the sole company of his daughter.

The inside of the hearse always smelled of leather and wilting flowers. On hot evenings, a faint stench would rise, like stagnant water left sitting too long in a vase. She found it strangely alluring to be out so late, without anyone else knowing – not even Mrs

Kite, who always slept soundly each night until dawn.

She never accompanied her father into the mortuaries and hospitals, but remained in the front seat of the hearse, breathing on the windscreen and writing her name over and over with her index finger. Eventually, he would appear, pushing a gurney, with a corpse inside a canvas bag, which he loaded into the back. On the way home, she would listen for any signs of life from the body that lay behind her – a cough, a cry, a timid sigh – so that her father wouldn't be like that man in the story who'd mistakenly buried a person alive.

The purpose of these trips, her father explained, was to help her to understand the difference between the living and the dead, between a human being and a corpse. Unlike the nineteenth century, he continued, today a body had to be examined by a raft of experts – a medical examiner, a coroner, a mortician like himself – before being declared officially dead.

The problem, Ginger soon realised, was that even a genuine corpse often refused to remain silent. Once, on their way home from a pick-up, she was startled to hear a sound, like a distant, faulty vacuum cleaner, whistling from the rear of the hearse. Another time, she heard a moan, as if the body was having a nightmare. Yet another time, she heard what sounded like a brief explosion, and her father explained to her that the dead are full of stale air and wind desperate to escape back into the atmosphere of the living.

One morning, when she admitted to him that she was still confused, that she still feared her mother had been buried alive, her father began chewing on the inside of his cheeks. He glanced around the room for what seemed like a long time, as if someone might appear to give him some advice on what to do.

Eventually, he cleared his throat, as if preparing to make a speech.

'Trust me,' he said. 'Your mother has not been buried alive.'
She sniffed and looked away, shaking her head.

Her father tugged on his beard several times and sighed. She glanced up into his eyes and to her they seemed watery and unusually grey. And then he did something he'd never done before: he took her hand firmly and began leading her down four flights of stairs, to the basement. His hand around hers was warm and reassuring – as it had been when he'd walked her to her first day at school. And, with every step she took with him – she couldn't tell why – she felt her anxiety diminishing.

*

The sandstone walls were lined with wooden cabinets, painted white, with glass doors through which she could see various bottles and jars of what looked like pale yellow powder. Surgical instruments were lined up beside a double sink: needles, scalpels, tubes and forceps.

In the centre of the room was a steel table with a narrow drainage gutter running around the sides. Lying on the table was a body – one she and her father had collected the night before from the Royal Prince Alfred Hospital. Until that moment, she hadn't seen the corpse, a young woman with matted green hair whose collarbones and ribcage jutted through her skin. Her eyes were closed and her skin had a bluish sheen to it, like the early swelling of a bruise. Her father lit a candle and held it over the body. She flinched as she watched him lower it towards the woman's arm and held the flame against her wrist. Ginger smelled a hint of singed hair but, as she watched the woman's skin redden, she heard no cry of pain, not even a whimper.

Her father explained that, in the olden days, there were other ways of proving that a body was no longer alive: cutting off fingers, rigging bells to limbs, placing pennies on eyelids for three days before burial. Now, what with the advances in modern science, the chances of such an accident occurring were virtually impossible.

Ginger frowned. She grasped a hank of the woman's green hair and pulled on it. The woman didn't make a sound, nor did she move. 'Can we dig up Mum?' she asked. 'Just to be sure?'

Her father pursed his lips and shook his head. When she asked why they couldn't, he explained that exhuming bodies, without consent from the authorities, was against the law.

'What if we don't get caught?' she persisted. 'We could do it in the middle of the night, when everyone's asleep.'

And that was when he sat her down on the wooden bench and told her he had something else very important to share with her. He had wanted to wait until she was older, he explained, at least until she was a teenager, but now seemed as good a time as any. Ginger crossed her ankles, unsure if she wanted him to continue or not. He put his hands behind his back and began pacing around the steel table, the lifeless body, staring at the concrete floor, as if following the path of a cockroach.

Finally, he paused, looked up, and announced that if she wanted to see her mother again she should not look among the dead, but the living.

*

As the years passed, Ginger slowly became inured to her own sense of loss, and to the grief of the funeral mourners who filed through her home. She continued to accompany her father on his pick-ups, helped him fill out paperwork, and watched with practised nonchalance as he drained blood from bodies, powdered the faces of corpses, and stitched their lips together. Sometimes she helped with the rouge and eyeliner, though she never failed to be surprised by how cold the face of a cadaver could become.

What had begun as an introduction to the cycles of life and death gradually became a part of her daily routine, as normal and regular as brushing her teeth or watering the front garden. She gradually stopped fearing that her father would preside over a premature burial. Now that she knew that her mother and father weren't her real parents – that she'd been adopted at the age of eight weeks old – she no longer pined so much for the dead woman who'd raised her, but for the woman who'd given birth to her, the one who was still alive.

She looked for this woman in the faces of shop assistants, bus drivers and stallholders at the local market. She searched the glazed eyes of young mothers pushing strollers, the smiles of barmaids who worked in the pub across the road from where she lived. She listened to the soft voices of librarians and the banter of gossiping women at outdoor cafés, wondering if any one of them could be the one, the mysterious woman who'd made her.

Her father – for that is how she still referred to him – did not know many details about the identities of her birth parents, only that they had both been very young and that her mother had lived locally, having given birth at St Vincent's Hospital only two blocks away. For Ginger, the mixture of anonymity and close proximity was both tantalising and exasperating. Why, she could have walked past her own mother every day for many years, without even recognising her. She had learnt from her father that the name 'Ginger' had been chosen specifically by the woman who'd given birth to her.

When Ginger asked why, her father merely smiled, and touched her long ponytail of reddish-blonde hair. She smiled back, and the thought that her mother's hair might be the same colour as her own made her shiver. Her father had showed her a copy of her own birth certificate: *Mother: Sonia Darling. Father: Unknown.*

By the time she was nine she realised that it was possible that she was no longer an only child. It occurred to her that she could have younger brothers and sisters who lived in the area, who maybe even went to her own school – children that her mother had decided to keep instead of giving away to strangers.

This possibility caused her to study local families even closer. Each afternoon, she scrutinised every fair-haired mother who picked up her kids from school. There was a cheery woman in her early thirties who wore sequined gypsy skirts and red boots, who collected her five-year-old son on a bicycle that had a second seat on the back. One day, Ginger found herself running towards her, stopping just short of the bike's front wheel. 'What's your name?' she blurted out, dropping her school case. Her son suddenly appeared and the woman put one arm around him and kissed him on the head. 'Caroline,' she replied. 'What's yours?'

*

There was also a very young, thin woman whose twin boy and girl never wore a uniform to school; every afternoon, she would stand at the gate, smiling, and holding two cones of strawberry ice-cream. Ginger didn't bother to ask what her name was: she wore a silver necklace with letters hanging from it that spelled out 'KAREN.' And then there was a glamorous woman – quite a bit older – who wore her blonde hair pinned up into a lacquered beehive, and who picked up her first-grade daughter in a dark-blue convertible that she always double-parked. One afternoon, Ginger summoned the courage to ask the woman her name. But the woman merely looked away and pushed a button on the dashboard. The roof of the car began to rise, enclosing the woman, and she began to wind her window up. Her daughter climbed into the car and they drove away.

After a few months, this imaginary life – this pretend mother – no longer preoccupied her, and she began to resent the conventional families she witnessed each day, with their ice-creams, bicycles and easy laughter. She dreaded the usual questions from the kids at school: What does your dad do? How many brothers and sisters have you got? What's your mum baking for the annual fete? Often her reply was silence, or she disappeared into the toilet block.

She decided that not one of the mothers she saw at the school gate would have given her baby away. The love and tenderness they exuded was too obvious.

*

By her tenth birthday she'd realised that the dead were much easier to get to know than those who were still alive. In calloused hands she recognised a hard life spent labouring; in dark, leathery faces, permanently suntanned, she sensed years whiled away on a fishing boat; caesarean scars revealed the births of offspring; a thin and hairless body told stories of incurable cancer.

Ginger also grew to understand that you could learn a lot about a corpse from the kinds of mourners it attracted. For example, a few scruffy men with beards and oversized shoes usually meant that the deceased had been homeless and had probably died in a nearby lane. It was on these occasions that her father usually performed the ceremony alone, delivering a short, general eulogy, in lieu of the usual family members and friends.

Women in black suits and pearls, with matching handbags and shoes, usually mourned a corpse that had acquired some wealth, one who had lived in Double Bay or Vaucluse – probably a former socialite or the mistress of a CEO who'd died of leaking breast implants or too many sessions at a tanning salon.

One day, the parlour was packed with over 200 people – some with dreadlocks, others with shaved heads, teenagers with tattooed arms and hands. The air, she remembered, had been thick with the smell of incense. She'd even noticed a handcuffed female prisoner wearing an orange jumpsuit, flanked by two male guards, sitting in the back row, and a huge grey dog the size of a Shetland pony panting away beside the coffin. At the time, she sensed that the service would be for a local criminal. This was confirmed when, before the ceremony began, she walked down a side aisle, tripped on an outstretched foot, and bumped into a man wearing a dark suit. At once, she glimpsed the inside of his open jacket and the gun in a holster strapped to his chest. When she looked up she noticed he had a hooked nose and smelled strongly of a minty aftershave. He seemed like a man who would hunt down criminals, she thought, one of those policemen you can't recognise because they try to dress like everyone else.

She eyed the gun, frowning. 'What are you doing here?' she asked, before she could stop herself.

He buttoned his jacket, concealing the gun. 'Just wanna make sure the bastard's really dead.'

When she thought about it, she understood that she could easily learn more about the background of a corpse than she could about her own. The deceased always came with a death certificate, stating its date and place of birth, its parents and grandparents, and of course the cause and date of death. A corpse usually attracted a big family of close and distant relatives, best friends and casual acquaintances, those who were inconsolable and others who feigned grief by bowing their heads and clutching tissues and handkerchiefs. Death gave a person a complete identity of a kind that it probably hadn't achieved in life. The dead knew who they were.

She now flitted between the embalming room and the funeral parlour, between mourners and flower arrangers, with a detached, almost world-weary air. She thought she'd seen everything: bullet wounds the size of saucers, gangrenous legs, and once – on Christmas Day – a complete decapitation, with the woman's head in a separate plastic bag from the one in which her body was stored.

Then, late one night, in the first month of winter, her father received a summons from the morgue at St Vincent's Hospital. Even though it was only a hundred metres up the road, her father insisted that Ginger accompany him. The last time he'd left the hearse unattended outside the hospital, in order to sign paperwork, a man had jumped into the driver's seat and driven off on a joyride, with the corpse still in the back.

Wearing her flannelette pyjamas, dressing gown and slippers, she waited in the front passenger seat, watching a patient wearing only a thin green hospital gown standing in the icy wind, hooked up to an IV, smoking a cigarette. She looked at his sunken face, his rounded, almost collapsed shoulders, and knew the next time she'd see this man would probably be in the basement of her home. She was surprised to realise these thoughts no longer disturbed her.

She was further surprised when her father walked through the automatic sliding doors without pushing the usual gurney or stretcher. At first, she thought there'd been some mistake, that the body they were to collect had been stored at another hospital. As her father drew closer, however, and as he moved briefly through a pool of yellow light from a passing car, she noticed he was carrying a tiny package in his arm – no bigger than a loaf of bread. He was lurching slightly and seemed to be finding it hard to breathe.

*

The organist played 'Amazing Grace', slower than usual, as downcast people – some dressed casually in jeans, others in dark wool and pearls – filed into the candlelit parlour. Mrs Kite was arranging some flowers beside the front dais and Ginger was passing out the Order of Service cards. Earlier, her father had handed her a pair of old-fashioned dressmaking scissors, which had once belonged to his mother. He'd whispered instructions about what she was to do with them following the ceremony, and she'd nodded and slipped them into the pocket of her dress.

In the back row sat a group of men whom Ginger recognised immediately from the beer garden across the road, clutching caps in their fists, wearing overalls and work boots covered in dried concrete. The local shopkeeper, who was always dressed in black, sat alone in the corner – an Italian woman who sometimes had to have her teenage son translate for customers. There were a few pale-faced women in a middle row cradling gurgling babies and softly berating their restless toddlers. Then the Lord Mayor swept through the door with a photographer and two suited men – Ginger had seen her picture in the paper many times. She was wearing a grey pinstripe suit and her neck was ringed with her usual leather choker dotted with silver studs. By now, it was standing-room only and some fold-out chairs had to be wedged against the wall.

Standing an arm's length away from Ginger was a tall man in a blue suit, studying the crowd. It was only when she caught a whiff of mint aftershave, and glimpsed the hook nose, that she recognised him. She could just make out the impression that his gun made through his jacket.

She frowned and glanced about, wondering why he was attending the service. After a minute or so, she recognised another man, similarly suited and groomed, standing closer to the front, his eyes roving like spotlights across the crowd of teary mourners. Ginger glanced back at the hooked-nosed one, at the slight lump protruding from the left side of his jacket, and wondered if he planned to shoot one of the mourners. It seemed strange to have detectives attend such a ceremony, as if her father were about to commit an act of terrorism rather than conduct a short funeral.

She handed out the last of the Order of Service cards and tiptoed up the middle aisle, between rows of bowed heads, through whispered prayers in what sounded like several different languages. She sat in the front row between an Aboriginal woman and a young man taking notes. The organist was now playing 'Just a Closer Walk with Thee'. On the front dais sat the usual wooden rectangular stand, but instead of supporting a two-metre casket, half-open for viewing, it presented a tiny white coffin, no longer than her own arm, surrounded by fragrant lilies.

It was only when her father appeared from behind the curtains, when he assumed his place behind the lectern and began his eulogy, that she began to understand why this funeral seemed so different from the others.

'No doubt you've all read about this tragedy in the press,' her father announced in an unusually quiet voice. 'And I thank you sincerely for gathering here today, to mourn this anonymous soul, this tiny angel, whose presence on earth was such a brief flicker.'

Even though she had her eyes on her father, standing tall behind the lectern, she could hear people softly weeping, the rustle of tissues, a deep cough. The detective at the front of the room uncrossed his arms and raised one hand to his face.

Her father turned a page on the lectern and seemed to be reading from his notes.

'The poor child,' he continued, 'did not even have a name by which we can farewell her.' He also added she had no accurate date of birth, no known address.

Ginger slid to the edge of her chair and crossed her ankles, confused. In her experience, just about every corpse had been accompanied by a name and date of birth. It was customary, at the very least, for some tattered pension card, dole form or ATM receipt to identify a body. She had seen her own birth certificate, though it was incomplete.

Her father shifted and cleared his throat. 'This nameless newborn,' he continued, 'deserves our prayers and greatest sympathy, for her few days of life here on earth were no doubt filled with suffering and pain.'

The parlour door slammed open and she looked around to see a few more women, barely out of their teens, filing into the room. The hook-nosed detective scrutinised them each briefly before turning his attention back to the service.

'This poor child,' her father explained, gesturing to the coffin, 'was not even a week old when she was found—' he paused and caught his breath '—when she was discovered inside a green recycling bag that had been dumped in a lane behind a local hotel.' A gust of sighs and low moans rose through the room and the candle flames trembled, casting shadows against the sandstone walls.

'She'd been wrapped in a towel and her umbilical cord had been crudely severed, possibly by a kitchen knife or garden shears – so much so that it had obviously become infected shortly after her birth.' Her father cleared his throat and ran his hand through his hair. 'But the infection was not what robbed this child of her short life,' he added. 'It was the hypothermia she suffered after she'd been abandoned in the lane.'

For a moment Ginger's eyes met her father's and she saw

that he was looking directly at her, as if there was no one else in the room.

She suddenly realised she was shivering, as if the temperature in the room had plummeted ten degrees. Her stomach tightened and she found it difficult to breathe. She realised, now, why the detectives were there, why they were closely examining all the funeral mourners, especially the women. Gazing at the coffin, she felt dizzy and nauseous at the same time.

Later, she hoped, she'd feel better, when she and her father, as planned, would stand outside, on the verandah of the parlour, together with the other mourners. They would watch the small white casket, no bigger than a toy box, being pushed into the back of the hearse, along with floral wreaths, notes, dolls and teddy bears. She knew her father's hand would be a warm glove around hers, as it always had been. When her father nodded, she would pull the ornate pair of scissors from her pocket and cut the strings of the twenty pink balloons tethered to the porch. And she'd watch them float up, beyond the chimneys where her angel mother no longer lived, and into the cloudy sky.

But for now she stood up, and pressed her back against the wall, her eyes, like those of the detectives, roving over each woman in the room – those who were crying and those who sat motionless, wondering who was the one.

ALL THAT WE KNOW OF DREAMING

PENNI RUSSON

It was the children who woke me this morning, tiptoeing in and out, peering at me sleeping. I could hear them talking in the hall, or rather I perceived a ceaseless humming that gradually became their voices. I rolled over and played possum until the youngest of the three sisters, Mimi, settled on the end of the bed, weighing down my legs, watching me. At night sometimes I hear her, somnambulating from room to room, rustling curtains, scratching her fingernails against the walls, bumping into furniture. She dreams with her eyes open. I have forgotten how to dream.

After some rapid whispering among themselves, the children refused to tell me where you had gone. So I left the breakfast unmade to show them I would not tolerate their tricksiness and went down to the orchard to check the pears. The little silver car – mine – sat in the carport, like some kind of domesticated pet. Your car was gone. The morning was dazzling and damp; a fine mist hovered over the opposite hills.

As I walked down the low stone steps into the orchard, I pictured you netting the twin pear trees at the beginning of summer, tossing the large white nets over the stretching body of each tree with a graceful gesture, like covering a bed with a sheet. Today, after weeks of alighting on the topmost branches and clambering over the mesh, the morning birds have found their way inside the net, and they're raucous with fruit.

The pears trouble me. A fortnight ago I went to touch one to see if it was ready to pick. One side was smooth, classical, like the curve from waist to hip. Yet just as I laid my hand on the hardness of the pale green skin, I saw that the other side of the pear had been eaten out, and the fruit was filled with quivering wasps, entering and exiting, gorging on the interior. The wasps grew slow when the weather got cold, or perhaps the recalcitrant neighbour finally poisoned the nest on the boundary of his property – whatever the case, we haven't seen one for days; they no longer squeeze through gaps in the house, the husks of them no longer litter the window sills, baking dry in the sun. I returned to the house. The mist was rising from the hills; dry sunlight crept across the yard. In the house, Mimi, the baby, was crying and the other two stood over her, pinching her fiercely to make her stop. When she saw me she stopped anyway.

I took pity on them and cracked eggs into a bowl, frothed them with the whisk and swirled them into a pan. I made one omelette and cut it into three. The little girls ate obligingly but without appetite. When they were done I told them to go outside and play. The older ones made for the orchard, full of plans for catching a bird and making it a pet. Mimi stood at the open door, looking wistfully back over the threshold, but I knew she dared not come back inside. Not while I was there, haunting the rooms, waiting for you to come home.

I fixed up the beds, starting with the children's, vigorously shaking the last vestiges of sleep – flaked skin, dried insect scales – out of the blankets. Outside the birds were belling to each other. The older girls played in the orchard, cackling like hens. No sound from Mimi, probably nestled in the middle branches of a tree. Treelike herself: half of the soil, half of the sky, bending where the wind takes her but fixed in place by other, sturdier forces. Isn't she pale, like paperbark?

In our room I stood at the end of the unmade bed, looking over the shape of us, where we had been sleeping. I pulled hard at the bottom sheet, which peeled from the bed and billowed around me like a sail, filling the room. Under the sheet, time stood still. Outside, it sped up. The day travelled over the fields, rushing towards me, with unknown intentions. Mid-morning, my sister rang. She was not in the least sorry to hear about the pears – 'Three dollars a kilo at the supermarket!' – and she thought your absence unremarkable. 'Do you always keep tabs on each other?' I'm embarrassed to tell her that most of the time we do. It never occurred to me that marriages could go any other way. I stretched the phone as far as I could, uncurling the cord, so I could see out the window. The big girls flitted from tree to tree. Mimi hung solemnly on the gate, fingers gripping the mesh. A flock of cockatoos flew overhead.

'Sometimes I think it's us out there,' I said, 'playing under the trees. One of those games that stretched from summer to summer, that we could pick up and leave off for months at a time.'

'Oh, I see us all the time,' my sister replied, as if it were not news. 'Every time I look out the window when I'm riding the train into the city. There we are: stalking through the long grass in the wasted land by the tracks, scrambling over a fence, telling secrets, collecting stones. Long scratches on our arms, bruises on our legs, dried grass and leaves tangled in our hair.'

'But if they're us,' I said, watching as the older girls squatted down together and poked at something in the dirt, 'does that make me Mum?'

'Oh God, no!' my sister said. The older girls scooped up something apparently alive, then disappeared around the side of the house.

'Well then, who am I?' My voice sounded far more plaintive than I meant it to.

'You don't have to be Mum,' my sister said, as if we were in a game and she was in charge of delegating roles. 'You can be one of the godly matrons.'

'Great,' I said. 'Thanks a lot.'

She giggled, then suddenly: 'Is that really the time? Shit!' She hung up without saying goodbye. That was typical of Sofie. Or had it been Hillie? You always say we sound exactly the same, we three sisters, our voices high and sibilant, as if we were still children.

I took lunch outside, to the orchard. I spread out a blanket and ate with the girls. The autumn sunlight was warm, a bee droned in the lavender and a familiar faint boredom settled over me. They were like puppies, the girls, tumbling over and lying on top of each other. Their bodies spilled off the blanket; they tussled, fighting for territory.

Amid this jostle I saw our neighbour, Murray, pass by the gate. His dog sniffed around the fence and the girls attempted to entice it in with crusts of bread.

'Hello!' I called out.

'Car's gone off the road.'

'God, really? Where? Is it serious?'

'Up near Creek Road. Hit a roo. Big one too. Car's a write-off.'

'Is anyone hurt?'

He squinted at the sun. 'Couldn't see no one.'

'How awful!'

He shrugged and whistled his dog.

After lunch, the big girls disappeared again, to twitter in the trees or hide under the verandah. I left the back door open and put boxes of juice and a container of broken biscuits on the kitchen bench for the older ones. Mimi was too young to leave behind, so I strapped her into the car and drove up over the crest of the hill and down to the creek road. It wasn't far, but it would have been an impossible walk with Mimi. You could have done it, set Mimi on your broad shoulders and waltzed her down the road.

I saw the roo first, and I parked alongside it. 'Kanga's having big dreams,' I told Mimi as I unbuckled her straps. She looked down at it with wide eyes. 'Soon it will wake up and hop away home.' It's what she believes of death anyway. She believes any thing caught out in the world alone is on its way to Mummy. Every insect, spider, bird, human man or kangaroo she has ever encountered – living or dead – is a temporarily lost child.

Mimi wrapped her legs around me like a monkey and we stood beside the car together, looking down the bank between the road and the deep channel of the dry creek bed. This wreck had been here for years, for decades, its chassis rusting into the understorey. I'd seen it here before on my summer walks, when the evenings were long and mellow and the air creamy sweet. I'd even thought about photographing it, but I could never be bothered carrying the camera that far. And it wasn't that I wanted to photograph it exactly. It was more that, every time I passed, I told myself that I meant one day to look at it. Really look at it. Perhaps that was why I was compelled to stagger down the embankment now, hefting Mimi aside, so I could see past the child in my arms to the placement of my own feet. Or it might have been this: since I stopped dreaming, everything has taken on the same weight. The tissue of meaning that connects things has grown wild and dangerous, now everything is connected, everything is enmeshed.

I walked around the car's deteriorating exoskeleton. Its soft insides had long since rotted away. Long grass grew under the car roof and inside the bonnet. The steering wheel and the gear box, the entire engine, was gone, the tyre-stripped wheels sunk into the ground, which had formed a new hard surface around them, as if the car had grown there, and if you dug – I could see it in my mind like a botanical cross-section of a turnip – you'd find a complex network of mechanical roots branching far down into the earth.

Behind me, the bush murmured to itself: the tone-deaf song of a frog, the whirring of unseen insects, the bobbing throats of bellbirds, or simply the faintest whisper of leaves brushing together. I felt if I stood here long enough with Mimi, if we were still enough, someone would emerge from that sound, from the heart of the forest. The lost driver of that ancient car perhaps, in sepia tones like his rusted-out chassis, clutching a bleeding head. Or three little girls, living naked and wild in the bush, mud in their hair, fingernails grown like claws, hauling real human babies around like playthings. Or my mother, dressed for luncheon in her powdery-blue suit and coral-pink lipstick.

Mimi was heavy in my arms. She twirled a finger in her hair; her head drooped onto my shoulder. I put her gently down on the long silken grass. 'It's just for a moment,' I promised. 'Wait here.' I clambered up the embankment. I looked back at Mimi. She had settled herself down on the grass to wait patiently, a bird in a nest.

I followed the black marks on the road: looping skids, as if the car had been dancing with the kangaroo, with slow balletic grace. The other car was just around the bend.

It was a completely alien object; it may as well have fallen from the sky. Dazzling red and broken, its entire front had folded in, the windscreen a spider web of cracks. The wheels were badly bent and twisted, reminding me, with a visceral chill, of broken limbs. I hovered on the edge of the road. Now I had seen it, I wanted nothing to do with it.

I realised what I had intended was impossible: to come and look upon this wreck, to make some kind of sense of its existence, and then leave it behind me. What if someone was in that car, had slithered to the floor, gasping their last shallow breaths? Or another had been flung from the car and lay close by, quietly bleeding? I sidestepped down the rocky hill. Inside, it smelt strongly of aftershave, and also damp, like the soil was already creeping in. The glove box yawned open, its contents meticulously cleared out. There was nothing, not a drop of human presence.

With a jolt, I remembered Mimi. How long had I left her? I scrambled up the rocky hill and gravel escarpment. There was my car on the road, and the deflating body of the kangaroo. There, down in the rushes and the weeds, was the body of the rusted wreck. But where was Mimi?

I must have run down the bank, my shoes skidding on the loose ground, but as I compose this I remember it as freefalling, as if I kicked off the earth, threw off the shackles of gravity just for a moment, and let myself plummet safely to the spot where Mimi had been.

'Mimi?' I called but the forest threw my voice back. *Me?* it asked. *Me?*

Your search would have been methodical, circling in ever-increasing rings that would scorch themselves on the earth like a bullseye. I zigzagged frantically back and forth, always returning to the patch of dirt and grass where I had left her, as if I might have simply failed to see her. Space would unfold like a flower and reveal her sleeping in its heart.

Many thoughts entered me at the same time, one on top of the other. I was no longer one person, but many possible versions of myself, clumsily overlaid to occupy – more or less – the same space and time. One of me believed I must have left her at home accidentally, like I might a purse or a mobile phone, and brought only a phantom with me, a dream of Mimi, not the girl. One thought that you had come, seen the car, discovered her, scooped her up thoughtlessly and taken her away, like the pair of gloves we found pegged to the fence, weeks after they'd been lost. Or the forest had taken her, my third daughter of a third daughter; such a creature was destined to have a curious, wandering fate. Or the drivers of the two cars formed together in my mind into one misshapen, predatory thing and dragged her away for meat. I wondered if I even had a daughter – *Me? Me?* – or if she was just a conjuring trick? Was it a sister I was looking for all along? And which one – Hillie? Or Sofie? One thing was clear to all of my selves: if she was gone then my life was also gone; I too would disappear and begin again as something new.

In the end I gave up. I knew she wasn't there. Or if she was, she was somehow beyond my reach. I climbed back up the bank to our car, keys in hand.

I'd like to tell you that, as I climbed out of that deep ditch, everything fell silent, nothing stirred – not a twig, not a blade of grass. But the trees continued to murmur among themselves, frogs pipped, birds sang their same throatful of notes. 'Nothing to see here, folks,' the broken-down cars said. 'Keep moving. Keep on moving along.'

I opened the car door. And there was Mimi, between the back and front seats, curled up asleep on the floor. Her face when she's sleeping relaxes into the tiny baby she once was; her bones become soft and spongy. I scooped her up gently, without waking her. I placed her into her infant seat and buckled the straps. When I glanced into the rearview mirror she was awake, staring back at me with fierce dark eyes, but later when I turned around, I saw she had gone back to sleep, her head to one side, her mouth puckered into a rich full raspberry kiss.

She was still asleep, still buckled into the car, when you came home.

*

It's nighttime. You lie beside me. I cannot sleep, so I write this in my head. You will never read it; by daytime, these words will have been carried away, though I tell myself that, first thing, I will write them down. Our daughters sleep in the next room, three sisters, their legs curling up to protect their hearts. Somewhere in the city are my own sisters. They stand in front of their separate mirrors, putting on lipstick the way Mum used to, smearing the colour on and then rubbing their stretched lips together. Diva Red, Honey Shimmer, Cha Cha Cha.

Mimi is restless. I can hear her turning in her bed. When I close my eyes, darkness swirls. I crouch on the edge of a vertiginous night. When I sleep, I will not dream. But before sleep comes I see her stand up, on her roly-poly legs. She's looking around for me. I hear her faintly – 'Mummy?' and then again, 'Mum-*me!*' – but her tiny voice is swallowed by the forest as mine was. I see her climb the hill, hard work for such stout little legs; she slips back a little, she scrapes her knee. She is brave and does not cry. She makes it over the loose verge of the bank, hauling herself up by the bendy trunks of young trees.

She has to visit with the kanga first, to squat down and pat it with a flat open palm.

'Mummy back soon,' she says. 'Nigh-nigh, Kanga.'

She lifts the handle of the car door with both hands. Of course I've left it unlocked – I always do. A tidy child by nature, she pulls it closed behind her. She sits on the seat and slides on her bum to the car floor, and a giggle explodes out of her. She wants to do it again – again and again and again – but it's a lot of effort to get her top-heavy body back onto the seat. Anyway, something on the floor catches her attention, a toy one of the big girls has dropped: small and hard and plastic. A blue-grey cat, quite true to life. She lies down and looks at it, until her eyes blink closed. Nestled inside the husk of the car, like a fairy child scooped into a seed pod, lulled by the silver voices of the bellbirds, she's asleep before I've even noticed that she's gone.

LEBANON

FAVEL PARRETT

My brother and I were watching TV after school. I had a lot of homework to do – to get done – and it was worrying me like it always did, but I did not want to start. Not yet. I just wanted some time to not have to do anything.

My brother turned to me and asked me where Lebanon was. He was in year four and I was in my first year of high school. I told him I didn't know.

'A man came to talk to us about Peace,' he said. 'He was from Lebanon.'

There were often talks about Peace at our school. All I knew about being a Quaker was that there were minutes of silence when we were meant to think about Peace, and there was grey. Grey uniforms and grey walls.

I got up off the couch and walked over to the small bookcase that was really just a shelf squeezed in between the chimney and the wall. We had a two-volume edition of the World Book Encyclopaedia. They were brown and black, maybe they were leather, and WORLD BOOK was written in gold letters down the spine.

Mum had won them in a raffle and that was lucky because I often needed to use them for homework.

I took down the L–Z volume and carried it back to the couch. I opened it up to the beginning of L.

LEB.

Lebanon is a small independent republic at the eastern end of the Mediterranean Sea. The name of the country comes from the snow-capped Lebanon Mountains. In the Arabic language it is called LUB-NAN. Lebanon's capital and largest city is Beirut.

I read it out loud and my brother nodded like he knew, like he was being reminded of something that had just slipped his mind. There was a map of Lebanon – long and thin and by the sea. There were also a few black and white pictures. One of a giant cypress tree, and one of some ancient ruins with Roman-like columns standing tall without a roof. There was a photo of a smart-looking city with lots of cars and people walking in the streets and bright white art-deco buildings against the sky. One building had a sign on the rooftop that said RIVOLI in huge curly writing.

The caption read – *Place des Canons, Beirut – 1969.*

On the next page there was another picture of the city, only there were no cars and no people walking and the art-deco buildings were gone or so altered that there was nothing there to recognise. Smoke rose from missing rooftops and everything was blackened or grey. Everything different. The city had been smashed to pieces.

The caption read – *Beirut 1982: Operation Peace for Galilee.*

My eyes scrolled down the page then, down all the columns about all the wars in Lebanon. The Civil War and the War with

Israel and the War with the PLO. My brother had stopped looking at the pictures; he stopped looking at the book altogether
and rested back against the couch.

'No one wins a war,' he said, and he breathed in heavily.
'That's what the man said he had come to tell us. No one wins
a war, we just all lose. He showed us some photos of his family
and he passed them around and told us they were all gone.'

I closed the book and sat with it heavy on my lap. The TV
was still on but we were not watching it. Eventually I got up and
walked over to the bookcase. I stood there in the corner with
the World Book in my hands and the room was very still.

'Is the man going to stay here now?' I asked, and I meant
forever. I meant was the man going to stay here in Hobart
forever.

But my brother just shrugged. His eyes were back on the
TV and he wasn't thinking about the man from Lebanon
anymore.

Only I was.

The story was inside me now. I knew I would remember the
man even though I had never even seen him or heard him speak.
I didn't know if he was old or if he was young, but I would think
about him, here, living on this island without any of the people
he loved or even knew at all. Here, so far away from home, knowing that he could never return to the place he remembered
because it was gone.

J'AIME ROSE

TEGAN BENNETT DAYLIGHT

It was Thursday, and we had a free period before lunch. This gave us time to get to Ben's new house and watch *Days of Our Lives* before coming back for maths. The way to sneak out of school was not to sneak. You walked with your back straight, your head high, and you didn't look to see if you were being watched or followed. You had to believe no one had any reason to stop you.

Ben was short, with brown hair and a face that had been smooth and pretty when we were ten-year-olds. At sixteen he still had the same lush black eyelashes and brown almond eyes, but now he also had acne, and didn't wash his hair much.

Ben had always wanted me, even before we started high school. When we started French in year seven we were asked to write down and then read out loud the things we liked, starting *J'aime*. I can't remember my own list, only Ben's, which ended with *J'aime Rose*, with our special fake French trill on the R of my name. I wasn't really embarrassed. Ben was the sort of boy who could do things like that. He seemed quiet and even shy, but in fact he was clever, fierce and defiant, and he cared nothing for what other kids thought. He was the most entertaining friend I had. He was the only boy I knew who laughed when things were funny, rather than when they were meant to be funny, or when everyone else was laughing.

I had female friends at school, two of them, misfits like myself who read too many books or became spluttery about The Cure. I sat with them at lunchtime, and also with Ben and his friends. We were together as a group if you saw us from a distance, but in fact the girls sat in a circle of their own, on old pieces of sandstone, and the boys sat to one side, on milk crates they'd stolen from the canteen. Our spot was under a fig tree at the edge of the school where the land, briefly, became bush. It was private, neglected. It looked like an old campsite.

Ben and I didn't talk at recess or lunch. Neither of us knew how to cross from one side to the other, and Ben scorned my friends anyway, particularly Janice, whom he'd made cry by saying that the lead singer of The Cure was gay. That was a bad day. Through angry tears, Janice said that Robert Smith had been with his girlfriend, Mary, since they were teenagers. Ben, pretending to disbelieve her, said, *But there's nothing wrong with being gay*, and Janice couldn't deny it, because that was the code she lived by. This was what Ben could do, if he chose – lead you somewhere you didn't want to go, and leave you there.

I called us misfits before. I wasn't quite a misfit. I didn't have the courage for that. Not for me the glories of triple-pierced ears, or a radical devotion to a singer or a style. I couldn't commit to standing out like Janice did, with her black-ringed eyes and hair teased into a dyed dandelion. With her unconsummated marriage to Robert Smith. In this part of my life I was watching, and waiting. I was waiting to be transformed. I would be nobody until someone chose me.

*

I didn't like being alone with Ben, but this time I hadn't been able to think of an excuse.

Ben's father had died when he was six, and recently his mother had got married again, to an advertising executive. Now Ben had a stepfather and a stepbrother. Two weeks ago he and his mother had moved into their house, which was next to a wharf, and overlooked a stretch of river with boats clustered at its shores – yachts, and cruisers, which are like mansions on the water, only streamlined, a mass of architecture pointed at Sydney's bays and private beaches, at its harbourside restaurants.

Two weeks ago, too, Ben had given me an ultimatum. It had happened over the phone. Every afternoon after school, when I'd said hello to my mother and got myself something to eat, I used to sit in the study with my feet up on the tooled leather desk and phone Ben. I could tilt the office chair back and use my legs as pivot, as anchor, swinging myself back and forth as I stared at the ceiling. I'd been doing this for years, it seemed: talking over the day that had just passed with Ben, comparing the idiocies of our teachers, gossiping about the people we sat with, the kids in our classes.

This is what my parents were like when my father came home from work. They didn't wait for us to go to bed to begin comparing notes about their day; they talked over our heads, impatient to exchange impressions. I'd thought that perhaps Ben was meant to be my boyfriend because we had this too, this intense kinship, this shared bounty of laughter. I didn't want to wait much longer for a boyfriend, but something had stopped me settling for Ben.

Suddenly Ben said, 'I'm sick of this.'

'Sick of what?' I said.

'Waiting for you to make up your mind.'

So it had come. I didn't pretend not to know what he was talking about. I sat up in the office chair, and brought my feet down to the ground.

'It's obvious we were meant to be together,' said Ben. 'I know you better than anyone does. I know you better than you know yourself.'

He'd said this before. It made me feel small, and imprisoned.

'Just give it a go,' he said. 'See how you like it.'

I didn't need him to explain what he meant. He meant for me to let him hold my hand, to submit to his body, let him tell people we were together. He meant for us to sit apart at lunchtime, kissing.

'Just give it a try,' he said, and I agreed to.

*

We were not really going to his house to watch *Days of Our Lives*. This was Ben's way of cornering me into sex. Guess how I knew: I looked in the front pocket of his schoolbag. He had two condoms, things I'd seen before but never held in my hand. In their plastic packets they made me think of surgeon's gloves – as though he was preparing for an operation on me. Two weeks of being boyfriend and girlfriend had passed; two weeks of having my neck nuzzled by him in assembly; two weeks of my damp hand in his on the way home from school; two weeks of gaps and halts in our phone conversation and Janice and Vicky looking pityingly at me when I moved to a milk crate next to Ben's at lunch.

If only I had been pretty, I would have had more choices. Ben thought people were fools for not seeing how beautiful I was. I thought only someone very kind could love me, with my round, cheerful face and dark, thick, horsey hair, with my soft stomach and breasts. I dreamed of a pair of scissors that could cut off extra flesh. I would slice away the mound of my stomach. When Ben put his hand there I had to draw breath very suddenly, stiffening, holding it in.

The house was a stack of concrete rectangles with tinted windows looking onto the water. There was a tall security gate with a keypad. Ben pressed the numbered buttons and the gate slid to one side with a shriek of metal, making us check behind us as if we were intruders.

I always take a breath when I walk into a house for the first time. This one smelt of cleaning fluid. We dumped our bags in the wide front hall and went through the cool of the air conditioning into the kitchen. There were two boys, one blond, one dark, a little older than we were, standing in front of the open fridge. There was nothing in the fridge but drink: rows and rows of champagne, aimed at us like missiles.

As we came in the blond boy popped the cork on a bottle of champagne, laughing as it hit the ceiling with its pattern of downlights. Then he put the bottle to his lips and drank and drank, not seeming to mind the bubbles. He passed the bottle to his friend, gasping and grinning at us.

What I remember best about this moment is a sense of the boys' sleekness, their look of good health and pleasure in being; a look that Ben, with his acne and his skinny shoulders, lacked utterly. They were like beautiful dogs, or horses, well-fed and adored.

Ben said, 'This is Rose.' He pointed at the blond boy. 'That's Alex. Who lives here.'

'I'm Rob,' said the other boy, and held out the bottle. 'Alex's friend. Drink?'

I remember, also, a long moment of Alex looking curiously at me.

There was a TV in the kitchen, but Ben would not stay there to watch, or drink from the bottle of champagne. He led me down to his bedroom in the bowels of the house, the air becoming colder as we descended, and less fresh. His bedroom was a concrete box with French doors giving onto a courtyard that was a dark tangle of ivy. The doors looked as though they would not open. He had all the things from his old house: his stereo, his TV, his boxes of tapes and stacks of LPs. But he had a double bed now, that I couldn't look at, and a poster of Brigitte Bardot on the wall, astride a motor scooter. I stood in the doorway. The smell of his room was already the same as in the last house. Musty more than anything else. Not bad. I could hear Alex and Rob crashing round in the kitchen, shouting with laughter.

'Let's go back up,' I said. 'We could get drunk.'

'With those idiots?' Ben sat down on the bed and patted the mattress next to him. His sheets were new, black and horribly shiny. He smiled at me, and then pursed his lips, a kiss. I shook my head. The inside of his mouth tasted like sandwiches or baked beans.

I crossed my arms tight over my chest. 'I want to get drunk.'

'What about *Days*?'

'Come on,' I said and he stared at me, and crossed his own arms.

'Please.' If I could get him drunk I could get away, and put off the sex. 'It'll be fun.'

Ben gave a long, weary sigh and got to his feet. I was already out the door. He stumped up the stairs behind me. I was running, taking the steps two at a time – I had a feeling, a superstition, that if I reached the kitchen before he got to the top of the stairs I would be free of him. I swung, panting, into the kitchen and Alex and Rob turned to look at me.

'I want a drink,' I gasped.

44

We didn't go back to school that day. As the afternoon went on I got lighter and lighter. It was my dream, I think, to disappear. The more I drank the less substantial I felt, almost coming apart, like a rag of cloud in a breezy sky. I drank and listened to the boys, and didn't speak. Once, just once, Alex came to stand next to me. Then he took my hand, and looked down at me, his eyes as startled as mine must have been. Ben didn't see this. He had given up needling me about getting back to his room and was becoming incoherent, staggering around the kitchen, challenging us to drinking games.

None of them noticed when I took the bottle of champagne I was drinking from and went out into the hall. There was a set of metal spiral stairs leading up a concrete stairwell. The edges of the steps were irregular and the concrete was bare and grey. It was as though the house was not finished, was a shell, and that the family had moved in before it was ready. I started to climb, holding the bottle by the neck. Four floors up and I had reached the single room at the top, which I knew must be Alex's. From it you could see the Harbour Bridge, shimmering in the distance. The sun was behind us now. A breeze had sprung up. I could feel it on my hot face through the open window, and hear the tink of stays from the moored boats. I was drunk; it was a summer afternoon; there was an opening out, a flood of possibility.

I turned back to the room. In one corner there was a cricket bat, on the desk a pile of folded clothes, on the wall a poster with a picture of a red Porsche. There were no books. I finished the bottle of champagne sitting on Alex's bed, and then went down the metal stairs as quietly as I could. I grabbed my bag from the hall, let myself out, skipped through the shrieking gate, pressed the button to close it and was up the street and round the corner as fast as I could go, my heart beating quickly.

I walked home, my schoolbag on my back. The leaves on the trees were bright in the glassy air. There was no one around – there was a lull at that hour, when fathers had arrived home from work and mothers were making dinner. Televisions were on in the front rooms of houses. Perhaps it would be autumn soon, after this long, bright summer. When I got home my mother was cooking in the kitchen with the lights off, the twilight rounding the edges so the room was gentle, soft. She turned and smiled at me as I came in.

In maths on Friday, Ben passed me a note that said *How do you like my new big brother?*

I read the note and then wrote, *He could be worse*, and passed it back.

Ben looked, and then covered the note with his hand. I tried to think of something else to write about Alex, but he hadn't struck me as funny, as most things did when I was with Ben. Our friendship flourished in confinement, like maths class, where our notes to each other made us sick with laughing and sometimes caused the teacher to send us out. Then we would push each other in the corridor, stagger against the clapboard walls, knees bent with mirth. But today we did our maths. We did not even pretend to hide our answers from each other, the way we usually did, in imitation of Mary Ann Wilson, who would be dux eventually and didn't want anyone else to share it.

Walking from maths to history, I told Janice about Alex. She preferred punk boys, skinny ones with stick legs in black jeans and winkle pickers, but she understood the appeal of the private school boy. Every girl, even Janice, wanted to be asked to a private school formal, where, we believed, some thoughtful parent would arrange for a party beforehand with actual drink being served, where the boys would not wear pale grey tuxedos with pale blue bowties but proper black ones. Where the boys would be capable,

46

handing us in and out of a taxi, talking to us at the dance instead of getting so slaughtered that they spent most of the night vomiting in the car park. Janice said nothing about Ben.

On the way home from school I walked with Ben as far as his street, allowed him to kiss me and put his tongue in my mouth, and then took the back streets to my house. I liked the quiet, and not having to think about cars when I crossed the road. I could daydream so intensely that reaching home was a surprise; my body had carried me there without me knowing. I told myself a story as I walked, of Alex coming up from the ferry, inexplicably early from his turreted school, liking the back streets as much as I did, meeting me under the arch of leaves. Neither of us would go home. We would choose one of the streets that led down to the river, one that ended in a tiny reserve, we would sit on the bench next to each other and talk and kiss. We would still be there when it was dark.

*

On Sunday afternoon I was sitting at my desk in my room upstairs, trying to force myself to do my homework. I had a modern history essay due that week. I knew I'd be able to write it if I could just make myself start, but instead I was fiddling with the radio, trying to find a song that I could put onto the tape I was making. But there was nothing on. I leaned over to pick up my bag and take out my history book, and Ben's slipped out from between its covers. I must have picked it up on Friday afternoon, when we were making the usual rush for the door. He would be sitting down now, just as I was, to write the essay.

Without the textbook, he could write nothing. This is what I told myself. He would need it. I would take it over. The walk would do me good. Probably Alex would not be there; he would be with friends. But he might be there.

It would be a chance to tell Ben that I had given being his girlfriend a try, and did not like it. I had no idea how I was going to do this.

It took me half an hour to get dressed. No shoes, I decided. I was subject to a number of complicated and constantly changing rules about my clothes. The adjustments I made to my cut-off jeans and t-shirt in that half-hour were invisible to the naked eye, but absolutely necessary to me. If I had been asked to walk out of the house any earlier I would have been assailed by panic. I put my thick brown hair in a ponytail and drew eyeliner around my eyes. My t-shirt was my older brother's, and much too big for me, which was important, as my jeans were too small. They had fitted me last summer but now I had a good handful of fat over the waistband.

I pressed the doorbell next to the electronic gate and stood there, trying not to fiddle with my clothes. I held Ben's textbook over my stomach to flatten it. A voice from the little speaker said, 'Yeah?' and I said, 'It's Rose. I've got Ben's history book.'

There was no answer. The gate shrieked open and I went up to the front door, which swung wide to reveal Alex, also in cut-off jeans and a t-shirt, his blond hair flopping over his face, his feet bare. The lurch in my heart was like being pushed suddenly from behind. I said, 'I brought Ben's book. I took it home by accident,' and Alex said, 'Come in.'

Most boys, when they saw you, did not change their way of being for you. They were slack-bodied, unresponsive – you could make no difference to them. But Alex was electric. I stepped into the house and a prickly charge went through me, and through him. He stood upright, and seemed to be about to reach for me, when Ben appeared at the top of the hall stairs.

'I was just looking for that,' he said, and held his hand out for the book. He jerked his head in the direction of the stairs.

'Come on then.'

I looked at Alex. His arm was very close to mine. It was tanned, and his hands were big, like a man's. Ben said to him, 'Aren't you meant to be studying?'

Alex met my eye and shrugged, and Ben took hold of my arm and led me downstairs to his bedroom. He pulled an extra chair up to his desk and opened the history book. 'We'll get a start on it together,' he said.

That push that I had felt on seeing Alex again – that force behind me, like a hand at my back; this is what impelled me. The glittering, prickling surge in my body. Also the desperate need to be done with this experience, to be on its other side, to be free from the fear of it and the fear that I would never do it. To be free of having to do it with Ben.

Feeling only a thumping in my body, I said to Ben, 'I need to go to the toilet,' and left him where he was, sitting at his desk, the history book open in front of him. But I didn't go to the bathroom on the middle floor, near the kitchen. I went on up the metal stairs, past the enormous living room with its vast, flat leather sofas and its glass-topped table, past the bedroom with the huge Ken Done painting and the en suite glinting in the carpeted distance, up to Alex's bedroom. I stood at his open door, dazzled by exertion, and when he turned from his desk to look at me, could do nothing but cross my arms, and make a strange sort of face.

*

'What were you doing?' Ben said. 'You've been ages.' He was taking a Style Council record out of its sleeve. He stared suspiciously at me.

'Talking to Alex,' I said. There was a sudden wet slide in my underpants. 'I couldn't find the bathroom.'

He put the record on the turntable and lifted the needle onto it. For a second, I closed my eyes. My body was still thumping; shock, and pleasure, in equal measures.

'You look weird,' said Ben.

*

I was nearly late for school on Monday because I had walked there so slowly. An autumnal sparkle was almost visible in the air; the trees rattled in a breeze that was cool around my bare legs. I was not thinking, however; I was not trying to figure out what I might do next. I was simply borne along, like the leaves that blew ahead of me. As I came down the hill towards the school I could hear the headmaster on the megaphone, which meant they would be marking the roll. I slipped in through the back of the crowd of kids and stood next to Ben. I nudged him to say hello, and he moved away.

This was the first sign, if only I had taken account of it. But I was too preoccupied. What would happen now? I didn't know. My thighs hurt a little. I had hardly slept for thinking of Alex. It was such a pleasure, but not just a pleasure, an achievement: not just in love, but no longer a virgin. The problem I faced in breaking up with Ben – in order to go out with his stepbrother – seemed tiny, easy, as though he would just step aside, give way, when he understood how I felt. Later, when I was ready to tell him. Some part of me really did believe this.

In French, from my seat at the back of the room, I screwed up a little ball of paper and threw it at Ben. He turned round and looked at me. I made a face, a stupid, grinning face, and he shrugged and sighed, and turned away. Then he put up his hand and said to Miss Ryan, 'Miss, Rose is throwing stuff at me.'

Miss Ryan was used to our small conspiracies. She said, 'Rose, *ça suffit.*'

I hoped Ben would turn again and grin at me, to show me he'd won this round, but he didn't. He was bent uncharacteristically over his work, occasionally looking up to study the board. It was so elaborate that at first I thought he was doing it to make me laugh. I did no French. I didn't pretend to copy anything down. When I couldn't get Ben's attention by humming his most hated song or putting our special French singsong into my answers – Ben loved this, we used to chant at each other '*Je voudrais une disque de Rrrolling Stones*,' just like the tape – I gave up, and looked out the window. Our French class was in the senior block, high up. You could hear magpies carolling in the trees. The shouts of kids doing PE on the oval sounded innocuous, even comforting, from that distance. But I was beginning to feel a little frightened.

Maths was when I understood that Alex had told him. Ben was late to class and did not sit at our desk, instead scanning the room and eventually choosing the empty seat next to Anthony Myer. Anthony Myer was Mary Ann Wilson's rival for dux. He covered his work too, and kept his pens in a row in his shirt pocket. At lunch you saw him running for the library, desperate to be first to the school's only computer, one hand clutching his chest to stop the pens falling out.

I tried not to care. I sat on my own and lined my pens up on the desk in front of me, and did not look Ben's way. I tried to be brave.

*

At lunchtime the next day Ben was not sitting with our group. I asked one of the other boys where he was, and he looked at me in an amused sort of way and said, 'Down on the oval.'

On the oval was the big group, where everyone who could keep afloat in the mainstream sat. I would have sat there myself, if it had been possible. No one would have tried to stop me; not physically. Down there the girls sat among the boys, sometimes on their laps, smoking and laughing and teasing the teachers if they walked by. Ben had occasionally visited there. He was welcome anywhere because he was so funny, so quick to spot a weakness in a teacher or a student who was ridiculous. He used to do the Anthony Myer sprint, holding his hand over a row of imaginary pens, to howls of laughter.

It was clear that Ben was not going to walk home with me that afternoon. I saw him lingering with a group of boys, glancing in my direction, when I was waiting for him at the gate, but he did not come towards me. I set off on my own.

Our school was at the bottom of a steep hill, which the buses had to labour up. Often they broke down halfway. Nearly always, we walked faster than they could drive, shielding our faces from the billows of exhaust. On this afternoon a bus was caught near the top, its engine howling as the driver tried to force it into a lower gear. As I passed, Marco Giordano and Jonathan Lane blossomed suddenly out of the back window, like an obscene flower, shouting at me. I stared at them. Marco was moving his fist up and down and rolling his eyes in pretend pleasure; Jonathan bawled, 'Can you suck my cock, too, Rose?'

I put my head down and walked on, ignoring them. Their voices became incoherent under the roar of the bus. I didn't look back. My heart was beating very fast. I hadn't done anything like what they were describing. It had been as much as I could manage to submit to Alex's weight, to open my legs, to keep still as he moved up and down on top of me.

At home I drew a picture of the dress I would wear to Alex's formal. I wanted something sleek and tight-fitting around the bust, that would burst into a skirt like a flower, like a poppy, at my waist. I had an idea that Alex might lay me down somewhere soft, on the velvet grass of whichever golf club or yacht club was chosen by his school, and push my skirts aside to find that I was not wearing underpants. This was not my own fantasy. I had read this in one of my mother's books when I was drifting around the house, looking for something to do.

As the weeks went on things got worse at school. If I caught a boy's eye in class, he would immediately loll his tongue out and leer at me. When I was sitting thoughtlessly on a wall, waiting for Janice and Vicky, three girls from our year laughed at me; one of them said, 'Close your legs, Rose – for once.' There was sniggering from the benches when we played volleyball. This had me checking my skirt for blood, adjusting my underpants, trying not to turn my back on anyone.

I could not talk to Ben. He dared me to, staring at me during assembly or whenever he had other boys around him. Someone kept ringing our house and gasping down the phone. None of this was so obvious that anyone could do anything about it. Teachers did not notice the attention I was being paid at school, and it always seemed to be me who answered the phone to the gasper. I could not talk to Janice or Vicky about what was happening, because it was too shaming to acknowledge it.

Meanwhile Alex was as strong a presence as if he was really there. I took to walking every afternoon and dreaming him up. He was as vivid as a real boy, appearing by my side, or leaning out of a slowing car to call my name and smile at me: a smile that would pull me to him as though I were a fish on a line. I wanted him very much. I was ready for him again. I could remember the feel of his cheek sliding down the skin of my neck. When I breathed in I could smell him. But I couldn't think what to do next. Instead, I waited for him in a hum of stillness, trapped in honey, suspended, unable to move.

*

I was twenty-two when I saw Alex again. It was in the front room of a shared house, at a party in the inner city. I was cruising at that time, on one of the currents of confidence that occasionally came past during those years, that had to do with minor things: weight loss, a series of compliments, the weather. I had been listening to a friend whose boyfriend had been complicatedly, trickily unfaithful, first with a girl we didn't know, then with a girl who was in our circle and had been very helpful during the initial part of the break-up. When my friend finished howling into my dress I felt increased. Bigger. Swelled with love and importance. It was hot, and sweat as well as tears soaked my dress. I stood up and looked around, feeling my dress cling to my body, and then saw Alex, standing in a corner and talking to another boy.

He did not look very different. His clothes were cleaner and plainer than my friends' – a blue t-shirt, a pair of jeans – which made him look simpler, more stupid, less interesting. But his jeans were the right kind, his stomach was flat, and I was infinitely adaptable. He still looked like a lovely, strong animal. He'd cut his hair short. It was summer, and his skin looked brown and warm. I took a long swig of the beer I had been holding, but hadn't been able to drink while my friend wept into my chest, walked over to him and tapped him on the shoulder.

He looked around. Surprise – and a kind of terror – lit up his face, but before he could speak I said, 'Come with me. I want to tell you something.'

He raised his eyebrows at the boy he was talking to, and followed me out the front of the house. Once we were in the dark I turned, took hold of his shirt and kissed him. He responded straight away. That glittering, that prickling. I slid my hands behind his neck and brought him down to me. Both his hands came up and took hold of my breasts. He backed me further into the shadows, against a fig tree that grew over the path, its cold leaves embracing my body.

I was so overwhelmed by desire that I nearly went down on my knees, there in the garden. I wanted to. It was a fierce feeling. But we clawed apart and stood looking at each other, panting.

'We'll go to my house,' said Alex. He led me to his car, opened the door and pushed me in. It was an old Falcon with bench seats. He drove with one hand between my legs.

His house was a three-storey terrace owned by his father, in a suburb that was about to become very expensive. I had stood in front of many unfamiliar terrace houses in this way, brought there by someone whose life, however briefly, had opened up to include mine. Pretending to myself a kind of helplessness.

But there was no time for reflection. Alex was playing a part in a movie of lust: he caught my hand, dragging me in and up the stairs to his bedroom. I let him. I let him pull my dress over my head, I let him throw me on the bed, I let him climb onto me and fuck me without stopping to find out if I was ready. He had a move that he must have practised – he suddenly rolled over, gripping me, like a crocodile in the water with a body, so that I was sitting on top of him. It hurt, but it made him come, and I was able to collapse onto his chest, slide myself off to lie beside him. He passed me a handful of tissues to clean myself up.

We did not have much to say. We talked a little about Ben, who was living in London and working for a film company. His mother was still married to Alex's father. We did not look at each other as we talked, but stared out the window.

The view of the night from Alex's room was of trees, their leafy tops, swarming around streetlights, shifting in a slight, hot breeze that came through the open window. Every so often the breeze would break the leaves apart and the street light would flash into the dark room. I watched them, and pulled the sheet around my breasts, and drew my knees up, making a tent.

Finally, I said, 'Why did you tell him?'

'What?' Alex said.

I could smell wine and sweat, and semen.

'Why did you tell Ben? That we had sex?'

'I didn't. He guessed.'

I turned to look at him. His eyes were closing. 'Did you come?' he said, and then he was asleep.

I gathered my clothes quietly and put them on. I could not see the tissues in the dark, but I was leaking; I used a hand to wipe myself and then wiped the hand on Alex's sheets. He was beginning to snore.

It was a night so hot that it felt like daytime. Walking alone felt safe, not scary, not isolated. People were in the streets or sitting on their verandahs, the red ends of their cigarettes like animals' eyes in the darkness. A man who bumped into me smiled an apology and kept walking. I carried my boots and trod carefully across the cracks and leaves and gumnuts that littered the pavement.

There had been a party a few months after I'd first had sex with Alex, at Marco Giordano's. His parents were going away for the weekend. He lived in a huge pile down on the waterfront, bigger by far than Alex's father's, with grounds that reached right down to a little beach, and a boathouse that had couches in it, a bed, a fridge. Everyone was invited, and everyone was going, and Janice and Vicky convinced me that I should too. We would stick together, they said. We would get drunk.

We had been sitting by the water, drinking a mix of vodka, vermouth and scotch filched from our parents, watching an orange moon rise in the sky. It had begun to seem possible that I could be remade into someone fresher, happier. I'd needed to piss, and left Vicky and Janice to head up the long lawn to find a bathroom, grinning as I passed people. The bottom floor of the Giordanos' house opened onto the lawn through huge glass doors, which were all ajar. It was a big room with a slate floor, and wooden walls like a sauna. It smelt cold, and musty, as though this was the first time the doors had been opened. I went down a corridor and there was another door, wooden this time, and there was Ben, leaning against the wall with his hands behind his back. We had not spoken in three months.

'Is that the toilet?' I said after a moment.

He looked at me scornfully and said nothing.

'Hello?' I said, made stupid by the mixture of alcohol I had drunk. 'Anybody there?'

Ben made an explosive sound of disgust.

'Well?' I said. It might as well happen now.

'I've got nothing to say to you,' he said. I waited for him to say something more, but he looked away.

'Come on,' I said.

I felt a sudden rush of warmth towards him. It had not just been three months since I'd had sex with his stepbrother, or three months since we had spoken. It had been more than three months since he had moved into his stepfather's house. I allowed myself to think about this now. He had been dreading it so much that he had called me in the days before and cried, something I'd never known him to do. His asthma had got very bad.

'What's it like living by the river?' I said.

There was a long pause. I put my hands out to him, involuntarily, their palms up; a shrug, an apology.

'You really want to know?' he said, looking at me now.

I nodded, and looked back, properly.

'My stepdad keeps *Playboy*s on the coffee table. Guess what my mum does all day.'

'Drinks champagne?'

'Exactly. She drinks champagne and she dodges me whenever I come into a room. Just like you.'

'I don't think it's me avoiding you.'

'And guess what,' said Ben, ignoring me, 'the only good thing about the whole situation is Alex because, guess what again, or maybe you already know, he's nice.'

'You said he was an idiot,' I said.

'That was just to keep you off him.'

'What do you mean, *off him*?'

And then Ben gave me one of those tongue-lolling, leering looks that I'd been getting from all his new friends down on the oval. It was meant to be me, crazed with sex, and so I did the 1950s thing, for the first and the only time in my life, and slapped him across the face. And he slapped me back, so hard that my head hit the wooden wall behind me and the tears rushed into my eyes. And then the door at the end of the corridor opened and a girl burst out who I'd never seen before, a girl with her hair in a bundle of ribbons and little plaits and rags and beads, a girl in full Boy George costume, stinking of dope smoke. She laughed and stumbled into Ben's arms and kissed him all over the face and neck. Ben stared at me over her shoulder and started to kiss her back, in a way that made me feel sick, as though he was a mother bird feeding a baby. I backed away, too proud and ashamed to hold my stinging face, and then ran out onto the lawn and around the side of the house, into the dark, where no one could see me.

*

My boots banged against my leg. My dress was still damp from my friend's tears and my underpants from the sex with Alex. Ben had never spoken to me again; had finished school, taken Vicky to the formal, moved away, all without a word. He was capable of this, while I, it seemed, was capable of nothing but acquiescence, stillness, a kind of insidious, destructive passivity.

I turned up a darker street, a long one, which I would have to traverse in order to get home. Most of the people in this street were asleep. The only light came from the streetlights, which seemed a long way apart. It was cooler. The skin at my waist hurt where Alex had gripped it. This would be the last time, I said to myself, but it was not.

ANY DOG

SONYA HARTNETT

They're saying something about a dog. But there wasn't any dog.

Unless they mean old Taf. But Taf has been dead for years. There's no good reason to speak so loudly of Taf.

– The son kept mentioning this dog.

– The family's here?

– No, they're coming. I spoke to the son on the phone. He lives with the son's family, apparently.

– Did you tell them to hurry?

– I assume they're hurrying.

The boy in blue creases his nose. He shakes his head like a pony. He is a nervy and restless boy. His lungs must be like bellows, that big body full of air. God it's hot.

– The hottest day on record, they're saying on the radio.

– Yeah, well, it feels it.

Words roll from me before I can stop them. They flow down my chin like lava. It's not hot, I say. The men in blue both look at me. They are surprised. I've kept silent thus far.

I remember hotter days when I was a boy.

– Well, I don't know, Mr Collier. They're saying it's the hottest day on record. It's forty-four degrees Celsius out there.

– Forty-four! The boy clutches his head. Jesus Almighty! Forty-four?

The older one shifts closer. Mr Collier, your son said something about a dog. A golden retriever. Did you have a dog with you? Do you remember a dog?

He's staring at me earnestly. I gaze mildly back at him. Sweat is unpleasant on my skin, on my neck. The room which holds myself and the gentlemen is square and small and white. The furniture is cheap and itches. There is a NO SMOKING sign on the wall. Also a sign that says WHO IS WATCHING?

I've shut my mouth, I'm feigning ignorance, I'm saying no more. They're speaking of Taf, and Taf's not their business. Taf sleeps in my heart like a secret. Nobody knows he is there. I will not discuss him, disturb his peace. I will not let them put their thoughtless paws upon him. My memories are antiques, china-delicate: even I handle them only rarely, and then with utmost care.

It was a hot day, like this, the day I found him. I remember a sky like blue cream, free of clouds. I can, in fact, recall everything about that day, just as if I'm walking through it again. I'm twelve. It's a flea-market. There's grass underfoot. I am there.

The younger sighs heavily. We can't wait all day.

– It won't be all day. The son said he'd be here. Besides, would you rather be outside? It's a hundred times hotter out there than in here.

The young one's collar is an eel at his throat; he wrestles with it. Anyone's got the energy to break the law on a day like today, I admire them. Wouldn't you, Mr Collier?

– Mr Collier, can we get you anything? Something to eat, maybe?

My nostrils flare. I smell toffee. It's a thick sweet smell, a tooth-rot smell, making syrup out of the air. I see a crowd of faces, some grubby and leering, others church-white and mean. Music is playing, something cranked out of a box, four or five notes that trip over themselves like a hiccuping drunk on a road.

The younger one has his feet up on the seat. I have never sat in such a way. He is big as a colt, and impolite. He has the habit of thinking his own concerns are paramount. He's bored, he's hungry, he's hot, he's tired. He's not yet learned that nobody cares.

– What did the doctor say, anyway?

– He's a bit dehydrated. A bit sunburned. He's in pretty good shape, considering.

– Then he can't have been outside very long.

– Who knows.

– Well, he can't have been. Simple fact. I mean, it's hot.

I mean, this is killing weather. Walk around out there too long – especially wearing your Sunday get-up like he is – and you're going to die. Simple fact.

– Drink your water, Mr Collier.

I'm at the flea-market and the sun is on my head like honey, drizzling into my shoes. I'm wearing shoes and socks. Most boys wear bare feet. My mother says that I am not a ruffian and I will not appear as one. She has said DON'T GET INTO MISCHIEF, as if this is something I occasionally do. She's given me a handful of pennies. She stands behind the table of the parish cake stall. BE BACK BY LUNCHTIME, KEVIN.

I take a sip of water. It comes in a paper cup. The gentlemen are watching with proud, doting smiles. The older one should have his thyroid checked.

At the market the junk stalls face each other with a wide aisle in between. The aisles head north, south, east, west, they are tidy and angular as hedgerows – yet they also tangle like rambling roses, and soon I am lost. Perhaps, in truth, I know where I am, could return to my mother in moments if I chose, but when I stop and look around, I can't remember the twists and turns I've taken to this point, the stalls I've passed, the goods I've fingered, the people I've bumped against. All is commerce. All is noise. Doubtless there are shady deals being sealed in the shadows but, from where I stand, all is good-cheer. Babies howl. Children squabble. Glass is broken. Money rustles.

– So what did they say about the vehicle?

– The wife's car. A station wagon. Green. He took the keys from her handbag, apparently.

Pennies only buy things that I do not need. I have a room full of trinkets and trash; also other, more costly wares. Spinning tops, wooden toys, a train set, boxed soldiers. A leather ball, rocking horse, a tin engine, a marionette. I have these and countless more. I'm an only child, an only grandchild, an only nephew, inundated. I don't particularly care for this overflow of goods – but nor do I care to see my toys ill-treated and manhandled. When Mother invites boys over to visit, I am edgy. Too often, my possessions emerge from these visits the worse for wear. I feel the damage is done deliberately, it's jealousy or revenge or a show of strength. I don't know whether to be angry or impressed. I am clumsy with friendship, I know. I am shy, I lack conversation, I constantly feel the fool. I squirm, when Mother asks another CAN YOUR BOY COME OVER TO PLAY? Even worse: the boy squirms. I have begged her DON'T SAY THAT ANYMORE.

WHY, KEVIN? I remember everything about her, her smell, her teeth, her hair, her clothes. I could point her out in the street to you. I remember how her face twisted in pain when I said DON'T.

THINGS GET BROKEN, I say.

HE BREAKS MY HEART, she tells my father. HE'S SUCH A LONELY CHILD.

My father won't speak of anything emotional. He glances at the stove. Dinner is his emotion. Dessert has his heartfelt sympathy. WHAT DOES IT MATTER, he says, IF THE BOY IS HAPPIEST ALONE.

BUT HE'S NOT HAPPY. THAT'S THE POINT.

YOU'RE NOT HAPPY. THAT'S THE POINT. KEVIN SEEMS FINE TO ME.

And the predicament is that they are both right. I am happy alone. I am also lonely. I think I've been born inside a glass box. There's no place for me beyond its confines. But I am reasonably content inside my home. In privacy, I am almost perfect. It's the wider world which finds me distasteful. When my mother insists on cracking the walls, inviting the world, dismay and disaster must naturally follow.

– Did the son know where he was going, in the car?

– Wasn't sure. Said he's always agitating to go home, to the house where he grew up.

– Oh yeah? Where's the house?

– In Dublin.

The young one sprays laughter. Then gets a professional grip. Try to remember where you left the vehicle, Mr Collier. The green station wagon – remember? You were driving it. Then you stopped and got out and walked around. Did you leave the vehicle by the side of the road? Or in a carpark? Or maybe in somebody's garage?

– It could be anywhere.

– No, it couldn't. It must be close to where we picked him up. The doctor said he hadn't been in the sun very long.

– The doctor only said he's in good shape, considering.

– Mr Collier? Can you hear me? Mr Collier, do you remember the car? The station wagon? You were out driving today, remember?

– You're wasting your time. He's got dementia.

The young one's lip curls – I think he's frustrated. So what was he doing behind the wheel?

– He wasn't supposed to be. He stole the keys, I said.

The younger one says nothing. He shakes his head again. His mouth can't help twisting into a smile. He secretly likes theft. I look away.

Then I see Taf.

He's inside a wicker cage with four hearty siblings. Each of them is similar, but it is Taf I see. He's standing, his wisp of tail waving like a corn leaf in the breeze. His ears are folded like envelopes. He has a white stripe down his nose. The rest of him is the colour of toffee-apples – slightly red, slightly brown. His coat is short, but also long – enough to betray his lifelong tendency toward untidiness. I am the same myself. KEVIN, PICK UP YOUR CLOTHES. KEVIN, YOU'RE DROPPING PEAS.

I gaze at him and I know I will die without him. Already I know his name.

The man behind the table is selling second-hand novels.

The pups are his burden, not his merchandise.

HOW MUCH ARE THE PUPPIES?

He looks up. HOW MUCH HAVE YOU GOT?

I know without counting. She always gives me the same. TEN PENCE.

THAT'S NOT ENOUGH. EACH OF THESE PUPS COSTS TEN BOB AND A HANDSTAND.

A WHAT?

A HANDSTAND AND TEN BOB. ARE YOU DEAF? I COULD HAVE CHARGED SOME JUGGLING TOO, BUT THEY'RE NOT PUREBREED.

I have my fingers through the wicker. The pups are biting me. Their teeth are like talons. They cut to the bone. I WANT THAT ONE.

OH YER, HE'S MIGHTY.

I'LL HAVE TO ASK MY MOTHER.

GET GOING, THEN.

SHE'S OVER THERE. AT THE CAKE STALL. I'LL BE BACK IN A MINUTE.

DON'T LET ANYONE TAKE THAT ONE WITH THE STRIPE.

CAN'T MAKE PROMISES, BOY.

I can hardly bear to turn my back. I tear myself away. I speed like the wind through the crowd. I feel my feet strike the earth. I want to run, like a sheepdog, over shoulders and heads. My mother is not averse to animals. In fact, she likes them, as does my father. I have many books on the subject of the natural world. I've had a rabbit and a white mouse. I can identify many wild birds. But I've asked, before, for a dog, and my mother has said no. I don't know why she's taken this stand. I am not irresponsible, forgetful, or cruel. I am clever and obedient and accepting. Until today I have always taken no for an answer.

I run, dodge, weave. The crowd is bovine, slow, thick-boned. Waves of sickness and fear splash me. She'll say no and my life will veer irreversibly onto the wrong road. I will become criminal. I will become hollow. I will waste away.

At the cake stall, Mother is talking. I hop up and down distractingly. I fidget as if I have worms. Finally she looks at me. CAN I HAVE A PUP?

NO. HAVE YOU HAD LUNCH?

BUT MOTHER. THEY ONLY COST TEN BOB.

AND ALL THE REST. HAVE A SUGAR SLICE.

I stand back from the table, swallowing. I feel suspended, as if from a hook. In this moment there's only me in the world.

There is me and the cobwebbed, abandoned planet.

PLEASE, MOTHER.

She leans towards me. Her voice is hushed in the vain hope that the other mothers won't hear. WHY DO YOU NEED A DOG, KEVIN? WHY CAN'T YOU BE FRIENDS WITH OTHER BOYS?

My lips are cracking. BECAUSE I CAN'T BE.

I'm trembling. It's the truth. I can't be friends with the other boys. I will never. In my life there will be only me. I NEED A DOG BECAUSE I CAN'T BE FRIENDS.

MAYBE, IF YOU TRY – THEY'LL LIKE YOU, KEVIN –

NO THEY WON'T. THEY NEVER WILL. I'M TIRED OF TRYING. I'LL JUST BE ALONE, MAMA.

My mother glances at the cake stall women. They stand around nonchalantly. They are curious as hens to know what she will say. They have boisterous sons of their own who get smacked on the backs of the legs. This is a smacking situation. The women listen, because there's pleasure to be had in hearing a child denied.

My mother recognises the moment of decision. Perhaps she sees me standing at the junction of life's long roads, sees me wasting away. Her shoulders fall, her gaze subsides. She waves farewell to the child she hoped I would grow up to be. WHAT SORT OF DOG?

A hot knife goes through me. I do not look up from the cup-cakes and jam slice. I DON'T KNOW. NOT PUREBRED.

YOUR FATHER WILL BE ANGRY.

I'm about to fly. She stops me with cool fingers. Our eyes meet over the fruit-buns. KEVIN, she says, and nothing more. I know I disappoint and perhaps frighten her. It's not my fault.

I am who I am. I will never disappoint my dog.

He was still in the cage. He looked out at me.

MAKE ROOM, MAKE ROOM, sang the second-hand man. THIS

BOY MUST FLAWLESSLY PERFORM A HANDSTAND.

I was not particularly athletic or skilled. I thought the handstand would prove a second ordeal. But my legs swung up limberly when my palms pressed the dirt, and I never forget the upside-down sight of my shoes against the sky, dark as war, huge as planes, blotting out the sun.

*

Something makes a noise. A static cough. The man in blue speaks into a crackling box. When he lifts his arm I see great lakes have spread across his shirt. These men, this room, this furniture, it's repellent.

– The family's here.

– Thank God. We're not babysitters.

– Oh, I've seen worse. He hasn't been any trouble. Hasn't wrecked the place. You've been good company, haven't you, Mr Collier? You poor old thing.

– How did he know how to drive, anyway? He can't remember his name or address or how to tie his shoes. How could he drive?

– Oh, dementia's like that. Sometimes they remember stuff from years back, clear as crystal. They forget last week or a minute ago. He's probably been driving for sixty years. It's as natural as walking. But he can't remember the vehicle or the dog or whether he ate breakfast today. Those are just black holes.

I jolt in my chair. How dare they. Perhaps I've forgotten other things – inconsequential people, countless patients, the smell of my wife's hair – but never, ever my dog. The gentlemen reach out to calm me. I turn indignantly away.

Mind your own business. Don't touch me. There's plenty of memories I can happily do without, how dare they accuse me of forgetting the dog. That will never happen.

Of course, we don't like to hear that – that an animal can be as beloved, or more so, than any human being; that the company of an animal can be preferable and superior to the company of our own. Such notions dangerously expose our faults, so we ridicule them. We insist and insist that the animal is lesser. We point to their silence, their forgiveness, their stoicism, their peace. These traits make them lesser.

But sometimes – maybe often – an animal is more. Sometimes an animal is the sun which brings all that revolves around it into the light.

My father said WHAT'S THAT?

MY DOG.

Father glared at my wilful mother. Yet his softest spot was for dumb children and animals. Taf was mine, but my father loved him. My mother loved him. Taf bound our family. He belonged to me but had loyalty enough for each of us. He became our centre of affection and goodwill.

Each afternoon, when I came home from school, my mother would tell me the things he had done. His sleeping, his waking, his yawning, his barks. His watching through the wire fence, his sitting outside the store. His many admirers, his enemies. No dog had such charm. For her, he was a listening ear, a sharer of biscuits, the wiper of crumbs, the guard at the door. She babied him, mollycoddled him, brushed his silken coat. He once chased and apprehended a gypsy who'd been staring through the bathroom window.

My father was the Teacher of Tricks, and Taf liked to succeed. No dog could jump higher, run faster, turn tighter on a coin. When called upon to perform, Taf never made my father out to be a liar. On Sunday afternoons the pair of them walked for miles across the countryside. For Father, Taf was mischief. He chased birds and cows. He would vanish and reappear with a crafty smile on his face. Father would drum his palms on his thighs. WHO'S MY WICKED TAF THEN? WHO'S MY CLEVER FELLOW.

Myself, he was my shadow. Often I forgot to think of him as *dog*. Rarely did I call him anything but *Boy*. With Taf beside me, I became that respectable thing – a kid with his mutt. I stepped, with him, back from the brink. My life changed. I remained shy, awkward, and unbefriended at school – but I saw that I would be all right anyway, that I could survive nonetheless.

Lovely creature. You beautiful animal. After all these years I can still feel the warmth of you. My hand recollects the shape of your head, my eyes see your sunshined colour. You good, cheerful soul. How I loved you.

Part of me hardly dares even to think your name. Especially in these ugly surrounds. It's sacrilege. You dog, you holy relic.

You lived for fifteen years. A shambling wreck by the end.

Arthritic and bent, mornings were the worst time. You did not walk, you hobbled. Your eyes were blindly glazed with silver, your coat was powdered white. You were deaf, yet seemed to hear everything that nobody else could. You slept deeply, twitching, eyelids fluttering, moaning. In your sleep, you could see; in your sleep, you re-lived life.

You evoked pity. IT'S QUICK IT'S PAINLESS HE'LL THANK YOU FOR IT, YOU'D BE DOING HIM A KINDNESS YOU KNOW. I was heartless, because I refused. But I wanted you to die only when you were ready: for I would never be.

I was twenty-seven years old at the end. My calling was zoology, but my mother begged me to do medicine. Initially, I refused. I had no empathy or concern for my fellow man. I knew I would struggle to care sufficiently. But Mother wheedled. Medicine will save you, she said. Respect and prosperity are no bad thing.

You don't have to care. Just do it well. You can study nature on your days off.

I was at the hospital when Father rang. That morning Mother had found Taf down the side of the house, curled and colder than stone. My father had dug the grave by the time I got there. Mother had cut flowers from the garden. I wrapped you in a bedsheet and laid you in the hole. The three of us were stoic. Nobody cried. But neither my mother nor myself could watch the dirt tumble down on you. We walked away, not speaking, leaving Father to do it alone.

For weeks afterwards I found myself waking at night, anxious, aching. My bones felt hollow, my chest cribbed. I told no one that I was haunted by the desire to unearth you for a final glimpse. IT MUST BE A RELIEF, HE WAS OLD AND FRAIL. But it was no relief to think of him under the mud. I took him from its sodden grip and bid him lie down inside my heart. It was warm and safe there. Sleep, I invited him. Don't leave me.

A year after the funeral, I married. The bride was lovely, the wedding fine. Everybody said it was the happiest day of my life. I remembered the flea-market, the handstand, my boots against the sky.

– Look who's here, Mr Collier. Your son and grandson. They've come to collect you.

– Dad? Dad? It's James. How are you feeling? Do you remember what happened?

– Ask him about Luka, Dad.

– The older man leans closer. Dad? Listen to me. Do you remember what happened this morning? You took the car and drove around and then you must have parked the car and started walking. These policemen found you wandering around lost, remember? Dad, where did you leave the car?

This newcomer makes a lot of noise.

We had four children, I believe. I spent long hours working at the hospital. My specialty was lungs. I liked their determined deflate and revive, their canine faithfulness. I liked them for being the cleanest element of the system, their memories of the fresh air.

When I wasn't at work, I was out in the fields. Flora and fauna remained the sustaining interest in my life. I also owned dogs. Seamus, the laughing German shepherd. Flight, the quick-witted border collie. Good dogs, now with Taf. Sometimes I picture what my life would have been, were it not for the dogs. I imagine it as a habitable but sterile, unbroken, grassless land.

Of course, I taught my children to appreciate animals, and nature as a whole. I believe children learn such things best from a parent. To take a broad view of the world; to respect lives other than our own. I don't much like children – I find them, as I did in boyhood, discomforting – but I'm pleased I've passed on to others my abiding affiliation with a wilder world.

– Grandpa? Look at me. Where is Luka?

I gaze obediently at the youth who is the other newcomer to the room. His face is unfamiliar. I won't speak to him – he's impolite. His hair has not been brushed. I don't know who or what Luka is, and I wish he would go elsewhere.

– We've put the vehicle's description out over the radio. Everyone will be looking. No question, we'll find it soon.

The youth seems momentarily lost for words. He puts his hands over his face. It is an action of despair. I wonder why someone, so young and healthy, would think they had cause for despair. The indulgence of it. I could tell him some stories that might make him realise he isn't so badly off. From behind his hands, the youth speaks. We haven't got time.

She'll die.

– We don't even know if she is in the car –

– Where else could she be, Dad? Where else would she have gone? He's taken her. He's put her in the car and taken her for a drive, like he's always saying he will. And now he's lost the car, and he's lost my dog. And it's forty-four degrees out there!

He is shouting. He is an angry youth. I don't know why he's shouting. I don't know what he's got that's worth shouting about.

– Maybe he let her out of the car. We don't know that she's still inside it.

The youth gasps for air. He shakes his head. If he'd let her out, she would have stayed with him. She wouldn't have left him alone. She's locked in the car, Dad – you know it!

One of the men in blue speaks up. If your dog is trapped in the vehicle, it's possible a passer-by might see her there, and break a window to let her out. People are very aware of animals in distress.

The angry youth just stares at him. His face is very red. His eyes are filling with tears. My dog is locked in a car, he mutters. She's lost and locked in a burning-hot car.

One man moves to put a hand on him. The angry youth wheels away. He crosses the room and bends down to me. I shy in my chair. He's a disturbing stranger. He opens his mouth and words crawl out like adders. I hate you. I hate you, you revolting old man. I wish you had died years ago. You've lost my dog – you're killing her. You've left her to die in a burning-hot car. I'll hate you forever for this. Until the day I die, I promise, I will never forgive you.

– Don't, whispers the empty-handed man. He doesn't understand.

– He understands! the boy yelps. Where's my dog? he asks, and raises a hand. Where's my dog? he screams. You son of a bitch, *where's my dog?*

There are no dogs. Look around, you won't see any dogs. There's dogs in my heart, hidden away – I won't share them with anybody. The dogs of better times, that's what they are. The great and enduring loves of my life.

The man with empty hands leads the shouting youth out of the room. The youth is weeping now. It is not manly. Healthy, young, in the prime of life, he's got nothing worth crying about.

– Mr Collier, would you like some more water?

– Yes, I say. It's very hot; I'm thirsty.

The gentleman in blue hands me a paper cup. I drink the water slowly. It's refreshing. I'm sleepy.

It's been nice thinking of you again, Taf. Though there's years between us, these days I seem to remember you better than I have ever done. I hear you barking at the end of the street; I hear your claws click the footpath. Sometimes I believe I feel your loyal presence at my side. I've lived a full long life, Taf, but it has been a lonely one. When I die, and if there's any justice, may the first and last thing I see be you.

A CHINESE AFFAIR

ISABELLE LI

I dream of my mother again. She is sitting in front of the sewing machine, crying.

I press on the wooden blue door and it opens quietly. My father asks me to come in. He is lying in bed, looking at the ceiling, where cobwebs dangle at the corners. He is murmuring, but his voice is loud, echoed by the whitewashed walls. It is a winter morning before dawn. The fluorescent light tube is black on both ends, casting white light on my father's dark skin.

My mother wears a thick cotton vest. She hunches over the sewing machine, holding a piece of cloth with one hand and rolling the sewing wheel with the other, sobbing. Her tears are trickling down her plump face, her nose red. She grimaces in silence.

I cross the room and spread my arms to hold her, and I am woken up by a stabbing pain in my heart. My hands are on my stomach, sweating.

*

My husband is in his third stage of snoring, loud but even. The first stage is when he has just fallen asleep. He snores suddenly, waking himself up. He then turns on his side, starting the second stage, soft and varied. The third stage is now, when he is deeply asleep.

I get up and steady myself, feeling the soft hair of the carpet between my toes. I have become used to this – waking up suddenly in the middle of the night, as sleepy and as alert as a snoozing owl.

The hall is lit by the moonlight through the ceiling windows. Maybe moonlight has a slightly cooler temperature. I tighten my dressing gown.

On one side of the living area is an antique Mongolian chest in dark green and two Ming dynasty antique chairs in burgundy. Above the vase of artificial white roses and between two cast-iron golden candelabras, my husband's deceased wife is smiling at me. She is surrounded by other family photos, her eyes following my movements. I sit down on one of the antique chairs, feeling dizzy.

*

I told my mother I live in a house next to the beach. On sunny days I open the window and the white curtains blow in and out, depending on the direction of the wind. I sometimes put on a straw hat and a pair of sunglasses to take a walk among the beach-goers. I wear various shades of grey and blend into the surroundings. I become two-dimensional, a moving shadow, walking under the sun like a grey cat walking under the moon. On rainy days, I close all the windows and peep into the yellowish-grey sky and the greenish-grey ocean. Raindrops knock on the roof urgently like visitors keen to come in. I told my mother I live happily in an expensive house.

I told my mother I am an interpreter. When I was young, she hoped I would one day live overseas and work for the United Nations. I told her as an interpreter, I attend meetings, where people from different countries negotiate important matters. I interpret for businesses, educational institutions, and government agencies. I learn the jargon for macroeconomics, banking, insurance, fashion, medicine, including cochlear implants and IVF. I create Chinese names for expatriates going to China, and their wives and children. I find beautiful Chinese words from the dictionary, and explain the meanings to them, quoting Chinese poetry.

At night, I may be called in to interpret for counselling hotlines, when young mothers speak about losing their children to illnesses, middle-aged wives speak about losing their husbands to younger women in China, and old women speak about their loneliness at having no one. The counsellors sound as tired as I am, but they diligently ask the Chinese-speaking callers open-ended questions, reflect back the situations by paraphrasing, and name the callers' feelings. I hear 'What should I do? I cannot see a solution,' and I say 'What should I do? I cannot see a solution.' I hear 'Are you feeling trapped?', and I say 'Are you feeling trapped?' I speak for both parties as if I am having an internal dialogue, as if I am comforting myself, being simultaneously the suffering child and the hand that's combing through her hair.

I told my mother I was the interpreter at an international conference on a neurological condition in which two or more bodily senses are coupled. So I was not playing games when I told her the colours of people's surnames. I cornered our neighbour's youngest boy, not to bully him, but only to teach him the colours of numbers. I met a Chinese artist who painted lotus in crystal blue. In another painting he painted raindrops in yellow and he titled it *The Shower of Gold*. He painted me too.

*

I met my husband when I was interpreting at a writers' festival for a Chinese poet in exile. What the poet said did not make much sense but I tried my best to make it sound logical. At the request of an earnest audience, he read a poem from his latest volume. People applauded, not so much for his poetry because he read it in Chinese, but for his long hair and his animated voice. My husband came to talk to me afterwards.

I was in my Chinese costume, Prussian blue with gold and silver bamboo leaves. There seems to be some decorative value in a Chinese costume, which makes me feel like a porcelain vase, exquisite and brittle, to be treated with care, by others and by myself. So that day I walked with my chin high and my chest out.

My husband used to be a carpenter, known for his impeccable craftsmanship. After his wife's death, he studied a real estate course and worked in the property industry. After he retired, he started to learn to paint, visit art museums, and go to writers' festivals.

He has the look of a well-maintained and respectable gentleman. His jaw, once square, has lost its sharp edge. Like the furniture he made decades ago, he now looks subdued and reliable.

My husband's first wife died twenty years ago. She has large eyes, a prominent nose and a sensitive chin. She smiles contentedly in every photograph. Her last photo was taken on her forty-fifth birthday. She smiled from behind the elaborate square cake and the orange glow of the birthday candles, oblivious to the accident to happen a few days later.

My husband had been progressively reducing the number of her photographs in the house, until I noticed it and asked him not to. Instead I reframed some of them. My favourite is in an oval-shaped ivory frame displayed in a corner amid fine china. She wears a Chinese top and looks straight out of a 1920s movie. I also like an old photo of her mother and her six aunts sitting on the fence of their family farm. Seven young women, squinting under the sun, cheerful and relaxed, their frizzy hair and floral skirts flowing in the wind. I spend a lot of time walking around the house, feeling accompanied and blessed by the dead. I am safely buried in someone else's family history.

My husband's eldest son is a contractor for telecommunications projects. The second son is an accountant for a large chain of funeral companies. His daughter is a nurse in a mental-health hospital. She is the only one younger than me.

They are generally kind to me. Just like their father, they share a collective comical affection for me. My comments are exotic, amusing, controversial and not to be taken seriously. Once I told them an old neighbour of mine could read characters written inside folded paper. They all laughed. It has since become a standing joke.

I can afford to be controversial. I can blink my almond-shaped eyes and make provocative statements to peoples' faces. I once said, 'The world is made of strings of energies. A brick and I are made of the same basic elements. The strings vibrate differently to form different particles.' My husband stared at me, shaking his head, sighing, speechless. He did not speak to me for the rest of the evening, but he made me Masala Chai tea.

The next day coming back from the church, he said he was going to save a space for me in heaven. I looked up from my book and said, 'How do you know we are not in heaven already? Every realm has the same problem of increased population.' We were sitting in the garden under a weeping maple. The sunlight was filtered through the new leaves. My husband shuffled his newspaper but he did not turn the page for a long time.

My husband likes to think of me as coming from the middle of nowhere. He often mixes up my hometown with Inner Mongolia and he once believed I rode a camel to school.

I go back to China less often now. After each trip, I would be depressed for some weeks. I read Chinese books, browsed Chinese websites, listened to rock music from the pirate Chinese CDs, and talked to my friends in China on Skype. My husband asked why I did not listen to the equivalent rock music in English. I said rock is about anger and there is nothing to be angry about in his society. When probed further, I said I cannot explain because it is a Chinese affair. He was satisfied with my response; it confirmed me as his inscrutable oriental muse.

Going out with me is not without challenges for him. We walk on the street, and people look at us, older men with envy, older women with contempt, Chinese women with curiosity, and Chinese men with disgust. Those that are English-speaking talk to me in simple sentences. Those that are Chinese-speaking pretend to whisper knowing that I can hear and I understand. The funniest is when we see other mixed couples, mostly older white men with younger Chinese women, and we look into each other critically as if we are looking at ourselves in the mirror.

My husband took me on holiday one day. When we came back, we went to his house and it was repainted in crimson. A local landmark, it used to be called the white house. It is now called the red house. I accepted his proposal for marriage and the fact that he had a snip done years ago. I told my mother I am married to an older husband, just like Jane Eyre to Rochester, and we do not plan to have children.

*

I tell my mother many things, but I do not tell her everything. I do not tell my mother that I dream of her and the dreams are my worst nightmares. I dream of her being sick, being hurt, losing her way home, or falling. Even her smiles make me worry.

My mother is losing her memory. She hardly speaks and if she does it would be questions about the children or remembrance of the distant past. She walks very slowly and has great difficulty climbing up to their apartment. On winter afternoons, she often sits on the sofa in front of the television, and if asked, she says she is waiting for the weather forecast. She looks like a chubby child wrapped up in too many layers of clothing.

I have not written to my mother lately. I have not told her that I am nearly three months pregnant.

My mother once told me she was very hungry when she was pregnant with me. The only treat she had was three hardboiled eggs a day. She could not endure the intervals between peeling the eggs, so she always peeled them all before eating them in one go. She said she longed for fried rice during those days.

I have been hungry too, sometimes feeling a surge of hunger in the middle of a meal, and I have to start afresh. I often feel like a wolf wandering in the winter forest, tormented and isolated by my hunger. I feel like smashing the table when food is late and kissing the waiter or waitress when my food is carried down the aisle. When other people's food arrives ahead of mine, I regret every order I have not made. During the day, I give up my usual Vietnamese roll or sushi and go straight to chicken kebab. At home, my husband is delighted to see his hearty stew suddenly in demand. I pity the North Koreans – no one should suffer from hunger like that.

Sometimes I feel I am being eaten from the inside. Other times I feel like a ripe fruit, about to burst into something pulpy.

My nose seems sharper than usual. I walk by men on the street, and I account in my mind: beer; cigarette; Indian curry; onion; perspiration. What I consider natural smells are still better than some deodorants that smell like blunt knives, and some perfumes that hit me like broken glass.

I search the internet for articles and images. I know which day the egg was fertilised. It should have turned into a foetus this week with its sex apparent. I try to imagine a world where sound is muted. The blood flow the spring creek, the heartbeat the distant thunder, a rub on the tummy the autumn branches swaying in the wind.

I find myself talking to her, apologising for any stress I have put on her. I have become careful. As the bearer of a secret, I avoid stepping on manholes or walking under roof edges, I wait patiently for the lights to turn green at pedestrian crossings, and I move away discreetly from people who sneeze or cough. At home I keep away from the microwave oven when heating up soy milk and I wash my hands excessively.

I have put on weight, particularly around my mid-section. I have outgrown my pants and since the weather is warm, I wear skirts and dresses. Loose long tops with ruffles in front are the most deceiving. My body temperature is higher and I feel like a mini steamboat. My hands are warm and my forehead feverish. My husband says the extra weight I have put on suits me.

*

My husband is an experienced gardener but the only thing I can help with is the weeding. He mows the lawn, trims the rosemary hedge, applies fertiliser for the gardenia and cuts back roses, while I squat picking weeds from the garden beds or between the pavements and the gravel.

Every Saturday morning, when we are working in the garden, I wait to find the perfect moment. This is the time when I most want to tell, to confess, to unburden and expose. The calming new green, the fragrance of the spring flowers, the primitive labour, make me feel innocent. Sometimes I feel so tense that I almost cannot breathe. I have prepared a whole speech, but still I wait behind the curtain for the lights to dim and the spotlight to turn on. The audience will stop their polite conversations and turn their heads to the stage. Then I will go up, ready to be executed.

I did approach my husband once while he was cutting back the citrus trees. He was in his shorts and T-shirt, his knees and elbows looked dry, he was panting from manoeuvring the heavy-duty scissors. I asked him to follow me and sit in front of the lattice screen with star jasmines. The flowers had not opened but already the perfume was leaking from the rosy pink buds. I was in a green floral dress, a pair of sandals, my feet crossed at the ankles, my hands held together on my lap. I focused my eyes on the pavement, where a group of ants were carrying a dead bee. Just as I was about to start, he took my hand and held it between his palms. He said he had not been able to squat for a long time and luckily I could and it was very nice of me to do the weeding. Maybe we could use a gardener so we did not have to do everything ourselves. Then we would have more time to smell the roses.

*

The night air is damp and heavy, the moon has gone behind the cloud. The wind chime makes a timid sound, as if it too is afraid of breaking the silence.

I open the bedroom door as loudly as I can and switch on the light.

My husband raises his upper body on one elbow and squints under the sudden brightness. What is left of his hair is sticking up. His face is more wrinkled than usual, red from pressing on the pillow.

'I have something to tell you.'

'Come back to bed. You'll catch a cold. And turn off that light.'

I turn off the light and lie down. He reaches out his right arm under my neck and holds me from behind.

'We'll talk about it tomorrow,' he says. His left hand is on my belly.

ONE OF THE GIRLS

GILLIAN ESSEX

My bed's covered with clothes and I'm still not sure what to wear because it was only yesterday she rang and first I thought I hadn't heard it right that she wanted me to have lunch and listen to a band with her so then I had to rearrange things and I didn't even think about what to wear but I don't want to embarrass her though now it's too late so I settle for the skirt because at least it's black and I don't look so fat in it and then the doorbell rings and it's Emma and I haven't even put make-up on but I ask her if I look okay and she says fine without really looking then on the way I don't know what to say because it's been a while and she looks at the road because she's driving so I just gaze out the window then she asks me where I want to eat but I don't know so she picks somewhere and orders but I pay for it and then I eat most of hers as well as mine because all she's done is play with it just like when she was little and she gives me that look and it makes me try to hold my stomach in when we walk into the pub and she introduces me to the band and they're all flat-bellied skinny girls and I think about how bands always used to be boys

85

except maybe the singer but I call out hello to the girls then one of them comes right over and shakes my hand then Emma leads me over to a battered leather couch facing where the band is setting up and she tells me that this'll be comfortable for me as if I'm old or something but I think the stools off to the side might be better though I sit on the couch anyway and try to pull my skirt over my knees and think about how it would have been better if I'd worn jeans like everyone else here and I hope the band won't be too loud then she asks me if I want a drink and I do really but I tell her no because I'm off alcohol now and then I think I should have asked for a lemon lime and bitters but I don't even know if pubs do that anymore and she says she needs a drink so she goes to the bar and I think she'll come back but she perches on a stool and doesn't look my way again and I wonder if it'd be okay to get up and join her but it looks like she's chatting up the barman and at first I think she could do better than that but then I think it's a start and anyway maybe she's just relieved there's someone else to talk to besides me so I stay on the couch and wonder how long it's been since I've been in a bar and if all pubs are like this these days with fake wood panelling and mirrors and stainless steel fittings and metal furniture apart from the couch and hardly anyone here to listen to the band but it's only three o'clock on a Sunday afternoon and it's sunny outside and perhaps when they start to play people will come through the large doors that open onto the street and I suppose that's what the band's for but it looks like they're being paid in drinks instead of money by the way they're knocking back red wine in beer glasses and I wonder if they'll even be able to play and then in walks this woman and I think she's one of the girls because she's thin and she's wearing faded and ripped jeans and a T-shirt with writing on it and her hair's got different colours in it the way they do it these days only mine's the

86

same colour it always was except my roots are showing and she greets the girls in the band like they're all mates and hugs Emma but then she comes over to the couch and she says this must be the mothers' couch only I think she's said 'the mother's couch' but then she sits beside me and from close-up I see she's got wrinkles but they're covered in make-up and she looks fantastic and I wish I'd put mine on and she says you must be Emma's mother but I just nod and wait for her to go away because I'm hoping that Emma will come back and then she tells me she's Sophie's mother and I don't even know which one Sophie is because I didn't catch their names but Sophie's mother points out the girl who's adjusting the mike and it's the one who shook my hand and she tells me that Sophie's the lead singer and I think that'd be right and I look at Emma and think she must be just the groupie if that's what they still call them and then Sophie's mother tells me that Sophie's studying law but I didn't know you could be a lawyer with a ring through your nose and she says she didn't really want her to be a lawyer and I think why not and then she tells me that she supposes Sophie chose law because she's always been surrounded by lawyers and I guess if Sophie's parents are lawyers then that's how come Sophie's mother can afford to look so good and then she says she's worried about whether Sophie will have enough time to study with all the band practice she's doing but she tells me Sophie's just won a medal at the uni so I guess Sophie does all right and I just think about how Sophie's mother hugged Emma like it was the most natural thing in the world and Emma didn't even flinch or not that I could see and then Sophie's mother tells me Sophie's going off to work in an orphanage in Cambodia as soon as she's finished her degree and then she wants to work in human rights and I think oh God she's going to save the world as well and I wonder if Emma would have turned out better if I'd managed to stay with her father because then she wouldn't have been so angry and we would have had more money not that she's turned out badly it's just she hasn't worked out what to do with her life yet and she's never even had a boyfriend or not that I know of but I haven't been much of a role model there and I wonder if it's because of me but then Sophie's mother says she doesn't want Sophie to go overseas and I think why wouldn't you because I would have liked to and I think it would be great if Emma got to go like for me and then suddenly the band cranks up and Sophie's voice sounds like she's channelling Janis Joplin and yet she's so tiny and she plays the guitar as well and now the girls are singing songs they wrote themselves about women taking control of their lives and I don't know where they could have got that stuff from being so young and Sophie's mother's sitting there and she's mouthing the words like she knows all the songs by heart and she says she goes to all their gigs as if it wasn't obvious and I think Emma must too because Sophie's mother talks about Emma like she knows her really well and I didn't even meet Sophie until today and all the time Sophie's mother's been talking I haven't said a word but I suppose I'd better say something so I say you must be very proud of your daughter and I ask her if Sophie got her talent from her and she says God no so I say from your husband then and she laughs in a brittle kind of way and tells me that she hasn't got a husband and then I say are you a lawyer and she laughs again only this time it's more like a sob and she tells me she just works for a law firm that's all well actually she just files and cleans up a bit and makes them coffee but all the lawyers look out for Sophie and I wonder how Emma might have turned out if people like that were looking out for her or even if I'd just encouraged her more but there was always work and bills to pay though I suppose that's just an excuse really because I wanted to try and have a life before it was too late but then almost before I noticed she'd grown up and then she was gone and if I'd known it was going to be so quick I would have waited and we could have had more of a life together and perhaps if I'd taken her to music lessons she'd be on the stage like Sophie and I'd be the stage mother and now Sophie's mother is talking about how she and Sophie are close like sisters and I wonder what that would feel like and I ask how old Sophie was when her father left but she says there never was a father and then she starts to cry and she says that she was married once but she lost the baby then her husband left her and had babies with someone else and she was so upset she persuaded a friend to help her have one too but he wasn't too keen at first because he was worried about the legal stuff so she got a lawyer to draw up some papers and the lawyer took pity on her and he was the one who gave her a job because she didn't have one and wasn't qualified to be anything except a mother and now all the lawyers in the practice are good to Sophie but you know how lawyers are she says only I don't and I think that was some friendship she had but then she says she used a turkey baster to get herself pregnant and I didn't think people really did that but Sophie doesn't know because that was part of the deal and I think that anyone who tried that hard deserves to have a daughter like Sophie even if it is a bit weird so I put my arms around Sophie's mother because she's still crying and I tell her she must have been a good mother because Sophie's so clever and she cares about people but then Sophie's mother says she's really scared because she doesn't know what she'll do when Sophie goes overseas and what if the band becomes successful and goes on tour and she can't go with them and then she tells me she's on anti-depressants and the doctor keeps putting up the dose but it's still not working and she supposes that's why she's crying and she does it all the time and then I notice that Sophie and Emma are staring at us and I see the pub's filled up with people so I move my arms but I keep holding Sophie's mother's hand between us on the couch and I give her a tissue to wipe the mascara streaks off her face and then Sophie comes to the microphone and welcomes a new band member to the stage and it's Emma and she goes to the microphone and starts to sing and it's just backing vocals but I'm so proud and I have to let go of Sophie's mother's hand so I can clap but not too loudly and then Sophie's mother stops crying and says I didn't know Emma could sing and then I start to like her better so I tell her that it's time she started thinking about herself and that there's lots of things she can do now that Sophie doesn't need her so much but when I say this she looks kind of panicked and I think she must be scared of being alone and perhaps I should tell her that it's not so bad when you get used to it but then the band's packing up and Emma comes over and asks me what I think and I tell her the band was great and she was fantastic and I would have said more if I could have thought of better words but there's a look on her face like what I said's enough and then later in the car Emma thanks me for coming and she says it was good that I could keep Sophie's mother out of their hair because Sophie thinks her mother's embarrassing and she wishes she wouldn't come to the gigs but they noticed that I seemed to be getting on all right with her and she asks me what we were talking about but I just say stuff because I know that's what Emma would say and I don't think she really wants to know and then she tells me that the guy at the bar owns the pub and he encouraged her to sing otherwise she would've chickened out and that's why she had to have a drink because he told her it would help and that she should pretend I wasn't there until after she'd sung and then I start to think differently about him too but by the time she's said all this we're back at my place and I ask her in and she hesitates then shakes her head but then just as I'm getting out of the car she gets out too and she tells me how glad she is that I came to hear her first gig and she says she hopes I like Sophie because she and Sophie are an item but they can't tell Sophie's mother because she'll freak and she tells me she's going to Cambodia with Sophie and all the while she's looking at my face and I try to keep it the same but I tell her that I think I like Sophie a lot and going to Cambodia with her is a good idea and then she walks right round the car and gives me a hug and tells me I look great and she likes my skirt and she thanks me for lunch and says that maybe next time Sophie can come too and I say of course she can and then with a wave she's gone and I go into the bedroom and pick up the pile of clothes on the bed and carefully hang them in the wardrobe and then I catch sight of myself in the mirror and there's this little smile on my face and I sashay into the kitchen and make myself a cup of tea.

THAT VAIN WORD NO

BRENDA WALKER

> He said, repeating the opinion of Socrates in the
> Phaedrus, that a tree, so beautiful to look at, never
> spoke a word and that conversation was possible only
> in the city, between men.
>
> — SAUL BELLOW, *Ravelstein*

William is an old man, a surgeon, standing barefoot on a paved
driveway at dawn. He holds a hot-water bottle in his arms. He's
looking at his trees. Conifers trucked in from some place of
immediate forests. They're lined up along the driveway now,
deep in the earth, evenly spaced, shocked. These trees don't
show their misery yet, the foliage is firm and grey, but William
notices an unhealthy pliancy that wasn't there when they were
unloaded from the delivery truck. They will recover; they will
grow. In the meantime he breathes in the scent of Christmas
trees that reminds him of the smell of disinfectant in a dirty
urban train.

He was six years old, sitting by his mother, watching her take a square of chocolate from a man across the aisle, watching as she slid into a light diabetic coma that the other passengers mistook for sleep. The man folded the silver foil back over the remaining chocolate; his hands were white and small. William said *no, please no*, quietly, she heard him and she refused to listen and he lost her. As he sat alone beside her body he relaxed. If she could slip away then so would he. He noticed the disinfectant: pine-scented chemicals rising from something, vomit, blood, half wiped up by a railway cleaner days before, and closed his eyes. His mother began to stir at Central Station. So long ago, almost sixty years ago, and the smell of pine is waiting in his memory.

Birds sing, the sky turns white, then rose, then blue, the hot-water bottle cools against his chest. He hears the tearing sound of a blind spinning upward in Dan's kitchen, the empty voice of a politician from the radio inside the house where his coffee waits.

Dan helped him to plant the trees. They've been neighbours for a long time. William knows the details of Dan's illness, the name of the woman in Geneva who sometimes phones him in the night. Dan is vegan, thinner than William, lining up ten vegetables and five fruits on his kitchen bench each morning. It's kept him alive, kept the markers down in his blood. Dan says that if he doesn't die of cancer he'll die of starvation. He's a good cook, in spite of the restrictions. He often cooks for William. The trees were his idea; it's William's driveway but Dan organised the sudden view of the pine trees through his kitchen window.

The old men hacked at the roots with axes, freeing the young trees from their clenched and pot-bound state. Dan dug pits slowly and filled them with water and William steadied each tree in the earth. Then they ate together: black ragged mushrooms with chopped garlic for Dan, steak for William.

Late at night, back in his own house, William climbed the spiral staircase to his bedroom. At every step he had a new view of the room below: the cane rocking chair, the sisal mat. Photographs of his daughter, Nina. Alone, long after a long-exhausted marriage, he circled the few things he owned like a great bird moving upwards in the air, thanks to this staircase. And it carried him like a mother to his sleep.

*

William is driving by the river, later in the morning. Boats with firm white sails slip beside his car and veer away into greener ruffled water. The traffic has to slow so that cars can file past a cyclist on a fold-out bike. A tourist. A man who doesn't know his cycle paths, who has checked his folding bicycle through with the rest of his luggage in some truly distant city. Osaka. Dusseldorf. The cars slow, slice into the edge of the adjoining lane, ease past. The cyclist could slip and be destroyed in spite of all this irritated care. It's William's turn to pass. He guesses at the space the man will need, then looks in the rearview mirror and sees that the rider has a joyful hands-free smile. Each driver puts aside the light callousness of the morning rush, slows, then speeds away.

William gives the day's first patient his opinion of her illness. She sits with her husband beside her and William watches as the man's hands began to tremble. He smells fire, an electrical fire, just a faint smell, then he realises that the smell comes from the husband, from his skin and breath. It's fear. She listens calmly; almost everybody lapses into shock. That's why William draws diagrams; he writes instructions down. The patient tells him, quickly, that she has children. As if this will reverse his diagnosis. As if he'll change his mind. She's in jeans and running shoes. Some of his patients dress formally in black,

they make a funerary occasion of their appointments. I have a
rendezvous with Death. William tries to think of the cyclist,
smiling on the lethal metal highway. After she speaks she gath-
ers her things. In the waiting room William sees a child scramble to his feet, a boy about the same age as he was when he rode
in the train to Central Station beside his own unconscious
mother. This boy must belong to his patient. Her secret shield.
Surely a mother cannot be taken from her child. Surely even
Death plays by this rule: that a mother cannot be parted from
her child. The husband leaves first, then the woman with her
son's hand in her own. Quite often at the door he feels misgiv-
ings; he senses the vast appeal of simple denial; the refusal of
his surgery.

*

Once William's mother took him to a strange house in the city.
He remembers the narrow street, the shush of trains. His mother
left him alone with instructions not to follow her upstairs. He
was afraid to leave the room in case she disappeared. He pissed
in thimblefuls, thirsty but too frightened to look for a kitchen,
soaking the brocade and wadding of a chair, soaking his own
dark shorts. He was damp when she appeared at the foot of the
stairs. By nightfall the cloth barely rasped his skin. There was
no smell. His mother was at her sweetest, her most warm and
sad. He knew that she hadn't pulled it off, the new lipstick and
the astrakhan coat had been good for an afternoon upstairs but
nothing more. They were going to be alone, William and his
mother, or William would be alone in a wet chair guarding a
strange door.

He sees patient after patient with good news and bad, the
day slides into shadow, he takes a message on his mobile from
Dan. Dinner again, yes.

*

Dan's house smells of butter and polenta, of cornfields in summer. Or is it paper? Something good. William leaves his drink untouched; his hands are occupied with a metal lobster from Japan. Dan owns this kind of thing. Probably old. Yes, it's old, Dan tells him that it was made by a family in Kyoto who died, one after the other, leaving no descendants. Brown flanges clack into place as William curls the tail. It's a miracle. The legs are loose and jointed like early attempts at prosthetic hands.

Dan's phone rings. He takes the call in another room but William can still hear his voice, he's speaking a name over and over again, a single syllable, half-sung into the receiver to soothe or amuse the woman in Geneva on the other end of the line. Like a parent calling softly in the darkness. Dan at sixty-seven, dying, and in love. William suddenly realises that it's the voice Dan uses when he says his own name, which he does at times, dramatising a conversation, putting himself in the sentence. Dan loves this distant woman as he loves himself.

William remembers crowding into a lift in the city with his mother. He was too short to see her face. He reached for her hand and held it until the doors opened and she stepped out ahead of him and he found that he had been holding onto a pale man, who smiled but did not speak. Tonight there is nothing but his mother in his memory. Even his daughter Nina fades. Perhaps he should speak to Dan about all this.

Through the window, beneath the blind that he had heard Dan raise that morning, William sees his row of conifers and feels the relief of darkness for the foliage newly positioned in unsheltered sun, the relief of the slow restorative lift of dampness from the unfamiliar earth. He closes his eyes and listens to Dan's love, failing as his life will slowly fail but still musical with the confident failing music of all human love.

96

LA MOUSTIQUAIRE

GILLIAN MEARS

The girl crouches in front of a fire about the size and circular width of the leaf she intends to wrap around some of the beans that she has stolen from the man. She has his little silver flask too. The veins of the leaf seem to glow with a green fire that's nothing to do with the burning twigs. If I could become very thin, she thinks, thinner even than the man, then I'd slip through this leaf to become its sap. The beans are on a metal spoon, smoothed by the innumerable tongues and fingers of girls who've accompanied the stockman.

This girl has been with the stockman for nearly five years but sometimes they are still such strangers the girl thinks it's as if they've been sealed off from each other in candlewax. On other occasions, there's no separation between them. Being with the man then is like cantering on the smoothest horse imaginable. The man puts his nose against the girl's and holding only one nostril shut breathes out and in so that their breath becomes the breath of one creature – neither girl nor man but the animal whose shape she has seen only in dreams, or in the moving leaves of a tree against the stars. It has a horse's head but its ears are soft and round in a way that reminds the girl of the love poem the stockman once wrote. 'La moustiquaire', the man said it was called. 'For you,' he said, reciting, but the girl could understand nothing of it, as it was in the language he'd learned when he went away to the long ago war. Mosquito net girl, he says it means. Mozzie, he calls her or Ginny, the name he called the other girls.

Yet not even the night with the rodeo boy on the last full moon in town can equal what the girl feels for the old stockman. The man can't live much longer and although she hates the man more than she has ever hated anything, she also loves the man more than she has ever loved. With the boy she'd pretended to laugh at his jokes about old men but even as his hands were finding her again, she'd felt the pang of her betrayal. Wondering if the stockman was over his sudden sickness, she'd suddenly lost all interest in doing anything more with that rodeo boy. Even as he was throwing his leg over like she was another of his rides for the day, she was wishing she was inside a mosquito net with the stockman, listening to him reading.

*

The girl sighs. Already it's light enough to see a line of trees about fifty horse lengths to the right. Hovering in this way between day and night, the land looks downy, as if old stockmen have multiplied out there and lain down with their finely haired shoulders turned towards the sky. The three horses are tethered near another tree and look over. She takes a biscuit of hay over to them and, deftly, between her own knees, she picks up the hoof of the one who seemed yesterday to have a stone bruise.

At least there are no mosquitoes here. The girl puts the horse's hoof back on the ground. It isn't often when they travel away from the town that she doesn't have to stay up all night with the switch made of wild grass, waving mosquitoes off the man.

The old travelling net rotted about a year ago and although it could've easily been replaced, now the man prefers to call the girl, La Moustiquaire. Or 'Ginny,' he calls, stretching her out over him as if her skinny limbs are cotton net. He jokes that girls like her are more beautiful when tired, with the purple skin under the eyes deepening in the way of the coast at dusk. 'Your father must've been one of those really black black-fellas,' he speculates, but she won't ever say who that father might have been or where he got to or if she even remembers him.

*

She mashes the beans into a paste and pinches some salt out. Her hands come together. 'Thankyou beans. Thankyou leaf who is a little like me. Thankyou God.' She wraps the leaf into a parcel and eats.

For a moment the girl's jaw stops chewing and with alarm she listens. The air has filled with the moaning noise of insects. Then she looks up and grins. For it isn't mosquitoes after all. She's sitting under a tree full of flowers and it's just bees, floating around the yellow blossoms.

Everything seems to be playing with me! she laughs. In a spiderweb there seems to be a heart shape on a string. And look at the sun! The more she stares, the more the sun pokes out its tongue. Even the sun wants a go at me, she thinks. Then, worried by this thought, she picks up the hip flask.

The rum almost instantly dries out all extraneous thoughts. So that's why the man has never allowed her any. She tips it into her mouth again and rocks back on her heels. Selfish, selfish, she thinks. Crazy old slutfish. She utters a few more obscene words and suddenly hopes that when she returns to the tent, the man will not want to get up immediately but will order her to take off her clothes and lie down on the square of blue cloth. I will pretend I'm with the boy. I will suck his old so-and-so until it goes foamy like the sea. Although she hasn't seen the boy for a while, she feels he isn't far away and that his face, smiling this way, contains all the haziness of a summer.

As the vision of the boy fades, she drinks all the rum and lies down. Suddenly she feels the mixed animal whose name she doesn't know is very close. It half hops, half runs but no, it is clearly a young bridal veil wallaby, she sees that now. White people are killing wallabies with knives and clubs. It's the time of blood and in the distance she can hear human babies crying. She knows they are babies with skin as black as her own and that like the wallabies, they're going to be harmed.

Oh, but it's too much. White women laugh and show their teeth. Even though they are only watching their men, the girl sees the power that the killing bestows. Under their dresses, she senses their breasts becoming even whiter, like huge dampers rising, threatening to smother the land altogether.

She sees that the killing makes them powerful in the same way she feels power over all the mosquitoes she's destined to kill, or the mice in the horse's oats whose tails she sometimes seizes, swinging their heads against a stone with a sharp crack.

When she kills mice the stockman smiles and loves her and says she's like a bloody good dog. Good at anything. His best Ginny ever. And he tousles her hair like it is indeed the ruff of a dog.

The girl sits up and spits. The twig fire's gone out. It's time to creep back to the old man's tent. First she goes across to the horses who prick their ears hopeful of an early feed. She scratches their tails instead and the favourite spot behind the wither and tells them that probably by this time tomorrow, they'll be back in town. 'There,' she says, pulling off two bottle ticks, 'that must feel better.' She licks her horse's neck where the salt from yesterday's sweat has gathered, in the hope that it'll hide the taste of her mouth.

When the girl ducks down into the tent, she sees with horror that the stockman is as if carpeted in mosquitoes. He has come out from his cover, the better it seems to feed the numerous mosquitoes that have been feasting in the tent. Panic-struck, she picks up her switch but it's of utterly no use. It's simply a miracle that the man sleeps on through such moaning. Surely there can only be one explanation. The man has fallen into that which he has always most dreaded. He's in the mosquito fever from which there is no return.

The mosquitoes, at the presence of the girl, rise for a moment like little blood suns, like a multitude of demon spirits with fiery gold wings and red bellies. 'But I am to die first,' she says. The stockman has always said this. That it's the fate of her race. That if she leaves him she'll end up buried young in a shallow reserve grave the dogs'll dig up. She utters the man's name which even though it is ridiculous and ill-suited is the only one she has to use.

The girl puts her mouth onto the man's but there is no response. The girl slaps the man and shouts that at the very least he could've fallen into a normal fever first. 'They'll think I killed you and stole your booze and bible.' The girl lets forth a volley of violent words. The man seems deep in his own breath and has tucked his hands into his armpits in the way of a sick bird.

Now she holds the man in her arms, the way the man has never allowed. He is just a tiny little fella really. Without his boots on, not much more than her size. She cradles the face. She forces open the stockman's mouth, trying to induce him to take a nipple. At the touch of the old man's lips, one nipple forms a drop of whitish dew. She looks deeply and sees the face his mother must once have seen, when he was just a baby. For a moment it seems that the man's going to suck but his lips loosen and, skinny though he is, he's too heavy to hold up anymore. Then she wipes the brylcreem from his hair off her breasts with sudden disdain. 'Funny, seeing you without your hat on,' she comments but he doesn't reply.

The day inches along. Now the girl grows impatient, wishing that the man would hurry up in the taking of his last breath. And what a rotten breath it has become. If God is breath as the man has said, then God is surely rotten. The girl feels the familiar revulsion. A wasp flies down towards them and then out of the flap to the outside. Then another.

'The bible's hatching!' The girl in one leap is at the book, sealed up last visit to town by a pottery wasp building her nest along the pages. The man had taken it as a sign. That not until the wasplings had hatched and flown safely away would it be time to resume his readings.

Two perfect holes now pierce the mud and from within comes the humming noise. The girl goes back and leans down to the man's ear to convey her excitement. The hair of the man's ear shimmers as if traced in late evening water seen from a track, but he doesn't appear able to hear. The girl feels bitter. Her shoulders slump down in the most downcast of ways. After all their waiting, for the book to be released but for the reader to be dying.

Throughout the day, more wasps hatch and many memories come and go. Then, when the sun's right overhead, the man grows suddenly much older, before, just like that, just bloody like that, the little bay filly that got the lockjaw dies right before her very eyes. The girl spits at the man's feet because not once during the entire length of the day has the man so much as acknowledged her presence or joined in the excitement over the wasps.

'What do you do anyway, with such an old man?' the rodeo boy had wanted to know.

'We're waiting for a book to hatch,' she'd replied, completely sick of the boy and his fingers.

*

When she cries it's because she always knew much more than the man. She, not the man, has lain on the earth and felt the strong lines moving through her like God and the waterbird with wings as outspread as the big altar, flying through darkness to enter through her hands.

Now it's too late. She can never tell the man about this or look directly into his eyes. Cautiously, the girl pushes her thumbs over the lids and pulls them down. As soon as she lifts her fingers, though, the eyes come open again.

Remembering how the man once seeled the eyes of a brown hawk, she thinks that this is what'll have to be done. He'd found the book on French hunting birds in that green bedroom above the pub and for weeks had been determined to get a brown hawk to catch rabbits for them. The baby hawk he got out of a nest never did any hunting. 'It died didn't hit,' utters the girl sadly, not bothering to correct her pronunciation the way he'd liked. She searches around in the saddlebag for the mosquito-net mending needle and thread, hoping that the man has thrown it away, but it is more or less in the place where it always was. Grave now, she threads the needle. There's not much light left. Old man skin must be tougher than hawk lids. She cries. For the man. For that poor hawk and how its eyes got full of pus.

Another wasp finds its freedom and hangs low beside them. The girl wishes that she could read something from the book for the man. 'Well, you were quite a nice man,' she says instead but the words come out sounding like an accusation.

The bird the stockman used to call The Cup Overfloweth Bird begins to call and there comes the feeling of bright uncontained liquid running in every direction. It calls and calls like liquid and seems to belong to no specific time at all. It could be two thousand years ago or two thousand years ahead. The bird leaps out of the purple tree and its wings look to her like the rodeo boy's dark red shirt when he's in the shute for the last ride of the day. She drinks all the rum in the big bottle and feels so sick she thinks she too will lie down and die for a while.

Later, gulping down water at the tent's opening, trying to dissolve her uncertainty, she claps her hands and clicks her tongue. 'By and by,' she tells the man, 'we'll come back for you,' knowing that no such thing will happen and that after this night she'll never see the stockman again. 'I know,' she says, and finds his stash of black jellybeans. 'We'll leave you these.' But then one by one she eats them. 'I'll ride your horse,' she says, 'and you'll see how smoothly she travels for me.' She makes a dismissive gesture with her hand. 'I was always a better rider than you.' In the town she can sense it's that time when the dust is hanging in the air and the mandarins the man likes to eat from the tree by the travelling stock route would probably still be too green.

In the last light left she takes the bible into her hands and examines how perfect and round are the leave-taking holes of the insects. Nothing has ever looked so simultaneously complete but empty, so full of potential but so spent. One chamber was never filled and sealed and she pokes her finger into it before tapping the whole nest off the book. On the underneath of the nest she can see where the mud the wasp collected was dark and where it gleams with silvery river sand. She has covered the man in the blue blanket. When she looks underneath she jumps backwards, for the man's feet have taken a different position. Even when dead the man tries to keep his feet in the stirrups, thinks the girl and feels a grudging kind of admiration. The man's face looks like a rock now, blank but vast and excessively salty. She drops the bible that as much as it brought them violently together, helped shamefully to hold them apart.

In the light of the fire she builds, the horses look like they're preparing for an end of show parade, dancing at the end of their ropes. Below his forelock, Boney the white gelding's face looks rosy, as if his cheekbones have been rouged. Big horse yawns seize the girl. She hopes the fire will last until morning.

The mosquito when it comes towards the skin of the girl's arm comes tentatively at first, then more surely. I can feel the wings, she marvels. Like a small mouth blowing. Like a little breeze.

She watches the mosquito's beak tapping, then experiences a small sting. Gradually the abdomen of the insect fills with blood. When the girl sneezes in response, she feels every particle of moisture as it lands on her body and the mosquito flies off, only half full. If the stockman was alive the girl would have to hide that she's no longer the extraordinary black girl from the coast that mosquitoes won't touch. Now, like any other girl, the mosquitoes form in a spiral above her head. Now she just watches.

The unknown animal hops across the night without moving, formed of stars. The girl waits for morning which seems longer away than ever before. On the caps of her elbows, on the edges of her ears and toes, the welts of the mosquitoes are already rising and beginning to itch. More mosquitoes arrive. When she chucks the bible into the fire she is sad all over again. One day, she'd thought, like a perfect leap on old Boney over a fallen tree, their separation would be severed. Now all the possible moments have passed. Now the bible burns like a grey fan; the colour plate of Jesus in the Lily of the Fields going into ashes; red coals taking away all those little words in the way of ants taking eggs.

THE MOVIE PEOPLE

FIONA McFARLANE

When the movie people left, the town grew sad. An air of disaster lingered in the stunned streets – of cuckoldry, or grief. There was something shameful to it, like defeated virtue, and also something confidential, because people were so in need of consolation they turned to each other with all their private burdens of ecstasy and despair. There was at that time a run of extraordinary weather – as if the blank blue sky, the unshaded sun and the minor, pleasurable breeze had all been arranged by the movie people. The weather lasted for the duration of the filming and then began to turn, so that within a few weeks of the close of production, a stiff, mineral wind had swept television aerials from roofs and disorganised the fragile root systems of more recently imported shrubbery.

My main sense of this time is as a period of collective mourning in which the townspeople began to wear the clothes they had adopted as film extras and meet disconsolately on street corners to re-enact their past happiness. I didn't participate. I was happy the movie people had left. I was overjoyed, in fact, to see no more trucks in the streets, no more catering vans in the supermarket parking lot, no more microphones and boom lights standing in frail forests on corners or outside the town hall. The main street of town had been closed to traffic for the filming, and now the townspeople were reluctant to open it again. It's a broad street, lined with trees and old-fashioned gas lights (subtly electrified) and those slim, prudish, Victorian storefronts that huddle graciously together like people in church, and as I rode down the street on my scooter on those windy days after the movie people left, it struck me as looking more than ever like the picturesque period town, frozen in the nineteenth century, that brought the movie to us in the first place.

I rode my scooter to the disgust of women in crinolines with their hair braided and looped; men in waistcoats and top hats: citizens of some elderly republic that had been given an unexpected opportunity to sun itself in the wan light of the twenty-first century. I knew these people as butchers, plumbers, city commuters, waterers of thirsty lawns, walkers of imbecile dogs, washers of cars, postmen, and all the women who had ever taught me in school. They were so bereft that they stayed in the street all day. They eddied and flocked. Up the street, and then down again, as if they were following the same deep and certain instinct that drives herring through the North Sea. They consulted fob watches and pressed handkerchiefs to their sorrowful breasts. The wind blew out their hooped skirts and rolled the last of the plastic recycling bins down the street and out into the countryside, where they nestled lifelessly together in the scrub.

I rode my scooter to the home of my wife's parents. She was sheltering there, my wife – Alice – because the movie people had left. She loved them, see. Not her parents – that tranquil couple of bleached invertebrates – but the director, the key grip, the costume ladies, the hairdressers, the boom operators, most particularly the star. The whole town loved the star. Even I succumbed to it, just a little – to the risky and unpredictable feeling we all had in the weeks he was among us, that he might at any moment emerge from a dimly bulbed doorway or unfold his long legs from a rooftop. We'd never seen anyone so beautiful. He shone with a strange, interior, asexual light; and his head seemed to hang in mid-air, as if there was no body to attach it to – nothing so substantial. Looking at him was like entering a familiar room in which you see everything all at once; and at the same time, nothing.

I rode to my wife and said, 'Alice, darling, he's left now, they've all left, so can you please come home and love me forever; entangle your limbs in mine on the couch while watching television; comb your eyebrows in the bathroom mirror when I'm trying to shave; go running with me in the gorgeous mornings; and dance guiltily, ecstatically with me to bad disco music in the kitchen?'

But Alice, who now wore the costume of a sexy, spinsterly librarian, trim with repressed desire and lit, at her throat, by Edwardian lace, only sat on her parents' chaise longue embroidering silken roses with inconsolable fingers. Her parents sat nearby; her father, that placid old sinner, was now dressed as a country parson with a monocle in his crooked eye, and her mother peered out at me from the battered piano, which until recently had been nothing but a prop for picture frames. Now my mother-in-law played it with a watchful plink and plunk, with maternal suspicion tinkling over the expanse of her oatmeal-coloured face, and a frill of veil in her ornamental hair.

Other times I visited, the door was opened by a sour maid who informed me that my wife was not at home.

'Is she not at home?' I asked, 'Or is she not *at home*?'

The maid, with a grim, polite smile, shut the door in my face.

The mood of the town improved with the success of the movie. A special preview was held just for us, in the town hall;

we sat in the municipal pews and called out the names of everyone as they appeared on screen in a long and lustful litany. Each name we invoked brought laughter and teasing, but really we were all overcome with a kind of bashful pride, as if finally the world had reached a solicitous hand into our innermost beings and, liking what it found there, held us up for emulation and respect. We were so distracted that, afterwards, nobody was sure what had actually happened in the movie. A forbidden love, generally – something greenish and unrequited – one of those glacial *fin-de-siècle* stories in which the tiniest gestures provoke terrible consequences about which no one in polite company speaks.

At the premiere party, the townspeople danced the gavotte and the quadrille; they waltzed among potted palms with a slow, bucolic concentration; and they feasted on tremulous dishes of jellies and aspic. All throughout that strange, orchidaceous, combustible room, women fainted into arms and onto sofas, and a tiny orchestra of men with Civil War whiskers played endlessly into the night as Alice – my Alice – danced time and double time and time and again with the star, who appeared to have flown in especially for the occasion. Her parents nodded and smiled and accepted the nods and smiles of other doting gentry, and Alice flew over the carpets, her face alight.

I demanded of everyone I met: 'Who does he think he is? Just because he's famous, he can dance all night with another man's wife?'

Unlike that decorous crowd, I was insensible of my own dignity. Finally, the man who used to service my scooter (dressed now in the handsome uniform of an English corporal, which made of his red belly a regimental drum) drew me aside and told me that the man Alice was dancing with wasn't famous at all; he was, in fact, Edward Smith-Jones, a man of the law, and selected from among the population as the star's stand-in. Apparently it

was obvious to everyone that the entire scene in the stables featured this man and not the star, who was nervous around horses,
especially during thunderstorms. So there he danced, lordly
Eddy, with another man's wife and another man's haircut, and
I watched his hand rest on her supple back and my heart was
filled with hatred for the movie people.

When I asked Alice for a waltz she told me, with a demure
shake of her head, that her card was full.

I lost my job when my graphic-design firm was asked to move
elsewhere. Certain other sectors of the citizenry, too, were
politely dissuaded; the Greek fruit shop became a dapper green-
grocer's, manned by a portly ex-IT consultant with Irish cheeks
and a handlebar moustache. He stood jovially among his gleam-
ing bronze scales, measuring out damsons and quinces. Unless
they were willing to wear their hair in long ropes, the town's
Chinese population was encouraged to stay off the main street
between the hours of eight-thirty and six, and preferably to
remain invisible on weekends. The gym was forced to close for
lack of customers, and the Video Ezy. The tourists came in
excitable herds, transported from the nearest town in traps and
buggies. They mistook me for another tourist, and I was comfortable walking in among them, watching as my wife strolled
in the botanical gardens, her face in parasol twilight; a brass
band playing in the rotunda; a British flag afloat above the trum-
pets; nannies sitting with their neat ankles crossed on benches
as children toddled close to duck ponds. Alice walked with her
Edward, and her parents followed close behind. She tilted her
head this way and that. In the movie she had been one of those
extras who almost has a speaking part; the kind they focus on
to gauge the reaction of a comely crowd.

When I heard they were engaged, Alice and Mr Smith-Jones,
I retired my scooter. I took a job at a printing press, and the

tedious hours of setting type gave me finicky time to think things over. On the day of their wedding, I dressed in costume. In the movie I play the role of a man about town; you can see me in the lower right at 20:16, loafing with friends on a street corner while gauzy women flutter behind us, in and out of seedy cottages. Yes, right there – I'm the one watching the dog.

I walked to the church among apple carts and small sooty boys, and there was a yellow quality to the air, a kind of residual loveliness, as if the sun had gone down hours before but stayed for some time just below the horizon. The church doors swung open before me, revealing soft pale heads among bridal flowers. The parson – my father-in-law – trembled on the moment when I should speak or forever hold my peace. I spoke. Eddy and I met in the aisle; he swung and I dodged and I swung. Alice shook in her slim white dress, and roses fell from her hands. I floored Eddy; he pulled me down. We rolled on that ecclesiastical carpet, up and over and around and down, while flustered ushers danced around the edges of our combat. Ed would be on the verge of springing up, a lawyerly Lazarus, but I clawed him back down; I, on my knees, would be making my way altar-ward, only to find him wedded to my foot. The organ began to play. The congregation piped in alarm. An elderly woman keened among her millinery. Finally we exhausted ourselves, and it was me – me! – Alice came to comfort. I knew she would recognise my supplicant heart. Edward was banished, and loped away into the high noon of heartbreak. Her counterfeit father was ready to join them in mock matrimony, and so with a merry shake of his worldly head, he re-joined us instead. The sun set, and the moon rose. We ate ices at the reception, and great silver fish surrounded by lemons, and that night, as she withdrew her slender foot from a slender slipper, my wife shuddered with a virginal blush and laid her head upon the pillow.

There followed a happy time of croquet and boating expeditions; then Alice went through her suffragette period, which I pretended to disapprove of. Things are more settled now. We read Darwin together, without telling her parents, and she's discovered Marx. We take walks in the country, where my naturalist wife sends me scrambling into trees for birds' nests. Things aren't what they used to be, but there are consolations: a certain elegance to the way she stands at open windows, and longer, darker nights now that the town has switched from electricity to gas. But I've noticed in her lately a strange inability to see the resemblances between things: a tennis ball (she plays modestly, in white dresses) is nothing like the sun; a glass of water, she says, has no relation to the ocean; if I comment on the similarity between her neck and a swan's, she turns away. In fact she dislikes the similarity of things even without recognising their likeness, and can't bear, for example, to see a brown short-haired dog on brown short-haired grass.

The rest of the town is like this too. They have a horror of seeing photographs of themselves, even the hoary daguerreotypes they love so much. They've removed all the mirrors from their houses, and the paintings of jaded horses on hillsides, and the china that depicts, in blue and white, the far-flung tale of luckless lovers. It's as if they're allergic to the very idea of reproduction; or at the very least, don't wish to be reminded of it. What a singular world they all live in, in which no thing has any relation to another!

They no longer mention the movie. They no longer watch movies. They expect to live forever. They've taken up laudanum. They seem happy, however – timeless and happy. I watch them all, a little wistfully, in my fraudulent frock coat. Meanwhile, the trees shake out their leaves in the wind, and in the evening my wife walks through the spent garden. Her face is like a flag that says – *surrender.*

THE NEW DARK AGE

JOAN LONDON

Now that the long winter was over, and all the clues to his convalescence, the little table by the couch for his books and remote controls, the earthenware pot for Chinese herbs, the meditation tapes, had been packed away, now that he'd resumed his place in the world, George was conscious more and more of a twinge of misgiving, like guilt or nostalgia, as if for something or someone he missed.

In the shop, old customers and friends congratulated him on his recovery, with eyes that followed his to avoid looking at the thinness of his body. He said *cancer* whenever necessary, not 'sick' or 'unwell', in the same way that he'd said *die*, refusing 'pass away'. Back from the brink, he discovered that he had an urge to bear testimony. What was his message? What did he have to tell them?

Every time he tried to collect his thoughts, someone interrupted him. Of course he was tired. The lunchtime rush made him dizzy. There was also the Rip Van Winkle effect: he had just installed the computer when he left for hospital, leaving

Ulla to wage a single-handed battle with its teething problems, and she was now very much the expert. She'd even fed a 'Welcome Back George' logo onto their receipts, though he soon put a stop to that. In a return to their old sparring form, she accused George of being a Luddite. Not at all, he told her gravely, modern pharmacology had saved his life.

It was his tenth day back, but still the shop did not look like his. There was a subtle change of direction in the stock. Ulla, not having strong musical tastes herself, always responded to the market. They now sold a lot of that alternative pop rock, Alanis Morissette and Nirvana, and compilations of World Music, and more well-known classical pieces, especially if they'd become a movie theme. Meanwhile Country and Western, contemporary jazz, the avant-garde, had dwindled, gone ragged, lost their edge. Some of these he found in a newly labelled bin, 'Discount Discs'. Ulla had the print-outs to justify her decisions, but he noted that some of his favourite customers, the ones for whom he put aside new recordings if he thought they'd like them, had trickled away.

All this of course he could turn around in a few weeks. The thought made him weary. Although he'd always said that *George's* was just a way of making money to support his music habit, there was a time when he'd been happy to feed it all his energy and creativity, and taken pride in its success, but that seemed long ago. Now he wondered if he was really suited to being a businessman. Out the window the newly renovated arcade with its little trickling fountain looked like a film set. People ambled past, licking ice-creams, bathed in a kind of cathedral twilight. It all looked false to him, temporary, unreal. He'd preferred the old premises, between *Perretti Tailors* and the *Wing Lo Deli*. Perhaps the rot had started to set in a couple of years ago, when they moved into the smarter end of town.

But what would he rather be doing?

Late in the afternoon, on impulse, he put on the little Brahms intermezzo which he had listened to all through the winter. At once he was taken back, so intensely that he felt exposed, and went to listen in the office. What an austere, intense winter it had been, his season of reckoning. Day after day he lay on the couch as the leaves fell in the courtyard and his life unravelled before him. He was like a monk, in loose clothes, his bald head covered by the dark red Tibetan beanie Kristina had found for him. There seemed to be a ring of silence around him. Chaste, isolated, engrossed, he was cut off from everyone except Kristina. His daughter Grace sent him loving postcards from South America where she was travelling with her boyfriend. He had Kristina to himself. He waited all day for the sound of her key in the door and the sight of her tired, pale face with its new anxiety and kindness. He couldn't have survived without her.

In the cruel, colourless twilights he saw that all his time had been spent in accommodating people, keeping the show on the road, in compromise and self-deception. So here you are, the little melody seemed to say, this after all is how it is. He felt as if the most innocent part of him had sat down and wouldn't go on.

*

Before the piece had ended he realised that the shop was empty; no browser could bear too much of Brahms's penetrating sadness. Ulla had turned to look at him through the glass partition of the office. Their eyes met as she peered over the top of her tortoiseshell glasses and he saw the sharp, watchful query in them.

He watched her moving on along the shelves, with her cropped grey hair and her habitual white shirt and black slacks, her diligence like a reproach to him. She felt his distance, sensed that everything had changed. He knew her ethics, her sense of fitness. She had not received her due. Not that there hadn't been lavish thanks, and a generous bonus. But she deserved to share, however symbolically, in his recovery. She had contributed to it. She expected a gesture of acknowledgement.

Still affected by the spirit of the music, he walked out of the office and asked her home to dinner.

As soon as he issued the invitation, he regretted it. Ulla pulled out a bus timetable from her bag and pushing on her glasses, consulted it. She announced she would have to catch two buses. He'd forgotten the whole painful ritual. Ulla, for reasons of her own, did not drive, but utilised very ingeniously the scanty public transport system. She tackled travelling arrangements with an air of moral challenge. She was skilled at arranging lifts from neighbours, friends, even customers. Also she walked great distances. She was solid and fit with tanned sandalled feet and a healthy flush on her cheeks.

Years ago, when he first opened *George's*, she often used to come to dinner with Grace and him. She always arrived early, sometimes hours early, so that she ended up chopping parsley, walking the dog, reading bedtime stories to Grace.

He'd just come from a bad divorce and knew nothing of business. In that first year there was no detail of his new life, from invoices to child-rearing, that he did not discuss with Ulla. That was twelve years ago, long before Kristina. When he was about Kristina's age.

He went back in to the office to stop himself offering her a lift. Because he wanted to go home by himself. He wanted to shower, put on some music, cook slowly, without talking. Spend a little time alone with Kristina.

*

Kristina said: 'Why tonight?' George was ringing her from the car on his way home.

'Why not?'

'Jerzy is coming, don't you remember?'

'They might like each other.' At least he wouldn't be alone with Ulla and Kristina.

'They might *not*.'

'Ulla really held the fort, you know. For all those months.'

'Well, you're the cook,' Kristina said. 'You can ask who you want.'

He'd noticed that Kristina was very sensitive to any reference to last winter. It always softened her, she immediately gave way. He tried not to take advantage of this. He should have rung earlier, but he didn't want Ulla to hear him deal with Kristina's prevarications. She would consider that he was asking Kristina's permission. Even if he shut the office door Ulla had the knack of barging in at the wrong moment. She doesn't even knock, Kristina said. Sometimes he caught himself believing that Ulla read his thoughts.

He turned off the highway onto the ocean road. The black shore was crusted with swimmers, the sky above the horizon was watermelon red. He was playing Theodorakis's *Canto General* and ought to have been uplifted – the summer night, the sensual people, the heroic landscape . . . The triumph of survival. What had he thought he'd learnt from his ordeal? Life was becoming the same old dutiful, half-hearted scramble. Already he'd forgotten what he'd been so certain about. And with it the old question resurfaced: Why? Why me? Medical opinion shrugged its shoulders, but he couldn't help recalling his old suspicion that in his life there was some chronic underlying lie.

*

Kristina said that she would only come to live with him and Grace if she had a space of her own. The house was very small, a two-bedroomed worker's cottage, one of eight identical houses all joined up in a row. So he converted the old shed at the back fence into a studio for her. It would be a place where she could draw – she liked botanical drawing – or study or simply be by herself. She made it clear that she wasn't going to make any concessions to family life. She had a horror of doing what she didn't want to. But when she started her research at the hospital, she worked so hard that most nights she fell asleep in front of television and in the weekends she napped and read the newspapers. She lived like the daughter of the house, while Grace had always acted like a little wife.

In the end Kristina never used the studio. They started to dump broken chairs there, old bike helmets, collections of *Gramophone* going back ten years, things they no longer needed but were too lazy to throw out. Last winter George cleared himself a path from the door to the desk. It became the place where he went to focus, to attempt to still his mind. He'd been trying to practise this every evening after work.

Something in the room's damp smell and shadowy light seemed to be waiting for him when he opened the door. He sat down, positioned himself. He closed his eyes and saw himself straight-backed at the desk under the window. Beyond the window was the courtyard, the last in the row of courtyards that ran up the street to Monument Hill. He breathed in deeply, and out. He soared above the palm trees and the War Memorial, circled the rising sun of the giant AIF badge . . .

The kitchen flywire door slammed. He opened his eyes. Kristina came into the courtyard. She stood with one hand cradling the elbow of the other, which held a cigarette. Two crows were sitting among the sticky leaves of the fig tree. Normally she would have paid them a little scientific attention, but tonight she just kept staring into the twilight. If she were happy she wouldn't be smoking. She kept a packet of Drum for emergencies in a tin on the kitchen shelf.

He might as well give up now. His meditation sessions became shorter every day. Although she refused to look at the studio, something about the way she stood seemed like an appeal. Besides he couldn't stop watching her. He loved the look of her standing in the greenish light, her shoulders high with tension, her hair pinned up for the heat, her vulnerable collarbones, her shining narrow arms. Whenever he saw her he had a feeling of wellbeing.

*

She wasn't going to tell him about it. In the kitchen he poured a small glass of white wine for them both and put on Ella Fitzgerald. As he prepared to cook he discovered they were nearly out of olive oil. At once Kristina snatched up the car keys and said she felt like a drive. Surely it wasn't the prospect of Ulla that was upsetting her so much? He looked into her face. He'd noticed recently that she looked older. Her long eyes had become more deep-set, as if she'd gone further inside her own head. There were frown lines in the fine weave of her forehead. These past six months had been as hard on her as him. He thought these signs of care ennobled her. Besides, he liked to think that she was catching up with him, that their age difference wouldn't be so marked. He heard the car roar off up the street. She was in the grip of something. He knew how easily she became obsessed. She might park by the ocean for a while, or at the Monument and look down over the city.

*

'Where's the mobile?' Grace had come into the kitchen in her red silk kimono, her hair in a towel. 'Can I borrow it tonight?' Wafts of flower scents followed her from the shower. He could hear the thud of House music coming from her room.

'In the car. Kristina has taken it.'

Grace came to his elbow at the chopping board. He braced himself, a reflex action. Once she would have said something like: 'I see. And left you to do the cooking. Typical.' She would have used this moment alone with him to warn him that Kristina was selfish and he didn't see it. That she wasn't to be trusted and would let him down one day. But Grace was altogether gentler since she returned from South America. She had left her father in Kristina's care and Kristina had proved her colours. Like a miracle, like sun after rain, there was peace at last in his household.

Grace puzzled up her beautiful plucked eyebrows at George. 'What do you think this means? Denny had a dream last night that he was being unfaithful to me and he was *devastated*.'

'He's afraid of losing you.'

'Why?'

'He's fallen in love with you.'

She half-laughed, pleased. 'Wasn't he before, in the beginning?'

'That was only the beginning.'

*

It was so long since they'd had guests that George and Kristina were shy and out of practice. Suddenly their small, hot rooms seemed cluttered, on display. They bumped into each other in the hallway as they each rushed to answer the door. In the doorway Jerzy's eyes flicked over George, to make his own prognosis. He'd just come back from long-service leave, six months travelling the world. All winter long his sardonic postcards, ignorant of George's drama, had dropped through the door. *Travelling is like death*, he'd written, *you see your old life with new affection . . .*

Now he surprised George with a bear hug, hampered by an armful of beer.

Ulla arrived loaded with gifts, though it was a long walk from the bus stop. She and George allowed themselves a peck on the cheek. She offered him a large bunch of orange zinnias – the colour of life, she murmured, to no one in particular. Also some bottles of cider – she was now a teetotaller – and a Swedish crispbread for which Kristina had once expressed a liking. Later Kristina would realise she'd forgotten to thank Ulla for this.

Jerzy's hair was longer and greyer, slicked back from his sallow face. He strode through the house to the courtyard, like a Polish cowboy bringing news home to the ranch. Old Perth wasn't so different from other places, he said, opening one of his cans at the courtyard table, there was mediocrity and complacency all over the world.

'But the air isn't as clear,' said Ulla, smiling primly across the table. When feeling shy she often adopted a contrary stance. She was wearing evening glasses with a rhinestone in each corner and a Nordic-looking embroidered shirt. Ulla always looked a little at a loss away from the workplace, sitting still, her hands idle.

Jerzy ignored her. George could see that he didn't warm to Ulla. He would sum her up as bossy: he suspected all middle-aged women of being bossy. George remembered that Jerzy, eternal bachelor, liked women with leather miniskirts and blonde tousled hair. He leaned across to Ulla and asked her to select some dinner music.

*

Grace stood in the doorway to say goodbye. She kissed George and told him she'd stay the night at Denny's. Soon she would move out with him. She kissed Ulla and for a moment Ulla came alive, beaming, her brown eyes moist behind her glasses. They were all silent for a moment after this vision of radiant youth had disappeared. The fragrance of George's char-grilled capsicum and eggplant wafted over the table like a consolation for the middle-aged. From within the house came the rich strains of *Les Nuits d'été*. A three-star disc. George signalled his approval to Ulla. Was this her taste, or did she know he'd planned to select it?

In the dark courtyard next door he could hear lushly flowing water. Connie was watering. A year ago her husband Sam had died of Alzheimer's and Connie had not yet lost the habit of nurture. She could be heard watering Sam's garden at all hours of the day.

*

What they had to understand, Jerzy was saying, was that the whole world had entered a new epoch. That this was just the beginning. In these last days of the millennium they were in the grip of historic change. The forces of pragmatism had finally taken over. It was the end of history, the end of knowledge. Knowledge had been replaced with information.

'One thing never changes,' Ulla said. 'Human nature.' She meant: like half-drunk men who hold forth. After dinner, Kristina had muttered something about making coffee and wandered off into the house. Long ago she had given up on Jerzy, had pronounced him sexist, irredeemable, Polish, like her father, the worst kind. He was a colleague of hers in the laboratory, and used to be a mate, but she had handed him over to George. George and Jerzy used to meet for drinks on Friday night.

Jerzy propped his boots up on Kristina's empty chair and addressed himself entirely to George. He had visited laboratories in hospitals and universities all over the world. All you needed now were networks and publicists, he said. It was global. He'd visited his cousins in Poland and they had given him their name for it. The new Dark Age.

'I've heard that before,' Ulla said. She was less and less discreetly slapping at the mosquitos that loved her healthy flesh.

George felt achingly tired. Kristina was probably asleep. Ulla was not appeased. The evening was a dud. A bore, a waste of time. As all things were which didn't come from the heart.

When Ulla gathered up her bag for the last bus, George rose at once and insisted he would drive her home. Jerzy could stay and wait for his return if he liked. But Jerzy, taken aback, took his boots off the chair and said he'd find a late-night bar.

Jerzy would have travelled the world from bar to bar. George envied him that careless trust of his own body. They used to talk of going to Cuba together. Now George knew he would never make a trip like that, whisky and cigars and reeling down crumbling avenues at dawn. He had lost the necessary bravado, the necessary romantic belief. Some quota of his mortal energy had been used up. What was left he needed for something else.

Kristina was lying on the bed, a dark shape washed up beneath the fan, as George ushered Ulla out.

*

He and Jerzy would grow apart, George thought as he drove away from the house. Jerzy would think that George had had the stuffing knocked out of him: the stoic response was to carry on as if nothing had happened. And in some ways he was right. But what George wanted, more than anything else, was to change. George had never quite understood why Jerzy persisted in liking him. He would miss him more because of that.

It was pleasant bowling though the night streets. Ulla was relaxed, looking out the window with her own thoughts, a little smile on her lips. The old ease was back between them. She was pleased with him again.

Over the years he'd probably spent more waking hours with Ulla than with Grace or Kristina, but there were many things he did not know about her. Ulla did not give reasons. Why she'd migrated to Australia, for instance – he suspected a love affair. Why, with her energy and acumen, she continued to work for him.

For a moment he felt nostalgic for their friendship too as it used to be. When he had been raw and lost, the shop a desperate gamble, only Ulla had believed in him. When the sight of Ulla, in her neat black and white, had been pleasing to him every morning. The customers had commented on the good vibe in the shop. On *George's* first anniversary there was champagne for everyone at closing time. Afterwards he and Ulla allowed themselves a little sentimental self-congratulation and finished off the bottles. For some reason, Ulla pulled out from her bag a photograph of herself at seventeen and showed it to him, and he remembered being touched to see how soft her eyes were then, in the round face of a mid-sixties European schoolgirl. It was very late and somehow they ended up on the floor of the office. There had been laughter, an upturned wastepaper basket, carpet burn. George had blotted out most of the details. A last-minute intimation of danger on his part. Ulla's patience. A subdued brushing down. They must never drink again at work! They said the next day. He was relieved they both felt the same. After all, he told himself, he and Ulla came from the same generation. Those were rough-and-ready, more forgiving days.

*

When did he understand the grip that some people's love could have on you? Its weight, even its peril. In the hospital, Ulla's bunch of wattle had a scent of such virulent sweetness that it seemed to penetrate his brain. He couldn't have peace until, dragging his post-operative drip with him on its trolley, he carried the vase out of his room down the corridor and left it on the reception desk. But back in bed the scent found its way to him. Off he trundled again, this time to dump the flowers in a bin marked 'Hospital Waste'. It took a night for the scent to drift away.

'Of course you'll have to live differently,' Ulla said when she sat by his bed. 'Diet, exercise. No drinking or smoking. A more natural life.' *You caused this. You did this to yourself.* He didn't look at her. 'Does Kristina understand this?' she said.

*

'I'm re-thinking everything at the moment,' he said suddenly to Ulla when they were a few blocks from her place. 'About my involvement in the shop. The sort of hours I want to put in, the sort of commitment. Even whether to close the shop and turn the whole business into mail order, work alone from home, have a catalogue on the Web, that sort of thing.'

'What aren't you happy with?'

'Nothing. I just want to simplify my life.'

'You're good with customers, George. Much better than with computers. You need people.'

'Maybe,' he said as he pulled up. 'Anyway, I'm giving it some thought.'

As usual, Ulla offered him a crumpled five dollar bill to pay for the lift, though she knew this annoyed him. He shook his head at her and pushed her hand away. She walked slowly up the pathway to her dark-brick home unit through its drab bush garden.

He knew as he drove off how cruel he'd been. She didn't deserve this. For years her first thoughts had been for the shop. She really deserved to be made a partner. Or perhaps she'd known all along how it would end. On the freeway he opened his window to a rush of weedy river breeze. He felt cool and hard and savagely light-hearted.

It was clear at last that it must happen. Ulla would have to go.

*

Kristina was sitting on the front steps of the verandah, her bare feet on the footpath. The road was awash with the yellow light of the streetlamps. Behind her the black zigzag roof line of the row of houses ran like a spine up the hill.

Kristina said she felt stifled in the house. She couldn't sleep. He sat down next to her. How unhappy she was, hugging her knees, not able to look at him, her mouth too set to speak. He wished she would tell him what was wrong. They were often at their closest when Kristina had a problem. An insult at work. What a colleague had said. She seemed to attract jealousy. He was very good at helping her.

'Did Jerzy say goodbye?'

'Yes. By the way, he wants to invite you to a game of squash.'

'Good God. I didn't know Jerzy played squash.'

'He doesn't. But he thought it might be good for you. Build you up a bit.'

In spite of herself Kristina laughed. George laughed too, warmed by Jerzy's loyalty.

They heard a trickle of water on the verandah next door and looked at each other: Connie, giving her rubber plant its late-night drink.

Connie had lived in her house all her life. She had seen many occupants come and go in the row. George would be one of the oldest residents now. When he first moved in, Des, in the furthest house, used to organise street Christmas parties, but nine years ago he died of AIDS. In the next house down, a couple of academics, Clare and James, had moved out to a serviced apartment when Clare became crippled with arthritis. Ted, of Ted and Mavis, had a stroke and died in a nursing home. Sweet Mary Van Beem died three years ago of breast cancer. After she died, Kristina had seen a white heron circling over the roofs of the terrace. Then Connie's Sam. Then George.

Every two years. You had to wonder if it was higher than the national average. Or if there was a reason why this row of houses had attracted the attention of a particularly vengeful angel. Death Row, George privately called it. One night last winter he asked Kristina if she ever thought of this. 'It's coming our way,' he said.

'No it's not,' Kristina said instantly. 'It jumps around. Ted and Mavis lived further down than the Van Beems, remember?'

So she had thought of it. She was surprisingly superstitious for a scientist.

When he opened his eyes from the anaesthetic, the first thing he saw was Kristina picking out the corned beef from a hospital sandwich, looking haggard and exasperated. She was wearing the little gold cross from her long-repudiated Catholic childhood, which she'd always worn to interviews and exams.

His mood had turned sombre. He felt his limbs grow heavier by the moment. He touched her shoulder. 'I'm off to bed.'

*

Before he left, Jerzy had stood at the bedroom door and called into the darkness: 'Is he going to be all right?'

Kristina said that no one knew. If he made it through five years, his chances were good. He was in remission for the time being.

'Don't do anything to upset him,' Jerzy said suddenly.

In one bound Kristina rose up from the bed and stood blinking in the hall. She didn't dare ask Jerzy what he meant. They talked about George.

She'd been sitting on the steps since Jerzy drove off. From down the hill came the distant static of Fremantle on Friday night, shouts and crashes, feral drumbeats, the pulse of car radios. Her stomach hurt.

This afternoon, the man who used to be her lover had phoned her at work. He was a doctor at the same hospital. They'd had a long infrequent affair that she ended when George was diagnosed with cancer. No contact at all, she had said. She didn't tell him about the pact she'd made, giving him up for George's survival.

The doctor said today that he'd heard George had recovered. He wanted to see her again. Just for a walk or a drink, to see how she was. He said he missed her. In fact – his voice broke and he whispered – he was beginning to think he couldn't live without her. And Kristina croaked back that she never stopped thinking about him either. A hoarse craving voice seemed to be speaking through her. At the same time she was filled with foreboding.

Later she rang him from the car at the Monument to tell him she wouldn't meet him. They agreed to try not to meet.

The more they denied themselves, the more they desired. Kristina knew this. She also knew that the doctor wasn't as nice as he was charming. When she first met him she thought he would be funny, with his long upper lip and ironic hangdog look. But he wasn't funny, in fact he turned out not to have much of a sense of humour. He didn't like her to cry, or even to dress carelessly. He could have a whining tone when he talked about his colleagues. He had a capacity to sneer. For all his height and authority, it sometimes crossed her mind he was a sleaze.

The one person whose advice she'd trust she could not tell. Her lover was not half the man George was, she knew. And yet her thoughts returned to him, over and over, like a mantra.

One seagull circled silently over the street, lit up white in the darkness.

The angel had got it wrong. *It should have been her, not George.*
She had kept her pact and the angel had flown off again. But
it was watching. It had left its mark on the door.

Her lover said on the phone at the Monument that he was
leaving it up to her. How had it got to this point, so quickly? She
didn't know if she could find the conviction not to see him. She
didn't know how much longer she could bear it.

*

God how tired he was. He had just enough energy to slide a disc
into the player by his bedside, pull his clothes off and fall naked
onto the bed. But still his eyes remained open.

He'd put on Kancheli's *Abii Me Viderem.* He'd been longing
for it all evening. He was listening these days to composers from
small, almost forgotten countries on the outskirts of the old
Soviet Union. Countries which had known great suffering.

Kancheli was Georgian. There was something pure and
unsparing about this music, like walking over a strange harsh
landscape. *I turned away so as not to see,* that was what *Abii Me
Viderem* meant.

He saw suddenly the garden around the hospital, pretend
bushland that had probably once been landscaped, stunted bank-
sias and eucalypts, forlorn paths of grey sand, a picnic table and
benches that nobody ever sat on. Still, it had a certain delicate,
unassuming serenity. After rain you could smell the eucalypts.
Freesias appeared in early spring and magpies chortled around
the car park.

Inside was its own world, a lonely place, and yet there was
no face which did not smile at him. You sometimes glimpsed
children in pajamas running down the corridors, bald-headed
sprites surrounded by a sort of hush as all the adults held their
breath for them. Once he walked into a waiting room full of

women, old and young, in pastel floral gowns, and it seemed to
him as they looked up that their faces were like flowers. Strangers told each other their stories, sitting together in gowns. They
went very deep, very fast. Cancer had humbled them. Nothing
had protected them, not virtue or intelligence or good looks.
There was nothing left to separate them, nothing left to protect.
A young Chinese woman called Mrs Cheng, sitting next to
George, told him she had the Lord and that was all she needed.
When she received her diagnosis, she'd reached into her handbag for a tissue to wipe her eyes and pulled out a little handcard,
nicely printed, which said *The Lord Will Save You*. She had no
idea how it got there. It was like a blinding flash, she said.

Sometimes he felt he *had* died and woken up.

How could he tell Ulla that to the end of his days (an end on
which he now reflected daily), he would never pass a bus stop
without looking for her, waiting in her dusty sandals?

He was growing sleepy. He reached out one arm and switched
Kancheli off. Out of music comes silence. Once he fell asleep
(after listening to one of the Russians) and dreamt that he was
walking down a snowy street at night, lit by glowing, old-fashioned lanterns. How could he tell them that what he remembered
most was the pull he felt, strong as love or nostalgia, to give up,
lie down in the snow, and close his eyes.

FORGING FRIENDSHIP

KAREN HITCHCOCK

Hannah replied to my Facebook request for friendship by email.

Hey Keira, she said in the email. What's it been, one year, two?

She was no longer with Thomas, had moved interstate, was making a short film and she'd prefer – she wrote – not to use Facebook. She would close her account any day now, it was a nightmare, she knew way too many people, and they all wanted to friend her. Nothing personal; she hoped I didn't mind. She hoped she'd bump into me one day. We should catch up sometime, when she was in town and wasn't so crazy busy.

Which to my mind was a fancy way of saying: Please fuck off.

So I wrote back: I totally understand, Hannah, thanks so much for finding the time to respond to me, because I do appreciate how extra precious your time is. I know that you really should have a PA to handle all this Facebook rejecting for you; how horrible it must be to tear yourself away from your city-slicking, vegan-shoe-and-blood-red-lipstick-buying, la-de-dah filmic machinations just to compose little Facebook rejections designed to make everyone else feel like a piece of crap. I mean, HOW TAXING for you, Hannah.

*

Switching pages, I see that Xanadu658 is selling a silver crochet evening purse lined in pale-blue silk. It is 'no longer suitable, due to a change in lifestyle.'

What kind of lifestyle precludes evening purses? I check the other items Xanadu has for sale: three diamante belts (all size XS), red kitten heels (a bit scuffed), a six-pack of baby booties (NWOT).

I'm watching a couple of dresses, their prices creeping, I don't need them, I probably won't wear them, and yet . . . Maybe I should invest; maybe I need an evening purse. Who knows what the future may hold. Maybe this evening purse holds my future of evenings out clutching purses against perfect frocks over flawless skin, all clutched tight by a companion.

*

Hannah has dark brown eyes. We were once friends. Now we are not even 'friends.'

I have a lot of 'friends.'

I mean, we all know, or knew, or knew of, or wished we knew (like the-guy-from-the-bookshop), way too many people, don't we? I'd even found my dad listed on Facebook: the first time I'd seen him since I was eight. Late one night, call it the bottom of the barrel. He looked fatter, smaller and dumber than I remembered. Barrel bottom or not, I didn't ask him to be my friend.

What I really wrote to Hannah was this: Cool, Hann. Give me a call sometime if you're passing through town and we'll have a coffee and catch-up. Ciao xx

I don't need to tell you; she'd never call, kiss kiss, how are ya babe.

*

Hannah moved from South Africa to my school in year eleven. Something about the end of apartheid and its impact on cattle farming? Her dad – despised, pined after – went to New Zealand. Hannah and her mum came here.

Her first week at school she caught me smoking by myself, behind the woodwork shed. She asked for a light and said my tobacco was grown in Zimbabwe. I looked at my burning cigarette, then back at Hannah, unsure if she was taking the piss.

She lit up, blew smoke out of the corner of her mouth. 'I'm Hannah,' she said, as if I didn't know.

I made no assumptions, but from that moment on she'd find me each lunchtime and peel me away from my book. We'd nibble our crappy sandwiches, make fun of the other students and smoke our guts out. We never hung out on the weekends; she was seeing some older guy named Frank who took up all her time. But in year twelve they broke up and Hannah and I made the transition from smoking buddies to out-of-school buddies and she started sleeping over at my place.

Weekday, weekend, it made no difference to us, we'd stay awake half the night, gulping hot chocolate and leaning out the bedroom window to smoke. Hannah's appetite for hot chocolate was insatiable; we'd go through a litre of milk each night, at least. Hannah's mum would only allow cocoa made with water and a splash of skim milk, so when she got to my place – where my mum slept heavily and didn't give a damn what we drank – she'd cut loose, heat the full-cream milk in a saucepan till it boiled, add half the box of cocoa and an avalanche of brown sugar. Each week I'd scrawl cocoa and milk on the shopping-list notepad on the fridge.

'The amount of cocoa you girls go through,' my mum would

sigh in her distracted way as she tore the list from the pad and rushed off to the supermarket on Friday night.

Hannah's hot chocolates. Her mother was one of those petite, pointy-nosed women for whom eating nothing was a sign of refinement. The world was a great and mysterious place where nothing was certain except the superiority of looking like an old bag of bones. Hannah inherited her father's large frame and appetite and made her mother look like an icy-pole stick. As far as I could tell, Hannah's mum had spent Hannah's entire life trying to whittle her into a twig.

One morning towards the end of the school year we were walking to the bus stop when Hannah told me that I held her in my sleep. I would – she said – wrap my arms around her waist, press my head into her chest or her back and hold on tight. She said she didn't mind, but wondered if I was aware that I did it.

No, I told her, I was not aware.

Then I said: Jesus Christ, how embarrassing, I'm so sorry, I'll try to stop.

She said not to worry about it, she didn't much mind.

She sort of liked it, she said.

She found it sweet.

*

I once read that the reason we are able to walk down a crowded street without continually colliding into others is because we detect subtle movements in the eyes of the people coming towards us – movements that somewhere deep inside our brains we understand as an intended direction and make the necessary adjustment in our trajectory. We make way for each other through a mutual understanding. Perhaps this is why we can feel comforted by a crowd.

Our eyes send signals so we avoid the barest touch. Perhaps

this is why we can feel so lonely in a crowd.

Hannah? It had not been what, one year or two. It had been twenty-eight months plus three weeks. And Hannah? Never mind.

*

Facebook makes me sick. Hannah and I used to meet up in the flesh and walk along a real street and enter real live shops, staffed by fragrant, embodied individuals who – if you reached out and touched them – would feel warm and smooth, as human beings do. In such establishments we would try on clothes that were new and available in most sizes, including ours. And we would choose a frock from a rack and slip it on and spin for each other, our backs to the cool, hard mirrors. Then Hannah and I would sit face to face, look across the table into each other's eyes, and lips, and down into our coffees, slowly stirring the froth in, as we spoke words with pitch and waves that hit each other's tympanic membranes and sent physical signals of chemico-electric form zinging through each other's brains.

'Keira?' she'd say.

'Hannah?' I'd say. And we would answer each other – 'yes,' or 'yes?' – without the use of emoticons or excess punctuation. Without the need to ruminate over the difference in meaning of 'oooooooo' and 'oooooo!!!' and 'oooohhhhhhh.' We used gesture and eyes and sounds. We sat face to face, and a single look transmitted the equivalent of three hundred posts on Facebook. None of which rendered me sick.

That saying 'catch-up' makes me sick.

That saying 'I hope you don't mind' makes me sick.

Sometimes, people streak so far ahead that there can never be any catch-up and too bloody bad if you mind.

Other things that make me sick: hot chocolate, long macchiatos, catching buses, the smell of burning fabric, dark brown eyes.

One time with Hannah I bought a pale-blue silk dress from the Vintage Clothing Shop. It gripped my tits like a cold fist but made my arse irresistible. Around the neck was a ring of pearlised sequins. It was cut at just the right length, highlighting both the bones of the knee and the curve of the quadriceps, which for some reason always screams vagina. Hannah made me buy it, although its price was such a stunner that I had to pilfer money from my mum's purse to pay. But I wore that frock dressed up with fish-net stockings, and down with bare legs, with scarfs and brooches and belts, depending on whether we were going to a club or a show or a café. I wore it with jackets on top and skivvies underneath, I wore it with hats and long socks and gold sandals and gloves. I wore that dress with Hannah.

Also, eBay makes me sick. And spastic and insatiable for things just out of sight. It fuels something frantic, then leaves me gutted. Without getting out of bed, with the rhythmic twitch of one finger against the return button on my keyboard, I can have frock after frock. None of which, poured out of their postpacks, caught warm in my fingers, satisfies anything. Although, according to the vendors' descriptions, every dress on eBay is 'stunning.' They are stunning with tiny flaws, or stunning and unworn, or they are stunning and would look fabulous with heels and golden eyeshadow or equally so with ballet flats and a leather jacket; they are NWOT and stunning. You don't need to ask why the vendors are auctioning off their stunning crap because – like a con man – they tell you before you ask. There are three stories: wardrobe clearout; fluctuation in body weight; change in lifestyle. No one ever says that they are auctioning their kids' toys because they need a carton of fags or a crate of VB, or because the bank's about to foreclose. No one's selling their shit to raise funds for a holiday or to build a herb garden or a gazebo or buy a pet dog. No one's selling their shit because it's shit. They all regret horribly the necessity of the sale. They expect us to look at this detritus and be stunned.

Nothing to lose, I sign in.

There are currently seventy-four thousand, five hundred and thirty-one dresses listed for sale. Five thousand six hundred and twelve of them are pale blue. Seven hundred and forty are pale blue and vintage. I survey the capacity of my room. I turn back to my computer, flip pages.

Nothing to lose, I sign in.

I have a friend request from Nicky Winch, the guy in grade four who had the set of seventy-two Derwent pencils in a tin. I wonder if that's enough to forge a friendship. Nothing to lose, I accept, and the face of another stranger joins my library of friends.

*

So the pale-blue silk dress I bought and wore with Hannah was sleeveless? And it started to unravel under the armholes? At the part they call a gusset? I sewed the edges together, but I'm not much good with a needle and a gusset is a triangle of reinforcement that can only bear so much reinforcing. And then I ran out of pale-blue thread, used up all my white, moved on to pale green and et cetera until the underarms of the dress looked like psychedelic spiderwebs. At special events or where the light was quite bright, I tried to keep my arms pinned to my sides. Someone might flick a glance at my armpit during conversation and this served as a reminder for me to clamp that arm back down. Hannah told me to relax. She said the mass of threads were scary-beautiful. Those were her words: scary, beautiful.

Then, a few weeks later, she said the mending seemed desperate, overly optimistic, why didn't I just get another dress? Desperate, overly optimistic; a cause and its effect.

I'd seen Hannah ruin two striped tops from her prized collection: one with blue-black hair dye; one behind the bus stop
where a rusty nail stuck out of the fence. Both times she did the
exact same thing, no threads involved: she just chucked them in
the bin, like wet tissues.

*

There are three hundred and seventy-three pale blue + vintage
+ sleeveless dresses for sale on eBay. Forty-four are 'Buy it now!'
The rest are up for auction. All bids end between one minute
and eight days from now.

*

The plan was that we'd both do nursing and then volunteer as
aid workers abroad. That's what we called it: abroad, which to
our ear was far more sophisticated a term than overseas. We
enrolled – and then spent the summer around town, me in that
dress, Hannah in ballet flats, red lipstick and one of her striped
tops. We talked about moving in together as soon as we got
part-time jobs. Meanwhile she stayed over at mine. Full-cream
milk and cocoa. I held her warm body at night and pretended
to sleep.

*

I log in, compelled by the old What if?
    Nicky Winch the Derwent boy has sent me a message.
    Unusual. Normally you accumulate ancient artefacts and
never exchange a word. Befriend, read their inane and desperate
and overly optimistic daily updates, voyeurism, despair.
    The Westgate sucks, sooooo happy Masterchef's back, shiny,
happy, kid topped the class.
    But here in the stream was a message just for me. For a

fraction of a second, a tiny boy in a crowded school photo, his pursed little lips, calling across years.

Kieiria wots up? Remember the day you fell from the monkey bars landed on me and stuffed my knee my knee still kills me and I might need an op. Work in a sign shop which is pretty shit. Usual stuff, 2 kids, don't have much contact tho. How goes?

He'd spelt my name wrong and I did not remember that monkey bars incident.

Then I did remember the incident and the attending ambulance and the fact that it was a girl called Sonya Murne, the netball champion of the school, who landed on his knee, not me. I hated the monkey bars. I hated netball. I liked coloured pencils in tins, and books and other quiet stuff. Hello? You think you know me? I'm not fucking Sonya Murne.

*

Somehow that summer between school and uni, bisexual had emerged as the new normal, so unless you were a Nazi Christian you said you were bisexual. We discussed it. In theory, Hannah said, she could definitely be in love with a woman; love was love, after all; male, female, what's the diff? Keep in mind that it was me she was sitting with when she said it. She said it to my face, looking into my eyes. Then she said, 'And woman on woman avoids all the problematics of submission that go with penetrative sex, the prescribed male/female dynamic, et cetera, you know?'

I nodded, heart thumping, palms sweating, cheeks probably fucking purple, though I had no idea what she was talking about. All I knew about penetrative sex I had learned at fifteen from Jason Campbell. Over four weekends we'd exchanged a dozen words max and a few buckets of bodily fluids, mostly mouth-to-mouth, and he did penetrate me. If pressed I'd say it was neither pleasant nor unpleasant. Mostly I was on my back, thinking, 'This is penetration. I'm being penetrated. He is penetrating me.' Probably I thought 'fucking' rather than 'penetrating,' but you get the picture.

If penetration was a problem for Hannah then that was no prob for me. And how I leapt to agree with Hannah on the question of loving a woman. Oh boy, that was something I knew all about.

*

I study the eBay pictures one by one with an attitude forensic. My neck stiffens, my eyes ache, and none of the three hundred and seventy-three pale-blue vintage sleeveless dresses resembles mine in the slightest.

*

Then one day Hannah and I were in Degraves Street, drinking double macchiatos because we liked the way they made us look – sophisticated glass, black ink, dense white foam. We were drinking them even though we would have preferred massive mugs of cocoa, cream, sugar, a half litre of milk, and a boy called Andre Devonport (and what sort of name is that, anyways?) comes over to our table and goes, 'Hannah?'

To which the only possible answer was, 'Yes?'

And then he asks if she recognises him.

And she does recognise him: he's a guy from her high school in South Africa. A great looking guy, with flopping-in-his-eyes soft hair and you-are-the-only-person-in-the-world-Hannah eyes. He pulls up a stool without taking his eyes off her and they start exchanging relevant demographic data – me feeling increasingly uncomfortable, then left out, then grumpy – and when Hannah says the word 'nursing' Andre's face expands in surprise, then contracts, and what's left of his eyeballs direct their suspicion at me. He turns back to Hannah, 'But you were so . . . clever. So artistic.'

Call it the beginning of the end, if you will.

*

When an auction has less than sixty seconds to close, the timer switches to red numerals and you can watch the countdown in real time. This never fails to scramble my mind and shrink my world. Do I want it? Should I bid? How much is it worth to me? I am held in a 59-, 58-, 57-, 56-second fist where I am without past or future, where I have no idea what to do. I pounce and feel sick. Or I move on and feel sick. Uncertainty, desire and lost opportunities. It's all there in the countdown.

It's a bit different with Facebook. Less intense. Needless to say, I immediately deleted Nicky Winch from my list of friends.

*

We'd be meeting less frequently and Hannah would be saying things like, 'Oh Keira, you're so . . .' and finishing off with adjectives that sounded a bit South African to me. A bit male South African with floppy hair and an eye for the particular. This 'you're so . . .' made me feel disappointing and small. And when someone starts to point out what you're like with a decrescendo sigh, it's a sign to get ready 'cause they're shrinking you down flat into a face in an old album that can be snapped shut with one hand. And pretty soon, you just watch, the act of misrecognition will be complete.

*

Things I had not contemplated: flats without Hannah, summertime without Hannah, nursing without Hannah, developing nations without Hannah.

'We can still hang out!' she said, grinning fluoro from the lips but not the eyes, after she informed me that she'd landed a job at the food co-op, was switching from nursing to film studies and moving into Andre's share-house.

Andre this. Andre that. 'He's so . . .' Eyes heavenward. Crescendo sigh.

'I'll have my own room, though. At least . . . at the start . . .'

It has often been noted that catastrophes take place in slow-motion, hyper-real time. I can add that your body sucks inwards. Major arteries slap the underside of your skin like untethered hoses and in the face of all this you can remain surprisingly polite. You can, if you wish, find air for something small and inane: oh, gee, wow, congratulations. Then you can flee.

*

EBay. Facebook. Twitter and chat. Send, comment, respond and reply. I'll buy stuff I wouldn't touch. I'll comment on your post though I wouldn't cross the street to say hello. Things that are not acts will pretend to be acts; they will take the place of acts. I will search and I will trawl and I will neither catch you nor be caught.

*

What I did was walk home, into the house of my childhood, into my bedroom, and close the door. I lay still on my bed for a long time. I peed once, in a milk-crusted mug abandoned on the windowsill. My mum knocked, said my name with a question mark and then went away. The sun rose and set twice. Soon after the second setting, I had a small thought, call it a plan. I stood up, went to the kitchen, gathered a glass of lemon cordial and a cigarette, a lighter, my blue mended dress. I opened the back door and stepped out into the cool night-time breeze. I sat cross-legged in the backyard as standing made me dizzy, and I watched the threads catch and smoulder to a fine grey ash.

*

I read something else: your life has a single story that gets repeated over and over, with a succession of understudies playing the role of your first co-star.

Let's say it's true. My story might go like this: a beautiful dress held my chest in her fist, and when she started to unravel I incinerated her remains. Make way for the understudy, you might say. Let's get this story restarted, you might say.

I log in, check the new pale-blue listings. I log out, I log in, see if anyone wants to befriend.

But the problem is this: you can't force her out of the story. You can't delete her or incinerate her or send her to your trash. She's your co-star, after all. And she might be a tenacious fighting bitch.

I log out. I log in. Out in out in.

Try whatever you like. I wish you all the best. But believe me when I tell you: that bitch has to leave for your first story to end.

HONEYMOON

CHARLOTTE WOOD

The night they arrive at the house on the lake, Mandy slides
open the door to the deck and a tiny grey possum clambers down
a tree trunk, an arm's length from the railing.

'Matt, look,' she calls. She takes a step onto the deck. Another
possum, bigger than the first, darts down the tree behind it and
the two animals leap on to the wooden railing. Mandy stops.
The possums fix their gaze on her, lowering their small heads,
eyes shining. She steps forward again – and then both the animals thump gracelessly onto the wooden boards and pelt towards
her feet.

'Jesus!' she yelps, jumping back behind the screen door and
slinging it shut.

The possums stop still for one long second, watching her
again. Then they waddle about on the deck, sniffing.

Matthew appears behind her, 'Oh, wow.' He reaches for the
door.

'Don't go out there!' She grabs his arm. Then feels her face
colour. 'They ran at me. Somebody must feed them.'

Matthew stands on the hairy orange carpet next to her, his new wife. He takes her hand from his arm, smiles down at her.

'Mand, it's just a mum and her baby.' Then he puts an arm around her shoulders. 'I'll get them some fruit,' he says. But he begins stroking Mandy's arm in long, firm strokes. 'It's OK,' he says, his voice soothing.

She shrugs her shoulder away. 'I'm all right.'

*

When Mandy came home from uni to her parents' small town and told them she was getting married, her dad said, 'Christ.'

Matthew was coming the next day. He said she should wait for him before making the announcement, that it was selfish not to. She couldn't say she wanted to protect him.

Her mother said, 'Heavens.' Then, 'That's wonderful, isn't it Geoff!'

Her dad said, 'You're only twenty-one. There's plenty of time.'

Mandy had put down her glass of champagne – she'd brought the bottle herself, opened it while they watched on, nervous, expectant. She looked at her fingertips turning white from pressing the base of the glass, and said, 'How old were you, Dad?'

Her mother twittered. 'Wonderful!' she said, and sipped the drink, glassy-eyed already. But Mandy and her father locked gazes.

He said, 'It doesn't matter, because I wasn't doing anything important.'

Mandy threw her head back. 'Jesus! That's great.' She turned to her mother, who was blinking quickly, the way she did when she met someone new, or spoke to someone she thought important in some way – tilting her head back a little, smiling, but flitting her lashes so fast they were almost completely shut.

'Sorry, Mum.'

Her mum gave her head a little shake, still blinking and sipping.

Her dad growled, 'You know what I mean.'

He meant university. Honours, maybe even a medal. Mandy stretched her arms above her head, and closed her eyes tight for a second to force away the tears she could feel beginning.

'I'm not an idiot, Dad.'

Then she lifted her glass, said, 'Well, here's to us. Thanks for your enthusiasm. You can congratulate Matt when he gets here tomorrow.'

She drank and stood up. Her dad watched her, the glass stem dainty between his big fingers. 'I'm thinking about your future,' he said. Then he muttered, 'I don't want you to limit yourself.' He glanced towards his wife, and then quickly away again.

But Mandy was already striding across the room, leaning down to her mother.

'Thanks, Mum,' she whispered, and kissed her soft face while her mother began shuffling her body out of the chair.

In the kitchen Cathy was coming through the back door, breathless, in her school uniform, smelling of cigarettes. 'Hi,' the sisters both said, as Cathy slung her backpack to the floor. Mandy said, 'I'm going out,' and slammed the door.

*

At the lake house there is a garage with old surfboards and plastic skis, and a tinny with a heavy, sluggish outboard motor. On the first afternoon they take the boat out. Matthew knows how to work the motor and sits next to it, hugging it one-armed while they putter across the water. 'Let's do this every day,' he shouts as the green water slides beneath them.

But Mandy has seen the kayak. In the morning she eases herself out of bed without waking Matthew, and goes barefoot to the kitchen to make coffee. She frowns at the noise of the electric kettle as it boils.

She picks her way down through the prickly bush garden to the water and hoists the white and yellow kayak off the grass, holding it across her hips, tilting herself backwards to balance the weight. She steps over the stones, and then lowers it – *plop* – into the water. With her fingertips she directs it between some rocks so it won't float away in the mild slapping of the water. Then she wades ankle-deep to the furthest rock and sets down her coffee cup on its flattest part. She wades back and lowers herself into the kayak seat, making the boat rock wonkily. She shunts her bum forward and uses the white plastic oar to push off from the stones, feeling the kayak grazing the underwater pebbles. She reaches for the cup and then, holding it aloft in one hand, digs a few one-handed strokes with the other, out into the deeper water. Then she lays the bar of the paddle across her lap and sips from the cup, letting the kayak drift out into the vast grey sheet of the lake. Almost as far as she can see ahead and to each side, is the metallic water.

She sits back, closing her eyes against the sunlight, knees bent. The water shrugs beneath her. Then she drains the cup and sets it on the floor, and paddles a few neat strokes with the sun at her back. She drifts over to where she has seen some fish jumping and sits very still, listening for the tiny splash, scanning for the movement. Then there it is, the *plish*, the glimpse of small white fish arched in the air above the silver water.

Every morning she does this, paddling and drifting for an hour on the silent lake, before Matthew wakes.

*

The wedding had been the usual thing for her home town. Ceremony in the park by the river (not Saint Mark's, after several arguments with her mother). The celebrant was a woman in a cream nylon suit and an aqua blouse, they'd read something from Kahlil Gibran. Afterwards, at the reception in the Corroboree Room behind the civic hall, Mandy sat at the round bridal table with Matthew, her parents, and her sister Cathy.

The smell of the wood panelling in the Corroboree Room reminded her of their afternoons there as children when their father had supplied the sound system for football club functions. In his youth, he had wanted to be a sound engineer. So he owned a mixing board and many long extension cords, he owned big stippled silver cases with snap locks, amps and various players, folding stands, large black speakers in scratched black chipboard casings and three microphones with stands of varying heights. He didn't need these things for his job at the gas company, but he liked to have them. While he spent Saturday afternoons of their childhood laying out cables and saying 'check, check' into the microphones, Mandy and Cathy had the Corroboree Room to themselves, sliding on the polished green lino and sitting in the crook of the one wooden step up to the stage.

At the wedding Mandy wore a dress made by her university friends and her mother sat next to Matthew. Her mum had secretly liked Matthew from the start. He played up to her, teased her in a way that made Mandy wonder if her father had ever done this, because her mother flushed and looked younger whenever she and Matthew bantered. Mandy imagined her dad – young, slim, broad-shouldered – teasing her mother about her hips, or her tea towels, the way Matthew did.

*

The second night at the lake they set the outdoor table on the deck for dinner, sticking candles into wine bottles, the candle-light making the trees flicker. Matthew has made a big bowl of spaghetti and stands over Mandy like a waiter, using tongs to lift the pasta on to her plate. Then there's a noise, and they look up to see the big possum angling its way down the tree again, one side of its body moving forward then the other, its snout lifting in purposeful, rhythmic nods.

'Shit,' Mandy says.

'It's OK, it won't come near us,' says Matthew.

But the possum leaps on to the railing and stalks towards them. The smaller one has appeared now too, waddling behind its mother.

Mandy stands, scraping her chair loudly and shoving it in the animals' direction. 'Shoo!'

The candle flames wobble. The possums stop. They stare at her, their dingy feather-duster tails held up in the air.

Mandy drags the chair again, looks around for Matthew, who has disappeared. She feels stupid. The dinner is getting cold. But the mother possum begins to walk again, delicately, along the railing, stretching her face towards the table. Mandy steps back, thinks of the possum's mean little teeth, the tiny fleas and bacteria in its fur.

Matt appears with a long, spindly piece of eucalypt branch. He steps forward and whacks the stick down, hard, on the decking. The possums straighten, staring. He cracks the stick down again, harder, and the noise echoes up into the dark around the house. The possums turn and amble along the railing towards the bedroom at the end of the house, into the darkness.

Mandy pulls her chair back towards the table. 'Thanks,' she mumbles, glancing past Matthew into the gloom. She can't see them.

Matt grins and says, 'I'll put some music on.'

On the nights after this they each sit with a thin branch leaned against their chair. Every night the possums come, then retreat into the shadows at the cracking of the sticks.

Sometimes Mandy looks up from the table to see their eyes shining out of the dark.

*

Matthew was a city boy when they met at a party in her first weeks at university. 'Never been west of the Blue Mountains,' he'd said airily, lighting a cigarette.

He wore a black suit jacket with his black jeans, listened to The Cruel Sea. When she said she didn't know who The Cruel Sea were he was incredulous. 'Tex Perkins. The *Cruel Sea*.'

She was blank. 'Sorry.'

He took the cigarette from his mouth and blew a long stream of smoke. 'You really *are* a country girl,' he said, and then he smiled, a wide, city-boy smile. Later they had sex in his room in the dark, the party babbling outside his bedroom door, beneath the mournful music coming from his battered CD player.

'I like your body,' he whispered, propped on his elbow in the gloom. He said *breasts*, as though it were not a foreign word for a boy. He drew a sharp line down her breastbone with his fingernail. She liked his spiky confidence. He switched on a lamp with a sarong covering it – he had been to Asia – and low orange light washed the room. He sat up in bed and began rolling a joint.

She lay naked on top of the sheets, feeling on her skin an echo of the line he had traced down her sternum. A corner of her future was opening up.

*

Long before the wedding, the first time she brought Matthew home, her mother made up Cathy's room for him, with the good sheets, the new pillowcases. Mandy had snuck into the room after they'd all gone to bed, squeezed in beside him, snickering at his clump of black clothes and his motorbike boots heaped on the floor next to Cathy's pale pink chest of drawers. She touched his nipple.

'Don't,' he whispered. 'Your parents.'

She laughed again, bent to lick it.

'It's not fair on them,' he murmured, gently pushing her away. 'They're nice people.'

She stared at him in the dark, and then she stood up and padded back through the silent house to lie in her childhood bed, listening to her sister asleep, breathing slow and heavy on a mattress on the floor.

*

At the lake they spend the days sitting on the deck, looking out at the water through the trees, newspapers strewn about them, listening to seed pods dropping onto the corrugated iron roof. The house is full of ugly, comfortable furniture they sink into. Prehistoric-looking couches with the nap worn off the fake suede, with seat cushions so deep their feet don't touch the floor. There is a smoked-glass coffee table with battered board games on a shelf beneath. Scattergories and Monopoly and obscure, failed board games: Payday, and How to Be a Complete Bastard with Adrian Edmonson's face all over the box.

The maroon milk crate filled with their uni textbooks and foolscap notebooks stays by the front door, untouched.

Sometimes they have sex, quietly, on the clean white sheets with the sun falling into the room, only the screen door between them and the cicadas and the chittering of the lorikeets.

*

The next time he had gone home with her was for Easter.

'Do you want to go with them?' Matthew had asked her at

breakfast, while her mother scurried around the house before Mass, checking her handbag, putting on lipstick at the hallway mirror.

Mandy had only snorted, and poured another coffee. 'Have you got any cigarettes?' she asked him.

'Shhh,' he whispered, angling his head towards her mother, who was now in the kitchen prodding at a solid white-plasticked chicken defrosting on the sink.

Cathy grinned at Matthew over her Weet-Bix. 'Wuss,' she said with her mouth full, spoon aloft.

'Come on Cathy,' called their mother. 'And you shouldn't be eating breakfast so late.' Their parents never ate before Communion.

They went to buy Easter eggs and hot cross buns after collecting her parents from Mass. At the supermarket checkout they watched the coloured eggs and the plastic bags of buns moving along the conveyor belt.

Cathy said, 'There's Sue McInerney.'

At the next counter a thin girl from Cathy's year stood with a lanky, slightly older boy, lifting things from a trolley; frozen food boxes and bags of corn chips and sheets of pale sausages.

'I remember her,' Mandy said. 'Brainy.'

Cathy flicked a red egg, sending it spinning in circles on the conveyor belt. 'Pregnant, apparently.'

The sisters raised their eyebrows at each other.

Matthew took out his wallet, but Mandy's father was standing ahead of them, a fifty dollar note ready in his hand. He was watching Sue McInerney too, until Cathy nudged his elbow for the waiting checkout girl.

As they were driving home Matthew looked out of the window at the yellowing trees. He said, 'It's quite beautiful here really. I could live here.' He didn't look at Mandy, but was watching the back of her father's head. 'When we finish uni,' he added.

Dad looked only at the road.

After lunch that day the family drifted into silence. Dad was slouched in his armchair, reading a Thomas Keneally book with his glasses halfway down his nose. Cathy was at the end of the couch, with a little collection of nail polish remover and enamels and cuticle-softener bottles arranged before her on the coffee table. She had a foot up on the table, rubbing a nail with a cotton ball. Their mother had put on Handel's Messiah, as she did at every family occasion. Mandy lay on the carpet reading a magazine, propped up on her elbow. In quiet parts of the music she could hear her mother and Matthew chatting in the kitchen over the washing up. He was saying something about the local council and town planning jobs.

*

One morning out in the kayak she sees one of the enormous pale jellyfish they'd noticed much further out in the deeper water, from the boat. Now it glides alongside her. She wants to touch its fleshy, globular tentacles, the huge thickened dome of its head. She strokes the water once with the paddle to keep up, following its slow-motion dipping and surfacing. But after a while the jellyfish sinks deeper, and though she stares hard into the dark water as it lowers, it disappears.

The sun is hotter now. She turns to see the house in the distance, the shape of Matthew hunched over the railing of the deck, looking out across the lake towards her.

She waves, then dips the paddle straight down, feels the boat rotate, graceful as a dancer.

*

At the wedding her father talked into one of his microphones, huskily welcoming Matthew into the family, but looking at

Mandy. She smiled back at him. Later, father and daughter danced awkwardly together. She was a little drunk. She called, through a space in the song, into her father's ear, 'You've been happy, haven't you Dad?' He grunted, 'Oh, love. Course I have.' Then he said, 'I'm sorry about before.' And she put her head into his shoulder to stop herself from crying.

*

Over the week she teaches herself how to control the kayak, experimenting by keeping her elbows at her sides or lifting them, or by shifting her grip along the paddle. Sometimes she moves through the water smooth and fast, as though propelled by some force beyond herself. At other times she can't wield the paddle; it smacks at the water or bangs down on the side of the boat, causing it to wobble and rock. But on each outing she spends much of the time simply drifting, gazing into the water. Sometimes she comes across a single patch of bubbles. She tries to stare into the depths, but once again there's nothing to be seen except the sliding, bulbous surface of the water itself.

One morning she sees the small red swatch of a kite high in the air.

When she and Cathy were small their father had had a brief kite-flying craze, driving his reluctant girls to the highest of the bare hills near the town. He would lift his kites, delicate creations of dowel and bright tissue paper, from the boot of the car. Mandy would huddle in her nylon parka, hair whipping her face in the freezing wind. 'I told you to wear something warmer,' her father growled while he untangled a cord. But Mandy had insisted on her pink tartan skirt and bare legs, and the wind was icy. The girls had to stand, each holding a skein of nylon line in both hands, while their father strode up the hill ahead of them. Then he would throw up each of the kites and shout, 'Run!', and they had to run over the knobbly tussocky ground, holding the lines high above their heads. The kite would mostly swirl once or twice and arrow straight towards the stony ground. But sometimes, sometimes, it would lift, and the spool would whirl and tumble in her hands, the purple kite lifting higher and higher, and Mandy would begin to smile, and Cathy's green box kite would lift and she would shriek, her head thrown back and mouth wide open, and their father would stand and watch his children falling in love with the high space beyond that small town, with the possibilities of flight.

Now Mandy looks up at the distant red kite in the blue sky above the lake, anchored to somewhere on the distant shore. She remembers the rhythmic tug on the line, calibrating its pull against the weight of her own body, the pleasure of letting out the line, then resisting. She turns from it then, and paddles towards the centre of the lake. But all morning, it seems the kite stays with her, always above her, there in the outer corner of her sight.

The wind rises. She churns back through the water towards the house, breathing deep and rhythmically, pushing the high end of the paddle forward with all the strength of one arm as she dips deep and pulls the low end through the water with the other hand, the choppy little waves slapping over the prow of the kayak.

Afterwards she walks up the garden, her arms and legs pleasantly jittery from the last long stretch of effort.

When she slides open the glass door Matthew is reading the paper at the table.

'I said I was going to come with you,' he says crossly. 'But you didn't wake me up.'

The room feels small and airless after the wide gusty space of the lake, the red star of the kite stamped in the sky.

'Oh, sorry,' she says, as she passes his chair. 'I forgot.'

*

At noon they gather provisions to go out in the boat for the afternoon. Matthew waits on the deck, hands full with a fishing rod and one plastic shopping bag of bait, and another holding lunch things – a half-bottle of wine with a cork jammed into it, some bread and cheese. His straw hat dangles, sunglasses glint on his head.

Mandy puts a hand to the bench for the door keys, but they aren't there. Matthew watches her from outside, shifting his weight while she scrabbles through the things on the bench: coins, unopened envelopes, a banana, a bottle of sunscreen, three pens, some national park brochures.

'Hang on,' she calls, moving to the other end of the bench where the owners keep a basket full of miscellaneous stuff. She peers into it. Fishing lures, magnets, pens, more sunscreen, a computer disk, some cassettes with the brown tape knotted in loops, a plastic tub of moisturiser.

'Come on,' calls Matthew, irritated.

She straightens. 'I can't find the keys.' She walks to the door. 'Did you have them or did I?'

Matthew groans. 'You did, because when we got home you opened the door and I carried in the shopping.'

This is true. She turns back, hands on her hips, thinking, scanning the room. The keys have an enormous plastic Bananas in Pyjamas key ring. Impossible to lose. Suddenly she feels a wave of dislike for Matthew, standing there ready for a picnic.

'Are you going to help me look?' she asks, hands still on her hips.

He sighs, puts down the fishing rod and the bags, jostling them into a corner of shade by the door. She thinks she sees his eyebrows lift as he bends, pushing the things about noisily, but when he stands again he is smiling tightly. She wants, suddenly, to smack him on his smooth, shaven face.

'I don't know where the fucking things are,' she says viciously, and begins striding about the room, flipping cushions and snapping pieces of paper.

'Don't worry, we'll find them,' he says. But making it clear, in his tone, that the delay is her fault.

They each begin to wander round the house, bending and straightening as they search, and he calls out questions. 'Did you take them out of the front door?'

'*Yes.*' She hurries to check. Not there.

'What did you do then?'

From the hallway she can see him now in the bedroom, lifting shorts and shirts to shoulder height, listening for keys in pockets.

'I don't *know.*'

He keeps yelling out questions, which she doesn't answer.

She moves, her body bent, through the rooms, lifting every cushion again, running a hand beneath each one. When she comes back to the kitchen he's standing in front of the rubbish bin below the bench. 'I guess we should empty it. They could have fallen in.'

She does not think the keys could have fallen in. They would need to fall at a 45-degree angle, backwards and under the lip of the bench top. But she has nothing better to offer. 'Mmmm,' she says.

She can feel her temperature rising, a headache beginning. They have been looking for twenty minutes. Matthew is still standing at the bin, hands on hips, his back to her. She is beginning to feel a panicky pain beneath her ribs. But Matthew is quite calm, standing there watching the bin as though it were a view.

It *is* her fault. This fact makes her angrier.

'Where the – ' she lifts a pile of heavy books and then lets them fall from a height, slamming on to the table '–*fuck* are they!'

She falls into one of the chairs, grabbing shoes from the floor, shaking each one.

She looks across at Matthew. 'What if we don't find them?'

She hears her voice, the sound of her own panic. He doesn't turn around, doesn't answer.

'What are we going to *do*, *Matt*?'

Then as she watches him she sees his hands in his pockets. He turns around slowly. She stares at him, and he smiles.

He's got them.

'It's OK babe, calm down, we'll find them.' He takes his hands – carefully, it seems now – out of his pockets, steps towards her across the orange carpet that reminds her, suddenly, of pubic hair. He leans down and puts two hands on her shoulders. She feels her body stiffen, her head is hot.

'Are you sure you didn't put them in your pocket accidentally?' she asks slowly, keeping her voice even, looking him in the eyes. He rears back, making a face. 'Course I'm sure!' But his hands stay on her bare brown shoulders. She glances down at his pockets, trying to see any possible shape, but he moves off, soundless, back into the kitchen, and bends to open the fridge door. 'My flatmate once put keys in the fridge,' he says, squinting into the square of light, reaching in to shift jars and bottles.

Mandy goes to the bathroom. She feels sick. She remembers the possums, his stroking her arm.

Breathe. It's ridiculous; of course he doesn't have them.

They have just gotten married.

She hears the fridge door close and then another noise, his voice. She runs into the kitchen.

'Ah, shit. Sorry, nope. My car keys.' He holds them up.

But he's still smiling that odd little smile. She sees him glance back at the rubbish bin.

Mandy's heart begins to jolt in her chest. She walks to the bin.

'I'll do that,' Matthew says, but he stays where he is, running a hand lightly along the top of the fridge.

She feels all the blood has gone out of her somehow, she is suddenly exhausted. 'It's OK,' she murmurs. 'I lost them, I'll do it.'

He says, 'Babe, don't be like that.' But he doesn't move.

She hauls the heavy, thin plastic bag out of the bin, across the carpet and over the sharp lip of the metal frame of the sliding door. The bag tears and liquid oozes out. She grabs newspaper from the outdoor table and crawls around the deck, spreading the pages about. She does not care that Matthew is standing there, watching her.

On the hot boards of the deck she crouches, upends the sweating black plastic and the thick, foetid smell springs up at her as the chicken bones and rotten fruit and oyster shells and nameless bits of sludge slide out. She lifts the bag away and a last wad of prawn shells falls wetly on her bare foot. The pink shells, and now her foot, are covered with tiny crawling ants.

She kneels then, in the rubbish, not bothering to flick off the ants, picking through the sodden remnants of the garbage with her fingers, knowing she will not find the glint of metal there in the coffee grounds and onion skins and Band-Aids, among the screwed-up tissues and the black plastic trays dripping with red meat juice.

She thinks of her father's warm, rough hands over her own seven-year-old ones, holding the whirring kite spool. She thinks of all his disappointments.

She does not look up when she hears Matthew cry out triumphantly from the living room. He appears in the doorway, holding up the keys on their huge blue and yellow plastic glob. 'Would you believe it, under the bloody magazines! I'll just have a piss and then we can go.'

And smiling his smile, he tosses her the keys where she kneels.
She catches them in her two hands, cupped against her chest.
She feels the sharp edges hit her breastbone.

CLOUD BUSTING

TARA JUNE WINCH

We go cloud busting, Billy and me, down at the beach, belly up
to the big sky. We make rainbows that pour out from the tops
of our heads, squinting our eyes into the gathering. Fairy-flossed
pincushion clouds explode. We hold each other's hand; squeeze
really hard to build up the biggest brightest rainbow and bang!
Shoot it up to the sky, bursting cloud suds that scatter escaping
into the air alive.

We toss our bodies off the eelgrass-covered dunes and down
to the shore where seaweed beads trace the waterline. Little bronze
teardrops – we bust them too. Bubble-wrapped pennies.

We collect pipis, squirming our heels into the shallow water,
digging deeper under the sandy foam. Reaching down for our
prize, we find lantern shells, cockles, and sometimes periwin-
kles, bleached white. We snatch them up filling our pockets. We
find shark egg capsules like dried out leather corkscrews and
cuttlebones and sand snail skeletons, and branches, petrified to
stone. We find coral clumps, sponge tentacles and sea mats, and
bluebottles – we bust with a stick. We find weed ringlet dolls'

wigs and strings of brown pearls; I wear them as bracelets. We get drunk on the salt air and laughter. We dance, wiggling our bottoms from the dunes' heights. We crash into the surf, we swim, we dive, and we tumble. We empty our lungs and weight ourselves cross-legged to the seabed; there we have tea parties underwater. Quickly, before we swim up for mouthfuls of air.

We're not scared of the ocean, that doesn't come until later. When we're kids we have no fear, it gets sucked out in the rips. We swim with the current, like breeding turtles and hidden stingrays as we slither out onto the sand.

We climb the dunes again, covered in sticky sand and sea gifts. We ride home and string up dry sea urchins at our window. We break open our pipis and our mum places each half under the grill or fries them in the saucepan, with onion and tomatoes. We empty our pockets and line the seashells along the windowsill. My mum starts on about the saucepans; she wants to tell us stories even though we know most of them off by heart, over and over, every detail. The saucepans she says, the best bloody saucepans.

Billy and me sit at the window while she fries and begins her story. I'm still busting clouds through the kitchen pane, as they pass over the roof guttering and explode quietly in my rainbow.

It was Goulburn, 1967, Mum would begin. Where's that? We'd say. Somewhere far away, a Goulburn that doesn't exist anymore, she'd answer, and carry on with her story.

*

Anyway, Goulburn, '67. All my brothers and sisters had been put into missions by then, except Fred who went to live with my mother's sister. And me, I was with my mother, probably cos my skin's real dark, see, but that's another story, you don't need to know that. So old Mum and me, we're sent to Goulburn from the river, to live in these little flats, tiny things. Flatettes or something. Mum was working for a real nice family, at the house cooking and cleaning; they were so nice to old Mum.

I would go to work with her, used to sit outside and play and wait for her to finish. And when we came home Mum would throw her feet up on the balcony rail, roll off her stockings and smoke her cigarettes in the sun. Maybe talk with the other women, most of them were messed about, climbing those walls, trying to forget. It wasn't a good time for the women, losing their children.

Anyway, all us women folk were sitting up there this hot afternoon and down on the path arrived this white man, all suited up. Mum called down to him, I don't know why, she didn't know him. I remember she said, 'Hey there mister, what you got there?' A box was tucked under his arm. He looked up at all of us and smiled. He come dashing up the stairwell and onto our balcony. I think he would've been the only white person to ever step up there. He was smooth.

'Good afternoon to you ladies. In this box, I am carrying the best saucepans in the land.'

Mum sucked on her cigarette and stubbed it out in the tin. 'Give us a look then.'

The suit opened up the box and arranged the saucepans on the balcony, the stainless steel shining and twinkling in the sun. They were magical. All the women whooped and wooed at the saucepans. They really were perfect. Five different sizes and a Dutch oven, for cakes. Strong black grooved handles on the sides and the lids, the real deal.

'How much?' Mum said, getting straight to the point.

The suit started up then on his big speech about the saucepans: Rena ware, 18/10, only the best, and this and that, lifetime guarantee, all that sort of stuff. The women started laughing. They knew what the punchline was going to be, nothing that they could afford, ever. Their laughter cascaded over the balcony's rails as they followed each other back into the shade of their rooms. 'Steady there Alice, you got a little one to feed there too!' they said, seeing Mum still entranced as they went inside.

Mum sat there, watching his mouth move and the sun bouncing off the pans. He told her the price, something ridiculous, and Mum didn't even flinch. She lit up another fag, puffed away. I think he was surprised, maybe relieved that she didn't throw him out, and he rounded off his speech. Mum just sat there as he packed up the saucepans, getting himself together to leave. 'You not gunna let me buy 'em then?' Mum said, blowing smoke above our heads.

'Would you like to, Miss?'

'Of course I bloody do, wouldna sat here waiting for you to finish if I didn't!'

He laughed. Mum told him then that she couldn't afford it, but she wanted them. So they made a deal. Samuel, the travelling salesman, would come by once a month, when money would come from the family, and he would take a payment each time.

Mum worked extra hours from then on, sometimes taking home the ironing, hoping to get a little more from the lady of the house. And she did, just enough. And Samuel would come round and chat with Mum and the ladies and bring sweets for me. He and Mum would be chatting and drinking tea until it got dark outside. They became friends after all that time. Three years and seven months it took her. When Samuel came round on his last visit, with a box under his arm, just like the first time, Mum smiled big. He came into the flat and placed the box on the kitchen bench. 'Open it,' he said to Mum, and smiled down at me and winked.

Mum pressed down the sides of her uniform then folded open the flaps and lifted out each saucepan, weighing them in her hands and squinting over at Samuel, puzzled. With each lid she pulled off tears gathered and fell. 'What is it, what is it?' I was saying, as I pulled a chair up against the bench. Under one lid was a big leg of meat, under another potatoes and carrots, a shiny chopping knife, then a bunch of eggs, then bread. And in the Dutch oven, a wonky-looking steamed pudding. Mum was crying too much to laugh at the cake.

'I haven't got a hand for baking yet. Hope you don't mind I tested it out?' Mum just shook her head, she couldn't say a word and I think Samuel understood. He put on his smart hat, tilting it at Mum, and said, 'Good day to you, Alice, good day, young lady.'

And when Mum passed, she gave the pots to me.

*

When my mother finished her stories she'd be crying too, tiny streams down her cheekbones. I knew she would hock everything we ever owned, except the only things we did – five size-ranged saucepans, with Dutch oven. Still in their hard metal case, only a few handles chipped. I run my fingertips over fingerprints now, over years, generations. They haven't changed much, they still linger patiently. They still smell of friendship. I suppose that to my grandmother, Samuel was much like a cloud buster. Letting in some hope from the sun. Their rainbow had been their friendship. And I suppose that to my mum, Samuel was someone who she wanted to stay around, like a blue sky. To Samuel, my mum and grandmother, I don't know, maybe the exchange was even, and maybe when those clouds burst open, he got to feel the rain. A cleaning rain and maybe, that was enough.

WHITE SPIRIT

CATE KENNEDY

The woman artist, Mandy, tells me on the Tuesday they need another day to finish the clothing in the foreground of the mural. She's leaning against the table telling me this, rolling a cigarette. She's got a look I would call high-maintenance – hair with lots of startling colour, stiff with gel and arranged to slope here and there, multiple earrings up her ear, lace-up combat boots. It's a look designed to suggest she's impoverished yet bohemian and individualistic, and nobody round here wears anything like what she's got on. She and her boyfriend, the other artist, drive in each morning from another part of town, a suburb where you can get a double latte early in the morning sitting on an upturned milk-crate outside a café.

The residents of this estate took a few surreptitious looks at this pair when they first arrived, and have chosen to stay out of their way since. We'll have to invite some in specially, over the next couple of days, for the photo documentation we need. Some casual shots of the artists chatting and interacting with residents, facilitating important interchange. Community ownership. An appreciation of process. It's all there in the grant evaluation forms.

Mandy flips open some of the books she's brought and taps an illustration. It's of a couple of women in Turkey, standing at some festival in regional costumes, the embroidery on their blouses and hats and vests achingly bright.

'That's what we're after,' she says, dragging on her rollie. 'We're focusing on getting that design right. All the details and colours. See the women there?'

She gestures to the mural, where her partner's painting in the figures of three women. They're prominent, next to the four laughing Eritrean children, who are holding a basketball.

'Should that be a soccer ball?' I say, half to myself.

'Sorry?'

'Should those kids be holding a soccer ball instead? They've actually formed a whole team; they play on the oval on a Sunday afternoon. I think soccer's more their thing.'

I might be wrong. That might be the Somalis. But a furrow of concern appears on her brow.

'Do they? That wasn't in our brief. But we'll change it, don't worry. We'll just blank out the orange and make it black and white.'

'I don't want to put you out, or start telling you how to do your job.'

'Not at all,' she says, grinning. 'That's what we're here for. Cultural appropriateness.' She exhales smoke and calls, 'Jake! The African kids – it's soccer, not basketball.'

He stops painting, stands up and stretches, and frowns at the mural.

'Do you reckon we'll have to change their singlets then?'

They both stand silently for a few moments, considering the image before them.

'No,' she says finally. 'Leave the singlets. Nobody'll notice that.'

*

They'd said in their interview, these two, that meeting the local community was their chief interest in applying for the job. They'd done similar things elsewhere – one at the Koori health centre, one at the credit co-operative, a portfolio of photos from a wall mural at a community market up in Queensland – and they said what kept them doing it was the rich sense of connection you achieved working alongside the very people you were depicting in your mural, and the growing sense of community ownership through collaboration. When they talked about the celebration of diversity, and how excited they were about all the different cultural groups represented on the estate, I'd felt the centre director, on the interview panel beside me, mentally checking boxes.

Now I look in, sometimes, on my way to teaching a class or driving the community bus somewhere and I don't want to hang around. They don't seem too excited now. There's nobody there but the two of them, with their big paint-splattered tarps and their ghetto blaster, music echoing round the empty basketball court as the mural gradually takes shape. Even the kids who usually come in here to shoot baskets after school are giving them a wide berth. It makes me uncomfortable, like I've let them down somehow, like it's our process here at the centre which hasn't worked. It's awkward, this silence; tainted with failure that nobody wants to claim. We skirt around it, the three of us.

'You'll be finished by Thursday, won't you?' I say. 'Because the opening's on Friday night and we can't change it, there's local councillors coming, and the minister.'

'Yep. It'll be done. We're used to working through the night, aren't we Jake?'

He nods and grins back – easygoing, unthreatening, pleasant. And yet nobody's come in here and expressed an interest in
picking up one of those brushes and helping. Nobody.

I'll have to round up some of the primary kids in my after-
school club tomorrow and get them in here. Take the photos
then. We can give out some brushes and they can do some
background, or something. Grass. Sky. Paint in those skin tones,
all those larger-than-lifesize arms draped around shoulders.
They'll like that. At least, I hope they will. I hope they won't
bounce off the walls with hyperactivity; throwing paint, scrawl-
ing their names, going crazy.

*

I unlock the office to get my bag out and scrabble in it for money
to buy material for the women's fabric-painting class. I'm meant
to use cash from the kitty but it's such a business, writing out a
request form and waiting round for the admin officer to open
the cashbox to sign it off. Easier to just pay myself for the plain
cotton pillowcases and white T-shirts they like to paint. I park
outside Spotlight and race in, arriving back at the car just in
time to see a parking inspector writing me a ticket.

'Oh, come on, it's only two minutes past.'

'It's a clearway after 4 p.m., just like the sign says.'

'Look, I'm buying stuff for a class. For a group of refugee
women.' I hate trotting that out, and in any case technically it's
a bit of a white lie now, but this is my money we're talking about,
my free time, my goodwill.

He sighs and looks at me.

'See?' I say, showing him the discount pillowslips, the tiny
children's T-shirts. 'Please.'

'Get going then,' he says shortly, deleting something on his
machine and walking off. Angry with himself for giving in to

me. He'd be a boy off the estate, himself. I bet thirty years ago he came with his parents from Lebanon and grew up on those stairwells and in that glass-strewn park. I bet he could still tell me the number of his flat, if I asked him. The number, the smell, the noise outside, the silent resolution of his parents to get out.

'Thanks!' I call out, but he's already at the next car up the road, already disappearing in a gritty shimmer of peak-hour monoxide.

*

'What do you think of the mural?' I say to the women later as they bend over their paintings. 'The big picture, in the gym?'

They smile shyly. 'Good.'

'Do you think you'd like to go in and help them, just do a little bit of painting in there?'

I catch their quick, hidden glances of consternation.

'No, no.' They're all smiling hard. 'Is very nice, but no.'

'You don't want to paint, though?'

'With the girl with the . . . um, this?' Nahir gestures fleetingly to her tongue, where Mandy has a stud, and all the women giggle uncomfortably.

I smile back, and shrug. I thought they'd like it, a mural that showed their community's diversity. We can all reel the figures off, the workers here, with a sort of proprietary pride: fourteen distinct cultural groups! Nine different languages! We shake our heads in bemusement at the multicultural, multilingual, multi-tasking jobs we've landed in, where every newsletter and flier has to be in five different translations, where if we're not running to put up the nets for Vietnamese boys' volleyball we're busy setting up the cooking class for the East Timorese mothers' group.

Maybe there wasn't enough consultation, after all. It's hard, finding something everyone's happy with. Or maybe the artists' hair and big boots, their thumping music, has scared them off.

'You'll come on Friday, though? To the opening?' I cringe at the eager insistence in my voice. They smile, confer among themselves in low voices, and nod obligingly at me.

'Yes. We all come.'

'Because, you know, you can wear national costume, if you like. Your traditional dresses? That would be wonderful. The minister would love to see that.' Their faces grow wary and apologetic with unsayable things. The room is stiff with a charged awkwardness, with languages I can't speak.

'No. But we come.' They go back to their painting, murmuring and sorting through the photocopied pages of designs. I should get a photo of this, I think absently; this pile of embroidery patterns they've all brought from Turkey, Afghanistan and Iraq, all shared around and used as stencils. If I mentioned it to the centre manager, he'd want a photo for our annual general report. Still, at least they're all coming along to the same class, and God knows that took me a while. Maybe one day I'll convince them to share tables.

Here in Australia, the women don't embroider the designs, though. They paint them straight onto fabric instead, finishing several pillowcases or table napkins in one afternoon. Out in the gym, the mural artists are carefully painting their figures in traditional embroidered dresses copied from a library book; in here, in the craft room, the real women are outfitted in pastel windcheaters, some of them decorated with flowery borders of quick-drying fabric paint. I heat up the iron and press their pillow-cases flat to make the dyes permanent and washable. Steam billows up in my face; the hot, comforting smell of clean, pressed cotton, the same the world over.

*

Wednesday afternoon, and Mandy and Jake are still not finished. There's a couple of faces still just sketched in at the front, likenesses they're working on from the health centre's photo album of snapshots from last year's barbecue. It's a rainbow of faces now, the mural, a melting pot. A few Anglo faces are placed judiciously next to Laotian and Eritrean, Vietnamese alongside El Salvadorian and Iraqi and Aboriginal, all standing 'We Are the World' style with arms round each other, grinning as if the photographer's somehow cracked a joke they all find mutually hilarious, something that in real life would involve several simultaneous translators and a fair whack of fairy dust.

The centre director is thrilled, the minister's going to love it, the artists have a jaunty spring in their step because the mural itself, it must be said, is stunning. It's a multicultural vision to be proud of. Community workers from other centres and other estates are invited to the Friday opening to marvel and envy, and apply for their own grants.

'You look a bit flat,' says Mandy, raising her eyes from the photo album to glance my way.

'No, I'm great. It looks wonderful, it really does.'

'We've left that bit there for the kids to work on this afternoon,' she says, pointing to a blank section of sky.

'OK, good.' I'll have to choose five or six kids, I think, bribe them with chocolate not to wreck it, just paint the blue like they're told.

'Someone here to see you in the office,' a workmate tells me, putting her head round the door. The music's off, briefly, and her voice echoes in the big, empty space.

It's a guy in a suit. He steps forward to shake my hand.

'You phoned me,' he says, 'about the anti-graffiti sealant?

I'm here from Pro-Guard, just to inspect the wall surface to make sure you purchase the right product.'

'Oh, yes. Well, we want to treat a mural to protect it against graffiti.'

He nods. 'That's a real asset-management issue now. Our products give years of repeat protection, whether you choose the impregnation-style pore blocking penetrative sealer or something with a sacrificial surface . . .'

He keeps going like this until my head is swimming with compounds, polycarbons, two-packs and one-pot formulations. I keep nodding as he inspects the wall in the gym and talks about polysiloxane coatings versus silicone rubber, and finally I say, 'Look, I need something we can apply ourselves which is quick-drying. And if someone graffitis it, I want to be able to clean it off without too much fuss.'

'They won't graffiti it,' interjects Mandy, who's listening. She's walking along past each big smiling face, painstakingly adding a dot of white in each eye, so that they jump to life with a realistic twinkle. 'Nobody will graffiti anything they feel a sense of owner-ship and inclusion about.'

'Right,' says the sealant salesman, eyeing her briefly before turning back to me. 'Like I said, we're in the business of helping you maintain the value of your asset and protecting it from senseless defacing. So for your requirements, I'd recommend Armour-All.'

'Great!' I respond with a smile. I'm tired now.

'It's a urethane product. You mix in the solvent and apply two coats twelve hours apart; using masks and gloves and adequate ventilation there's no reason why you can't apply it yourself. And it has terrific anti-stick. You can just remove any graffiti with white spirit.'

'Wonderful. We'll take it.'

He says he can deliver it that afternoon and names a figure. I nod, toting up the remainder of the grant money in the account. Just enough left over for snacks at the opening, catered for by the Vietnamese social group. Everyone likes spring rolls, as long as we don't make them with pork. We're having bread and dips too, so the Turkish cooking-class members don't get their noses out of joint. And maybe I should get the East Timorese to sing something . . .

'I'll go and get the after-school club kids,' I tell the artists. 'We've got to get this done by tonight so we can make sure the sealant's dry by Friday afternoon. The Armour-All.'

Jake and Mandy say they'll help me apply it. They're nice people, really. I don't understand why this whole process hasn't worked out like I thought, like I said it would on my grant project description.

*

It's got to cure properly, the sealant. So we end up applying the second coat at midnight on Thursday, the three of us slapping our fat brushes into the wall corners, wiping up drops with a turps-soaked rag, seeing it go on shiny and slick and impenetrable. I'm light-headed and starry from the fumes, so that the Nick Cave CD they're playing tonight beats in my skull like a racing, roaring pulse.

I've never been here on the estate this late at night. As I splash the sealant on I listen to cars revving and residents shouting, doors slamming, a quick blooping siren as the police pull someone over, the thumping woofers of passing car stereos. And through it all, I hear a babel of voices; every language group we're so proud of, calling and greeting, arguing and yelling, nearly 2000 people I couldn't name and who have no use for me. Who glance at me, leaving in my car every afternoon, and look

174

away again, busy with the demands of getting by.

I dip my brush and grimly slop on the Armour-All, over the big smiles and laughing eyes and joined hands, sealing them all in behind a clear surface which promises to dry diamond-hard.

*

'What a great event,' says the minister, and surveying the gymnasium I can see that, yes, this is just the minister's kind of thing – authentic ethnic food on the trestle tables, a welcoming song by the East Timorese choir, real grassroots community development in the shape of 130 or so attendees. In an estate of 1800, that's hardly a throng, but the minister's delighted. And behind it all, towering across the long wall, the mural.

'Such a positive message,' the minister is saying, 'and I understand the community itself had a hand in creating it. Marvellous.'

A group of adolescents goes up to inspect the mural, pointing something out. These guys wanted pool tables with the grant money, and who can blame them? The two artists step up to engage them in some kind of conversation, Mandy passing a self-conscious hand through her outlandish hair as the boys look to the floor, sullen and cowed, and I think there must still be residual acetylene fumes in the air, because I'm feeling a faint itching behind the eyes, a crawling tight constriction in my throat.

'You've certainly acquitted your grant,' the minister says, as I fiddle with my drink and watch the Vietnamese women serving the spring rolls, wondering if they see their faces in the mural, or something approximating them. Then I turn my eyes away from his charcoal lapel to catch the wondrous sight of my fabric painting class filing into the room self-consciously and stopping the show in a blaze of embroidered hijabs and fringed shawls and gathered layered skirts, seeing me there and smiling the faint encouraging smiles of the truly dutiful, the truly kind. Yes, it's a grant acquittal to be proud of, a culturally diverse photographic wet dream, and I'm blaming the Armour-All for the pricking sting now in the corners of my eyes, for the way everyone here, all of these estate residents, seem to have formed themselves, for once, into one homogenous whole; one discreet and circumspect crowd carefully distancing themselves, with subtle and infinite dignity, from the huge sprawling image which blares at them from the wall, bright and simplistic as a colouring book.

'Thank you,' I say to the minister. 'I wonder if you'll excuse me.'

*

I'm on my way over to the women when the centre manager grabs my arm, flushed and expansive. 'Great!' he says, handing me the camera. He's beckoning to the minister, grinning, glancing up at the mural to find a good place to stand in front of.

'I noticed those empty solvent tins out by the bins,' he says distractedly. 'Can you dispose of them somewhere else, where the kids from round here won't find them and sniff them? Ta.'

Another thought strikes him. 'And can you get some of the ladies in your Turkish group to come over here for a photo too? In front of the mural?'

Local colour, is what he wants. A multicultural coup. Boxes ticked. Oh, here's our vision all right, sealed and impervious and safeguarded. And no matter what gets scrawled there, whatever message or denial or contradiction, you can just wipe it away. With white spirit.

I weave through the crowd, away from him. Over to Nahir and Mawiya and Jameela.

'Here,' I say, handing the camera, against all office equipment policy, to a surprised Jameela. 'I have to go soon, so you take this.'

Her eyes widen uncertainly. 'To take . . . what?'

'Whatever you like. Just point and press.'

I turn to go, heavy-footed across the gymnasium floor. To collect those empty cans from the skip and then drive home, head out the window, car full of dizzying, flammable solvent vapours. To sling them into my own bin, in my own less desperate suburb.

I'm at the door before I hear Jameela calling my name. She's suddenly behind me, reaching to take my arm firmly, steering me determinedly back into the waiting group of the painting class, who have assembled themselves excitedly in a quiet corner. I stand there in the middle in my jeans and black top, a dowdy, sad sparrow among peacocks. Then as Jameela raises the camera carefully I feel two arms on either side of me, stretching tentatively round my waist, drawing me tighter, and in spite of everything, I smile.

LETTER TO A

ALICE PUNG

You ripped down the wallpaper one day when you were fourteen, ripped it right off the walls all four of them and then stuck up posters all over the room to hide the scabby paint. One day it will get painted over, you told yourself. One day the broken window will get fixed. One day the carpets will get changed. One day the ceiling will not fall down. One day the cracks will not be there, one day the smell will not be there, and when that day comes you will be out. Out of there. You will not be there to see it all. One day you will be out of there and one day you will live a freshly whitewashed life. Yes you will, and the ceiling will no longer peel and fall on top of you and these four walls will no longer close in on you, and you will have cauterised your wants.

There is a depression in the wall. These depressions come about when your knuckles itch and your upper deltoids ache to exert themselves and your mind is nothing but a blank black hole screaming to see red, that is when you strike and don't think of the consequences. This is when your inarticulate rage causes you to bunch up your fist and punch the wall so hard that the clock falls down on the other side, since there is no one to listen to your choked half-finished sentences about a cousin, a cousin who was once like a brother but is now nothing more than crap for all you care, a cousin so far gone that you don't think of the money he has borrowed from you or the money he owes you, the money to get out, you do not think about it at all because you do not want to think about him. To think about him is to stumble down the path of despair and once you are on that path, you have to keep running, keep running or else if you stop and pause to see what direction you are going, you will sink to your knees and realise how much you need water, water like the water bottles they carry down the streets of Richmond and you can always tell which ones are the ones on the habit because of these water bottles.

We were powerpoints, powerpoints with the three holes, two that slanted upwards and one that was a straight stroke down, straight and narrow and sad, like the prospect of some of us spending the rest of our lives doing PowerPoint presentations because our names are Andrew Chan and we wear glasses and sit in front of our PCs after school each evening because our parents want us to study hard and become successful, because this is a land of great opportunity and we must not waste it, it is a land of great fairness where even Ah Chan selling BanCao at the market in Saigon can raise a son who can decipher strange symbols in front of a screen merely by pressing many buttons in different combinations on a black pad, and it assures him to hear the clackity clack noise like an old abacus coming from his son's room, because then he knows that his son knows more than he does. Old Ah Chan doesn't have a clue about what the information superhighway is, all he knows is that there are no casualties, none at all, and that it can only go up from here. And so he buys his son the magic machine with the clopclop buttons and with a few clackity clacks and clicks he can transport himself to a nice office and a house in the suburbs and a shiny new blue Mazda.

Chink is an insult, but chink is also the sound that money makes as it rattles in your father's pockets, it is also the sound that those machines at the casino make when he hits the jackpot, so chink is not necessarily too bad a word. Chink is the only word that governs the life of your father, chink chink chink of the coins in the gaming machine, chink chink chink one at a time and not all at once, and so he sits there to wait for the sound of all-at-once chinks, meanwhile at home the boy and the mother and the kid brother sit together for a dinner of rice and vegetables and bits of beef before parting to play computer games or watch Chinese serials in separate rooms. You go off to your room and turn up the music, real loud music, and you look at the white wall which you had determined to paint a mural on, 'cause your art teacher says that you have real talent, but what the hell, what now? What is determination now, when the father won't come back and when the father won't stop spending the money and won't stop believing in the glorious sound of the chinkchinkchink of the machine.

A steady beat of chinks from the coins in his pocket, waiting for the rapid succession of chinkchinkchinks like the quickening of a heartbeat until the glorious rushing sound cannot be separated into its individual tinkles but all pours forth like a mad gold rush.

This is a different gold rush from the gold rush of the nineteenth century when we men had to carry heavy buckets and sift away to find the little pieces, and we needed strong stomachs to swallow the pieces and keen eyes to sift through the processes of our digestive tracts to find that little hard lump.

Meanwhile, swallow that lump in your throat you big sook,

'cause big boys aren't sooks goddam it, and look at your comic books and pictures of *Dragonball Z* and pick up the phone to call the number of that little pale-faced girl with the dark eyes and the black hair, even if she makes you write her letters instead of wanting to talk in person. Let the phone ring and ring and goddam is there anyone home? Keep your finger on the little soft grey 'off' button on the cordless phone in case her parents pick up and interrogate you worse than those Mao guards during the bloody cultural revolution that would not leave your family alone, that sent them to Vietnam, and then to this new land where little white-faced girls with black hair laugh at your stories of killing chickens in the Guangzhou countryside, and all your history becomes a funny after-dinner anecdote. Others would see your acts as barbaric, and squeeze their clean faces into squished looks of shudder-shake – 'eww, how gross' – even as they are seated opposite you eating a McChicken burger or severing the joints of the skinny bones of KFC chicken-wings with shiny fingers.

And so you lie on your bed in your room waiting for the father to come home, and you can hear the sound of your mother's footsteps padding to the kitchen to wash the dishes from dinner. You sit up and decide to write the girl a letter, a poem even, although you know all of this means nothing to you even though the girl means something to you, little ivory-faced girl in a tower. Grab a few sheets of Reflex paper, A4, nothing fancy. Goddam if the girl is expecting perfumed notepaper, well this was the best she was going to get and she had better be happy with it. Bloody hell how are you going to do this when you couldn't give a damn about this decomposed Keats your English teacher keeps mentioning?

Words are there to convey action, not an endless quagmire of feelings, and whatever you are feeling is transformed into action. And that is why for the life of you, you can't understand why the girl will not go out with you and all she wants to do is to write these bloody letters to you and wants you to write these bloody letters back to her. The surest way to get to know a person is to meet them, and take them out in your car with your recently attained Ps, God you are proud of these plates, and ask her questions but not too many, and do something fun like going to a movie or something.

But this girl, she's a strange girl. You wonder whether you should pursue her, whether this stupid poem will persuade her to actually go out with you. Grant you that date so you can be with someone for once and not have to say a word and just forget about things and have fun. But this girl, this girl looks like she can't have fun. Something about the look in her eyes, as if she is a little scared of what she sees in the world around her. Like she spends a lot of time thinking about why it is all so terrifying, and keeping quiet about her answers. You have no time for enigmas, you want to get out there and get some action, although not necessarily from this girl, because she is a good girl. You are sick to death of sitting still, of doing nothing.

You pick up the phone again and dial the number of the girl. 'Hello?' Ah, the familiar voice, you can imagine her now, sitting at her desk, which is where you imagine her to be, if you are not imagining her in other more pleasant places that suit your fancy but probably not her reality. You have called to chat to get your mind off things, but she does not want to chat, this girl. She wants to talk, goddam it why is it that the stereotype is true, why do women always want to talk about feelings and shit as if these feelings will change anything?

Dingdong. That's the bell. The father is home, the mother must be lying in bed, wide awake. You swear you can almost hear the bedsprings creak as she gets up. Creak creak. You can certainly hear the footsteps, the creak creak snap snap of the tendons of her feet and ankles as she shuffles to the door. You wonder whether the little brother is asleep, and whether he is going to wake up this evening. You wait to hear the inevitable question. 'Where have you been?' Even though your mother knows the answer she asks it anyway.

She can see the chinkchinkchink in his eyes, see the bags beneath. Dark bags beneath carrying phantasmagoric gold coins. He blinks once or twice, and the illusion is gone. He is tired. So tired. The bags hang down to his cheekbones, they become bags of bones, he *is* a bag of bones. 'How much did you use?' your mother demands. 'How much did you lose?' the terms are interchangeable, and it doesn't matter which one comes out.

'I'm hungry, woman, haven't had dinner yet,' the sad man in the old brown leather jacket with the elastic at the bottom grumbles.

'If you came home earlier, you wouldn't have to eat leftovers,' grumbles the mother, as she shuffles to the kitchen, but she brings out the beef from the stove, the beef she would not let you eat too much of because she was saving it for him.

FLICKING THE FLINT

ANNA KRIEN

Dad smokes on the toilet. When he's done, he parts his knees wide and drops the butt between his thighs, lets it whoosh past his balls. Listens to it sizzle. A laxative ciggie, he calls it. Most of his cigarettes are called something – there's the post-wank ciggie, the knock-off ciggie, a keep-warm ciggie, the I'm-done-with-dinner-now-clear-the-plates ciggie. Sometimes he just stands in the yard, flicking the flint of his lighter under his thumb, cigarette burning low in the other hand, ghosts coming out of his mouth. The *chip-chip-chip* of the flint like a bird call. That's a fuck-off-I'm-thinking ciggie.

I wasn't sure if it was one of those ciggies when I stepped out the door, schoolbag in my hand, and found him on the porch. I froze like I'd seen a snake. He had been in the search party looking for a guest and we hadn't seen him for a couple days. It was part of his job at the resort. Mum and I listened to the radio reports about it last night until Mum told me to go to bed. The collar of his orange fluoro work jacket was flipped up, covering the back of his neck, his beanie pulled low over his brow, laces of his work boots undone. Cigarette cupped in his hand.

'Hi?' I said, a puff of cold air coming out of my mouth. Dad turned, his jacket rustling, to stare at me. He was silent.

'Did you find him?' I asked. Dad sucked on his cigarette and turned away. I shifted my schoolbag onto my shoulder. Mum was hovering in the doorway now, peering out at Dad nervously. 'The stupid idiot decided to go for a stroll in the blizzard,' Dad said suddenly, starting to laugh. 'He was so drunk he didn't even notice.' He described how they'd spotted the jacket, it was hanging on a branch, then a jumper, then a pair of boots placed side by side, and a little way off, a pair of jeans with socks peering out of the legs. Finally, under a mound of snow, there was the guest – curled up like a baby in his undies and a singlet, blue mouth stinking of sweet bourbon. 'Frozen so hard you could knock on him like a door.' Dad stood up, flicking his butt into the garden. It hissed as it landed in a patch of icy grass. 'So was he dead?' I asked, not wanting to break the spell but not quite getting it. Dad turned to look at me again, his eyes narrowing. 'Of course, you dimwit, what do you think? Anyway, long story short, fuck off kid. Don't you have any friends?'

*

Dad knew I didn't have any friends. It was one of his favourite things to ask me. 'Where are your friends?' he'd needle, or 'Who'd you play with at school today?' On the weekends it was, 'You got someone whose house you can go to so me and your mum can have some time without you?' Once I tried to explain that there was no one to play with, that we lived on the side of a mountain in a row of three houses and that was it and the only people who came through were tourists, and I did have a friend once, remember, back in Preston when we lived in the city, but Dad snapped his head at that. 'You sound like your mother, boy.

I'd watch that if I were you. Soon you'll be playing with dolls and growing a pair of tits.'

*

One day, I lied. I said I'd made a friend at school. School was at the bottom of the mountain. A few portable classrooms, an oval and about fifty kids. I caught the bus there. I called my friend Chet. Dad's face lit up and he insisted on driving me to school the next day. I felt sick. I tried to lie awake all night, as if by some power I could hold back the morning with my eyes, but I couldn't keep them open and when I woke it was light. I stayed in bed when Mum came in, clung to the sheets with my hands and said I felt sick. But then I heard Dad yelling at her, that she was too soft, that there was nothing wrong with me, that I was a mummy's boy. I got up. I pulled on my clothes with a grim sense of being filled with cement.

We drove down the mountain in silence. I watched the sunlight jump across my seatbelt like an animation as Dad sped around the bends until he drew up behind a little maroon car, an old woman, her little white head hunched over the steering wheel, carefully navigating the turns. Dad beeped and revved, then dropped back and beeped, and revved close again, almost nudging her boot. 'I don't have time for this,' he muttered. 'For Christ's sake,' he spat, grinding his fist into the horn. The old lady twisted in her seat, trying to look behind at us. 'C'mon!' Dad yelled. When the mountain levelled, he overtook her on a straight, almost skinning the side of her car. I sank low in my seat to avoid the old lady's gaze at she squinted at us, trying to make out who we were.

At the school gates, I grabbed my bag before Dad cut the engine and opened the door.

'Thanks, Dad,' I said, jumping out. 'See you,' I added, hopefully. Dad pulled the clutch and put the handbrake on. 'Oh no,

Gerard, I'm coming in with you, remember? I want to meet this new friend of yours.' He gave me a big smile. It didn't reach his eyes. They stayed cold like a lake that gets no sun. 'That still okay with you?' he said, as if it was my idea.

I nodded.

He got out of the car and walked into the yard with me. He looked around slowly and then settled on a group of boys my age. 'Chet?' he called out in a singsong voice. 'Any of you Chet?' When they shook their heads, he walked over to them. 'Where's Chet? My son here says he's friends with Chet.' He smiled at them slyly, as if sharing a joke with them. They shrugged. 'Never heard of him,' said Billy, a boy covered in freckles. 'That's odd, son,' he said, turning back to me. 'Never heard of him. Maybe I'll go inside and ask one of the teachers.'

I looked at my sneakers. 'There is no Chet.'

'What, son?' Dad said in his chipper voice.

'There is no Chet,' I said, louder, still looking down.

The other kids had moved away, eyes on us. It felt like the whole schoolyard had stopped. Past Dad's legs I could see Miss Munro next to the bin, her hand poised above it. Balls stopped bouncing. Even the litter flipping on the ground in the breeze – empty chip packets, fruit juice poppers, the leaves – had stopped.

'Look at me when you're speaking to me.'

I couldn't get my eyes off the gravel. I had to haul them up, lift them like they were rocks, make them grab hold of Dad's shoes and drag them up past his laces, his jeans, belt, his neck, thick with its tendons tight, and finally, his face.

'You know why you've got no friends, Gerard?' I shook my head. 'Because you're a liar. And no one wants to be friends with a liar.' He looked over at Billy. 'Isn't that right?' Billy quickly dropped his eyes, his face turning red. He shrugged.

Dad looked back at me. 'So what are you telling me, Gerard?

I took time out of my day to drive you here and this is what I get? Do you think I've nothing else to do? Do you?' I shook my head, my schoolbag slipping off my shoulder and landing on the ground at my sneakers. Dad's face folded in on itself as if he smelt something rotten, his nose flaring. He spat out a sigh. 'We'll finish this at home.' He walked past me to the car, the back of his hand brushing against my shoulder, the shock of it making me stumble. Only when he started the car did it feel like the yard started to move again. Miss Munro dropped her litter in the bin. I heard the *thunk* of aluminium as it hit the bottom. A basketball ricocheted off the backboard. A fruit juice popper rolled onto its side. My knees were shaking.

*

We live in a weatherboard house halfway up the mountain. When Dad told us he had got a job here he said it was full-time, that he'd be getting paid more than Mum had been getting. 'There'll be lots of kids for Gerry to play with and you won't have to get the train to work every day,' he'd said to Mum. We were living in a red-brick flat and he bought a bottle of champagne, letting me uncork it on the balcony. I aimed it at the window of the guy Dad was having a fight with about putting the bins out. He liked that, ruffling my hair. My entire chest flushed with warmth at his touch. I nodded at everything he said. 'Yeah! It'll be fun, Mum,' I said. Mum brought out two glasses, looked at them and went inside and came out with two different ones. She looked at them again, as if trying to judge them through Dad's eyes, and turned around again to change them. 'Oh for Christ's sake, Jean, they're fine,' snapped Dad. She put them on the table, her hands trembling. She was biting her lip, trying not to cry.

Mum had a typing job in a solicitor's office where Aunty Bron worked. She got it at the start of the year. Dad didn't like it. He said it was making her snobby, that she was starting to put on airs like her sister. But that evening, Dad had nothing but good things to say about Aunty Bron. 'She can come and stay with us. I'll make sure she gets a guest room, free of charge,' he said generously. 'And Gerry can learn how to ski.' I nodded my head, up and down, at Mum. Dad put his arm around me and drew me into his lap. Mum looked at the street below us and sipped the champagne.

*

That was two ski seasons ago and I haven't put on a pair of skis yet. And for a full-time job Dad does a lot of standing in the yard, the flint of the lighter going *chip-chip-chip*. Aunty Bron hasn't visited either. I don't think her and Mum talk anymore. The last time I saw her was in our flat. She stood in the tiny kitchen, her tall reedy frame like a plant that had outgrown its surroundings, arms bent and trying to fit in awkward places, the gap between the counter and the cupboard. Mum sat at the Laminex table, hands tugging at a paper napkin, face bent over a mug. Aunty Bron wouldn't take off her coat or sit down.

'Jean, just fucking once, I want a phone call from you that doesn't involve a cup of chamomile fucking tea,' she said, pacing. Mum nodded, eyes filling with steam from the tea.

'What I'd kill for a phone call like that. Instead I get the same old broken record. You know the rest of us have problems too, only we try to *do* something about them.' Mum put her hands on the mug. The napkin was in shreds. 'I'm sorry,' she said in a small voice. 'I didn't know things were hard for you too. How is Stuart? The kids?'

*

So when we moved here and Dad was only working a few hours a week, not full-time like he said and we had to go back on benefits,

Mum didn't call Aunty Bron to complain. When Mum brought it up with Dad one night, he put his knife and fork down real slow.

'You calling me a liar, Jean?' he said, chewing each word before spitting it out. I edged my chair back from the table and thinned my eyes so everything started to blur.

'No! I jus—'

'You think I'm not working hard enough?'

Even with my eyes like this, I knew how my mum looked. Her eyes wide, fingers clasping the edge of the table, mouth stammering.

'No—'

'You don't believe me? You want to check up on what I say?' He stood up and grabbed the portable phone. He started pressing numbers. I could hear them beep a little longer than usual, the buttons slowly recovering from the force of his fingers. 'You want to ask them at the resort?' He thrust the phone at her. 'It's ringing. Ask them if your husband is a liar. Go on.'

I opened my eyes. Mum was shaking, her mouth open, hands splayed over her heart. Dad stood over her, the phone thrust in her face. A little tinny 'Hello?' was coming out of the receiver. 'Hello? Breakfast Mountain Resort. Hello?'

With the phone still in her face, Dad pressed the hang-up button with his thumb, then swung it back, making out as if he was going to hit her with the phone. Mum and I screamed, the phone stopping an inch from her face, and Dad looked at us as if we were the most pathetic, predictable animals he'd ever seen. He dropped the phone on Mum's lap, her skirt swallowing the dial tone, and walked out.

*

I've started doing this thing when stuff like that happens. When Dad starts circling us like a shark. I crimp my eyes thin so everything is blurry and imagine I'm on the school bus, coming down the mountain with school still a way to go, and Miss Munro is sitting behind me. Her blonde hair short and neat like a helmet, folded over her ears and those red dangly earrings. She saw me looking at them once as I twisted in my seat to speak to her, and she took one off to show me, and let me run my finger over its chalky surface.

'It's coral. From the sea,' she said. 'I suppose they dye it.' When she put it back on, her fingers fiddling and fixed around her lobe, she tilted her head and the morning light flickering through the trees touched her cheek, tiny white hairs glowing for a moment before the bus turned round a bend. 'You ever been to the beach, Gerry?' she asked.

I snorted. 'Course I've been to the beach,' I said, turning back to face the front so she couldn't see my face. 'Oh, you're lucky,' she said. 'I never saw the beach till I was an adult.' Amazed, I turned back around.

'Really? Why?'

She shrugged. 'Oh, you know. We lived in the country and my family wasn't one of those families that did things together.'

It was the first inkling I got that other families weren't what I thought they were – perfect and having barbeques and going on holidays together.

'Oh, we do everything together,' I said, quickly. Miss Munro nodded at me, her eyes – they were green, I realised, not blue as I first thought – betrayed nothing. I turned to face the front, feeling my cheeks go warm. Did she think I was a liar? It was true though, we never did things on our own. Dad always found a reason for all of us to go to the shops when Mum needed to go to the supermarket, and at my last school, when Quentin Riley asked if I wanted to go to his house, Dad insisted on meeting him and his mum first. My heart sank when I saw Quentin's mum waiting at the gate to meet us. She was tall with short grey hair and thick black glasses. Her lips were painted bright red and she wore men's suit pants. Dad said right in front of them there was no way I was going to some lesbian's place to play with her fat kid. So in a way, we did do everything together; we weren't allowed to do anything else and we didn't do much.

*

The school bus collected Miss Munro and then me. We were the only ones on the bus until Jackson and his sisters who lived about a quarter way off the bottom of the mountain got on. The bus driver's name was Kevin. He was a sleaze. He was always looking in the rear mirror at Miss Munro. I think she was relieved when I got on. When she first started teaching she sat up front, to be polite probably and chat to Kev, but later she sat towards the back of the bus. She gave me a big smile when I got on, patting the seat in front of her for me to sit there, placing me between her and Kev's mirror.

*

She liked travel brochures. 'I love going into travel agents,' she once said. 'It's like going into a newsagent but all the magazines are free.' Brochures on Egypt, New York, the Aztecs, the Great Barrier Reef, Switzerland, Rome, African safaris, she had them all. With a pair of scissors she carefully cut the photos out and pasted them into a scrapbook. Scrapbooking was big around here. In the city it was all about making slideshows and movies on the computer. At school, the popular kids were always holding auditions and filming at lunchtimes before commandeering class time for special screenings in which they'd give each other standing ovations. But here, it was scrapbooking. There was a shop in the main street that sold only scrapbooks, glue, pens in different colours, puff paints, stickers, patterned borders, sachets of glitter and sequins. One Saturday, while Mum was in the supermarket and Dad was watching her from the footpath, I looked in the shop through the window. It was full of women, bustling with their purses and bags. There were scrapbooks on display in the window – pages filled out with photographs of grandchildren and babies, tiny handprints and paintings by five-year-olds. Others were scrawled with family trees and histories, and old black and white postcards. One had a pair of booties sewn onto the front cover. None were like Miss Munro's.

If the glue was dry, Miss Munro let me flick through the scrapbook. The pictures bubbled where the glue hadn't been put on properly and some of the pages stuck together. She had a map of the world at the start with dots made with a purple marker showing where she wanted to go. There were pictures of lions, great big turtles floating in blue water, black people with the whitest teeth and houseboats on old brown rivers. She had a section for places to stay. Fancy hotel rooms with fridges and minibars, thatched huts on an island somewhere. Even then, the scrapbook had seemed to me a bit of a dream. No way was she ever going to be able to afford those classy hotels and big cat tours. But even though it felt a bit like play-acting, I liked our time on the bus. When there was a good photo on both sides of a page, she asked me to decide which was best. I liked the discussions that went into that decision. 'I like this zebra,' I'd say, turning it over, 'but this picture of the village could be handy when you're there.' Or, 'The beach looks better in this picture, but you don't have the hut in the background.' Or, simply, 'The rodeo or the burger and fries?'

Sometimes Miss Munro handed me the scissors and covered her eyes with her hands. She was the only adult I knew who had no rings on her fingers.

'You decide, Gerry, I just can't choose,' she'd say. I'd nod solemnly, silently making my decision. Then after cutting out the picture, Miss Munro would take her hands away and beam. 'Good choice, Gerry, good choice.'

It got to the point that I started dreaming too. Dreaming of going places, though not the places Miss Munro mostly marked out on her map, places where the people looked strange and the food looked like it was still alive. I wanted to go to America with Miss Munro. I lay awake thinking about the big plates of chips we'd order, and burgers with thick buns and heaped with pickles and tomato sauce and melted cheese. The cowboys – men who looked like my dad but they smiled easy – would take one look at me and decide that I had talent. They'd come over to us in the diner, their jeans held up by belts and wide metal buckles, walking as if they had invisible horses between their thighs, and we'd finish our burgers and then we'd go to a ranch. I'd have my own horse and the cowboys would ruffle my hair as we rode out together. Sometimes I dreamed so hard I could feel their fingers in my hair, catching on the odd knot, my head tingling.

Miss Munro started to save the brochures on America for me. 'It's not just cowboys,' she'd explain. 'There's cities with famous buildings and celebrities. Mountains too, like we have here – but bigger.' I nodded, fingers holding the glossy pages tight, but my eyes kept shifting back to the middle of America where I knew the horses and the cattle and the cowboys were. I put the brochures in my bag carefully and took them out again at night, looking at the photos in bed as the TV blared cop shows from the front room. Sirens and guns and yelling got in the way of the *clop-clop-clop* of horseshoes, the spit of whips and 'whoa, whoa' of cowboys. Usually I kept an ear out for footsteps so I could hide the brochures and pretend to be asleep but one night Dad came in quietly. The TV was going and I was staring at a picture of a cowboy on a horse trying to corral a cow back into its herd. 'What's this?' he said, grabbing a corner and pulling it toward him. I looked up at him, mouth open. I didn't even hear him come in. He started to flick through the brochure and stopped at the page where the tours were listed with prices. I'd circled the three-week tour, which involved sleeping out with cowboys and riding alongside them.

'$4320,' he said slowly, 'plus taxes.' He looked at me. 'Who gave you this?'

'It's for school,' I said, stammering slightly.

'And you think you're going to go? Leave your mother and me while we work and pay for you to have a good time?'

I shook my head. I was going to pay for it. I was going to find a job.

'You reckon you could earn this kind of money, do you? You reckon someone would give you money? To do what? What can you do, Gerry?'

I shrugged.

'No, really, Gerry, I want to know. What do you think you can do?'

I looked out the bedroom door into the hallway. I heard the volume go down on the television. I could feel Mum sitting up straight on the couch, straining to hear what was happening.

'Answer me, Gerry. What. Can. You. Do?'

I smelled grass. Cow shit. I could see the red and white chequered shirt of a cowboy, his flanks sweaty with horse. I saw Miss Munro sitting beside a campfire.

'Nothing, Dad. Nothing.' The smell disappeared. The cowboy too.

'You got any more of these?' asked Dad, holding up the brochure. I nodded and reached under my bed. I pulled out the other brochures Miss Munro had given me and handed them to him. Again he flicked through them and again he stopped at the pages where I'd circled what I'd planned to do. He laughed and walked out of the room with them. I lay there staring at the black rectangle of the open doorway.

In the morning when I stepped outside, Dad was chopping wood. I watched as he swung the axe high over his head, his jacket riding up and showing his white back, and his legs bowed like a cowboy's. He stopped when he saw me and leaned the axe up against the porch. He bent over and pulled the brochures out from behind the chopping block. Then the bus pulled up. Not saying anything, he walked towards the bus, Kev opening the doors and looking out, confused. I followed slowly. Dad nodded at Kev and stepped onto the bus. He looked down the aisle at Miss Munro. She looked up at him. Dad held up the brochures.

'This what you're teaching my son?'

Miss Munro opened her mouth but Dad wouldn't let her speak.

'That life is just about holidays? That while the rest of us are breaking our backs working, he can gallivant around the world?'

'No, Mr Colpitt,' Miss Munro started. 'It's about understanding different cult—'

Dad cut her off. 'Don't give me that bullshit. It's about leeching off the rest of us who are busting our balls trying to make a living.' He looked at Kev. 'Right, Kev?'

Kev had his hands on the steering wheel. They were knotted white around the plastic. He stared at Dad and nodded. Miss Munro peered around Dad at me. I looked at the floor.

'Don't give my son any more of this bullshit!' Dad flung the brochures at the floor near Miss Munro's seat. 'Teach him something fucking useful.' He turned around and I was in his way. I panicked, my schoolbag getting jammed against the seats. Eventually I tugged it free and moved to the side.

When Dad was off the bus, Kev cleared his throat and looked back at Miss Munro but she avoided his eyes. He closed the door and let out a low whistle, trying to catch my eye in the mirror. I looked away. The brochures lay on the floor until we got near Jackson's house. Then Miss Munro leaned over and picked them up, and put them in her bag.

The scrapbooking stopped after that. Well, my helping out did. I could hear Miss Munro cutting out the pictures with her scissors and gluing them into her book, but she never asked me to help her choose a photo. From that day on I sat closer to the door and Kev went back to glancing at Miss Munro in his mirror.

*

The mornings got lighter and the snow beside the road melted away. Dad started working on our car in the driveway. People stopped needing chains for their tyres and he took ours off, hanging them on a hook on the side of the porch. He let me stand and watch while he worked under the bonnet so I'd learn something useful.

He showed me how to change the oil. As the days got hotter, Mum would bring us cold drinks. She'd sit with us as we drank them and she and Dad would smile. He would drain his glass and tip it at me. 'You better appreciate your mum, Gerry,' he'd say, 'Ain't another one as good as her.' Then, 'Got any biscuits, honey?' and Mum would run inside and return with a plate of biscuits. Sometimes the man next door would lean on the fence and try to chat. Under the bonnet Dad would roll his eyes at me and I'd grin. Once I even made as if I'd fallen asleep at the man's boringness and Dad laughed out loud. Then one Sunday it was so hot that sweat poured off Dad's face as he leaned over the engine trying to tighten a bolt that kept slipping out of the spanner's grip. The man next door leaned on the fence and peered over at us.

'Hot enough for ya, son?' he asked me.

I turned to answer him, then heard the spanner slip again and Dad swear. I looked back and Dad was out from under the bonnet, his face shining with oil.

'Would you stop leaning on the fucking fence, you fat fuck?' The man looked at Dad, startled. 'Well that's a bit—'

'It's not gunna hold you every goddamn day.' Dad bent down and scooped up a burnt-out spark plug from the ground. 'Fuck off,' he yelled and threw it at the fence. The man ducked and disappeared. I started to laugh but then Dad walked up to me, whacked me over the head and went inside.

*

It was Mum's small tight smile that warned me, her eyes shifting to the side like a horse's do when it gets skittish. I was in my pyjamas, standing in the corridor when she stepped out of the kitchen to look down the hall at me. I could hear Dad in the bathroom, his belt shifting on the floor as he sat on the toilet and smoked. I stood there for a moment. I needed to pee but when I heard him flush, cough and the mirror cabinet door slam shut, I quickly stepped back into my room and hid behind the door. I listened to his footsteps go past and into the kitchen. I dressed and went to the toilet, trying not to breathe in the stink of shit and smoke.

In the kitchen I kept my head down, only looking at him sideways. His eyes were black. It was as if he was growing in his chair, gathering and growing and getting darker by the second. Mum looked at the floor as well. She carefully placed his toast on a plate at the edge of the newspaper, but it was either going to be her or me. I poured the milk over my cereal, careful for none of it to splash over the side of the bowl. I balanced the spoon on the inside rim of the bowl where there was no chance of me accidentally knocking it out of the bowl and splattering cereal on the table. I made sure my schoolbag was out of the way so he couldn't trip over it. But then, as I was leaving I took an apple out of the fruit bowl for lunch. It was the last one. I don't think I'd ever seen Dad eat an apple.

'What about the rest of us?' Dad snarled, looking up from the paper, his top lip curling. 'Ever consider that someone else might want that apple?' I looked up, the waxy soft not-worth-it apple in my hand. Then I felt something snap, like the jaws of a trap, or the clasp of an elastic band. Dad had found what he was sniffing around for. And something else snapped into focus. I realised it didn't matter what I said, it didn't matter if I opened my hand and let the apple fall back into the bowl, none of it mattered. Dad had made his choice and set his sights on me. So I dropped the apple into my schoolbag, hefted it onto my shoulder and ran.

It all went fast and slow at the same time. I heard him leap up, tipping the chair onto the floor while Mum let out a low moan. I pushed open the door and jumped off the porch, over the steps. I could see the bus pull up at the kerb, its engine shuddering as Kev, not seeing me, wondered if he needed to shut it down and wait for me. I hollered to get his attention, and kept running.

Dad was behind me. I could feel his weight, the bulk of him, the jangle of his belt, his keys and lighter and coins, his shoes on the gravel, the rasp of his breath and the sound of something else, something heavy clunking along the ground. I looked behind me and his face reared up like a wolf, his features all jumbled, mouth torn, eyes twisted, nose flared. And in his hand, the axe. He'd grabbed it on his way. I felt everything catch, the air in my throat, my legs against my shorts. My stomach heaved. I somehow lost time, the rhythm of my running, two steps became one. The bus doors were open and I scrambled in,

falling on my hands and knocking my chin against the gear-
stick.

'Go!' I yelled at Kev, who was staring past me at Dad. 'Go, go,
go!'

Dad was halfway down the drive. 'Don't you fucking drive
away, Kev!' he yelled. 'He's my fucking son, don't you dare fucking drive—'

'Just go!' I screamed. I stood up and started pummelling
Kev's shoulder. 'Go, go, go!'

Miss Munro was standing up. Her face was white, lips pink like
the underbelly of a shell. She stared at Dad through the window.

'Go, Kevin,' she said, quietly, and then louder when he didn't
respond. 'Go, for Christ's sake, Kevin! He's got a fucking *axe*!'

With that, the accordion doors squeezed shut and we lurched
forward. Dad was running beside us now and he swung the axe
into the side of the bus. The sound of it made me want to vomit.
A strip of metal tore and was flapping furiously as Kev put his
foot down on the accelerator. Miss Munro and I looked through
the back window at Dad who stopped, threw the axe onto the
road and then picked it up and threw it into a tree where it stuck.

'You're dead, Gerard!' he yelled at us. 'You too, Kevin! And
you too, *you fucking bitch!*'

*

I began to shiver. I was still standing, holding onto the back of
Kev's seat. My arms shook. I wanted a cigarette. I'd never wanted
a cigarette before but now I wanted one. I closed my eyes and
imagined one in my hand. Felt its heat lick my fingers. Miss
Munro came up behind me and put her hand on my shoulder. I
jumped and she turned me around, sat me down.

Kev wanted to call the police. It was a one-cop town so that
meant he wanted to call Gary. The thought of Gary hauling

Dad down to the station made me wish I'd not run and simply laid my neck down on the wooden block for Dad. Miss Munro looked at me and then back at Kev. 'Can you hold off calling him?' she said.

Kev jerked his head angrily. 'How am I gonna explain the side of my bus?'

When we were sure there was enough distance between us and Dad, Kev pulled over on the road and got out to inspect the gash. Dad had managed to swing the blade right through the panelling and had torn a strip of it away.

Miss Munro shrugged. 'Look, the last thing Gerry needs right now is Gary.'

Kev spat out his window, shifting the gears down as we took a corner. 'Yeah, and the last thing I need is a bloody gash in the side of my bus. What the hell have you got against Gary?'

I curled my hands into fists and leaned forward, letting out a moan. Dad had a run-in with Gary not long after we'd arrived when Gary had pulled us over. He'd made us sit in our car beside the road waiting for ten minutes or so, not getting out of his patrol car, lights flashing until Dad got jack of it. He got out and stretched, relaxed and easy like a cat. Then he lit a cigarette and strolled up to the police car, leaning in Gary's window as if he were the cop. 'You got a problem, mate?' I heard him say. Gary was furious. Mum and me watched as the cop pushed his door open and sprang out, yelling so much we could see the spray of spit from where we sat. Dad loved every second of it. 'Best thousand bucks I've ever spent,' he said later that evening, Gary's traffic fines proudly stuck on the fridge.

Oh God, not Gary. My knees jerked up and down they were trembling so hard. Miss Munro put her hands on them and forced them still. She looked at me, bending so her eyes were level with mine and I could see Kev watching us in his mirror.

'Gary's a shit, Kevin. He'll make things worse for Gerry.'

Kev sneered. 'And you? What are you going to do for the boy? Getting cosy?' Miss Munro reddened and pulled her hands away from my knees. When Jackson and his sisters got on, we rode the rest of the way in silence.

At recess I was sitting on the bench next to the drinking taps when Miss Munro came and got me. 'Gerard, can you come with me?' She tried to smile at me but I could tell something was wrong. When I followed her back into our classroom, I froze in the doorway. Gary and Kev were sitting in there, Kev talking fast and his hands flailing. 'My bus, it's bloody ruined, the bloody psycho—'

Miss Munro coughed. 'That's enough now, Kev, Gerard's here.' Both men looked at us, Gary's eyes running the length of Miss Munro, then me, then back to Kev. 'Keep going, Kev,' he said, ignoring us. I felt Miss Munro stiffen as Kev picked up where he left off.

'So bloody Colpitt, he fucking put his axe through the side of my bus. Tore the panelling off. Going to cost me a thousand at least.'

Gary raised his eyebrow. 'An *axe*?' A smile ghosted around the corner of his mouth. He turned to me, his blue leather police jacket squeaking as he twisted in the desk he was sitting at. 'An *axe*?' he asked again. I shrugged. I had liked it on the bus when Miss Munro emphasised *axe*. Kev had kept saying, 'Man, what did you do, kid?' But Miss Munro would correct him each time, 'It was an *axe*, Kev, no kid does anything to justify an *axe*.' But the way Gary was saying *'axe'* made me nervous. He was excited. He was practically jumping-out-of-his-seat happy.

'We were just mucking around,' I said quickly. 'It was just a joke.'

Kev snorted. 'A joke? A fucking joke?' His voice was high and whiny. Miss Munro put her hand on my shoulder. 'Gerry, you don't have to—' I flexed my arm, made it hard and tense and shrugged her off. Gary thinned his eyes, slats of grey in his small face, acne scars like rat bites clustering around his mouth.

'Well, your dad's a pretty funny guy, isn't he?'

I nodded. 'Sure is. Made you laugh a couple times, hasn't he?'

It went quiet when I said that. No one said a word and scraps of the schoolyard came in through the window. A group of girls were singing the lyrics to a song I'd heard a hundred times on the radio, then started screaming at one of them for getting the words wrong, a boy kept yelling, 'Here, here, here,' and the sound of a footy being kicked, the boy still yelling, 'Here! I'm here! Pass it to me!' And then Mr Thacker, the school maintenance man, and his dog wandered into view. A bunch of kids ran a wide berth around him and the dog, a brindle with clumps of its winter coat still hanging off its ribs. It was mean to everyone but Mr Thacker and he kicked it and it still loved him.

'Gerard?' It was Miss Munro. It felt like she was calling to me from a very long way off. 'Gerard?' she said again. The classroom sucked back into focus. Gary was standing now, his fists clenched at his side. Kev was staring at me. 'Gerard,' said Miss Munro, her eyes pleading, 'tell Sergeant Henning why your father was chasing you with an *axe*.' And I started to laugh. I thought it didn't matter why, I thought that because it was an *axe*, nothing else mattered.

'You rude little prick,' said Gary and suddenly his face was right there, his mouth with its teeth all overlapping as if crowding for a better view. I breathed it in, the taste of his uselessness, and laughed harder.

'Stop grinning, you little shit,' he spat. I bent over, holding my ribs it hurt so much, and when it didn't stop hurting, I turned and ran out of the room. It was dark and cool and hushed in the corridor, jackets hanging off hooks, bags piled into unlocked lockers, an open packet of orange Twisties strewn and stamped into the carpet. In the classroom I could hear Miss Munro and the men start to talk, their voices muffled; I couldn't make out what they were saying. I touched my face. It was wet. I walked over to my schoolbag and took out the apple.

*

In the yard I stood near Mr Thacker as he dug out the dirt from around a fence post, swearing each time his spade got stuck in the clay. The dog sat a metre or so away, eyes on his master. I stepped a little closer to it and it lowered its bottom lip, baring its yellow teeth. I rolled the apple in my hands before shining it on my shorts. I took a bite and spat it out. The apple was bad. It was brown and floury. I took another bite to check and spat it out again. I looked down at the apple in my hand and held it out to the dog. It looked at me, then warily over at Mr Thacker who was engrossed in the fence. Getting up on its legs, the dog stepped towards me and the apple quivered in the flat of my palm.

THE INTIMACY OF THE TABLE

DELIA FALCONER

But here I am in Sydney
At the age of sixty-one
With the clock at a quarter to bedtime
And my homework still not done.
— KENNETH SLESSOR

I was twenty when I met the great poet. It seemed to me then that I would always live in a narrow flat in a street between two steeples, that there would always be a bright arm of the harbour glimpsed sidelong through the eye's corner as I read in trams or trains. All that year I wore a shabby cream suit with a crimson handkerchief folded at the breast and a hipflask in one pocket. This day I had a nervous quiver at the corner of my mouth, my hair was brilliantined and combed. Is it possible that I also clutched a sheaf of my own poems, in a buckram folio, marked with the date and place of their composition, in the hope that he might notice them? I admit I did.

It was late on a summer afternoon when I climbed the steps to the Journalists' Club at the back of Central Station. The bar was dark; the sun squeezed in transverse cracks of heat through the edges of the blinds. The air was close and thick, as if it had been strained through dirty corduroy.

I saw him immediately at a table in the furthest corner, the thin neck and browless eyes I recognised from photographs, that broad and wizened head, the blue bow tie. There was a claret and a paper and a jug of water on the table. He wore a double-breasted suit, fastidiously buttoned. He made notes as he read the paper with a crabbed hand in a tiny notebook. From where I stood, ten feet away, I could hear the sharp, swift indentations of the pencil. I leant at the bar and sipped my schooner for now that I was here I had no idea how I should approach him. Although the temperature was less fierce than it had been outside in the street I seemed to sweat more. I had walked the full distance from my lodgings.

I wonder now exactly what I expected from him. I still imagined then that each writer knew himself as part of a club, that one great writer would always recognise another. I had come across his famous poem for the first time in my school reader where it had been placed, miraculously, among the work of well-known, foreign poets; I could still recite it. I knew that he had rarely published another poem since.

At last he put away his heavy spectacles and came up to the bar where he placed a pound note folded neatly into quarters on the counter.

'Which do you think is quickest transport up to the University, the train or bus?' he asked the barman. 'I believe I'm to deliver a paper there at the English Department in an hour.'

'No you're not,' I said.

He turned; his glare was quick and blank, the appalled expression of the recognised and put-upon which to my shame I feel sometimes flash across my own face if some reader taps me on the shoulder while I am standing at a festival with my literary friends, or if I meet a student in the street. His mouth was the same grim line which I saw on the faces of my father's friends, and I also recognised something of their brittleness, which, with some fear, I considered a symptom of the office life, as if the atmosphere of heavy ashtrays and high-backed leather chairs had permanently pressed itself upon them.

'It's next week. You can take my word for it.' I fished the crumpled flyer from my folio with shaking hands. I could not stop. 'It's true. I study there. Believe me, if there was a change of date I'd know about it.'

He nodded as he read, then shook my hand and thanked me. His palm was hard and surprisingly boney, for he was not a small man. He smiled faintly as he appraised me. He had the formal kindness I was later to associate with men who spent long periods of time alone, the outback reserve of country gentlemen or mining engineers. 'I've been dying to read your next collection,' I said.

'Not dying, I hope.' His eyes had lost a little of their flint. 'I'm sure there are better things to die for.'

We moved to the table he had just abandoned. 'Do you drink claret?' I nodded although I did not. 'Good,' he said, as he waved the bartender over. 'Rituals are the great comfort of growing older. It is important to remember that eating and drinking are also a kind of life. Some toast, or sandwiches? I knew a man once, a barrister, whose great pleasure in life was to go to the Lawyer's Club in Bridge Street – do you know it? – they served up English boarding school food, quite dreadful preparations: tapioca, sago, trifle with the hint of the stale and confiscated cake about it. The rest of us would amuse ourselves by making up new names for the dishes: Matron's Surprise, willow sausage, flannel soup. They were sold at tuckshop prices, the menu was scribbled on a blackboard mounted on the oak walls, between the portraits. My friend was a rather wealthy man, but I have never seen him happier than when he suggested we make an excursion there for their threepenny tart with custard.'

I could only nod, faced with the scrupulous mechanics of his conversation. The club began to fill. Occasionally, one of the men, with the lines of his hat still imprinted around his forehead, would greet him loudly, looming at our table. He responded quietly and introduced me to them as his 'friend'. Yet I could sense his eyes move across the backs lined up at the bar and felt that I would be soon dismissed. And I had not shown him my poems about flying foxes and Moreton Bay figs, or spoken with him about the cramped parks with their palms and memorial arches near my flat, or heard him speak about his great poems of the Harbour, or asked him why he did not write.

He asked me where young people 'went' these days. I said I did not know; that I was fairly solitary 'by choice' because I was 'too busy writing'; that I did go to the 'usual' bars around the university and the Greek cafeterias in Castlereagh Street; and that I went sometimes with my friend Robert who was a student politician to the branch meetings to which he was so frequently invited. He had no particular political calling, but had calculated that by this means we could save ourselves the price and preparation of around three meals a week. He had chosen the Liberal–Country Party because the women tended to be richer and the catering of a higher standard. The disadvantage was that we had often to travel up and down the North Shore train line to Lindfield or Wahroongah. We travelled to Willoughby only if the necessity was very great, for this required a bus, and the hostess at this particular branch lived in a house filled with uncleared mouse traps. She served without fail guacamole on a lettuce leaf balanced precariously on a piece of toast.

He had a charming way of laughing. He chuckled gently with his hands placed across his belly, bending back slightly, as if he took pleasure in gauging its vibrations.

I seized my chance. I told him where I lived, next to the Deaf Hospital in a pink federation villa which had been divided into bed-sits. I told him about the bathroom with its view of the railway tracks and the long ferny garden, the toilet pressed at an ungainly angle in the corner, the cantankerous water heater which I lit before each shower. I had been talked into minding a friend's axolotl which hung suspended in its green tank on the washstand and regarded my ablutions with the single lugubrious eye which remained in its possession.

'Is there a trombonist?' he asked. 'And an old lady with two sycophantic Pomeranians and an addiction to Epsom salts?'

There were no musicians, I said, but there was a thin American cartoonist who went out each Saturday evening and who, if he returned alone, played Mario Lanza on the gramophone and sang until the early morning. And once, I said, disturbed by his music which drifted unimpeded into my always-open windows, I had looked out of the bathroom at the grounds behind the Deaf Hospital and observed in the moonlight a game of naked rugby played in perfect silence.

The claret bottle was empty. The conversations around us seemed to have settled into more long-distance rhythms. 'Let's go to Holderigger's,' he said, and stood and wiped his eyes.

Outside the evening was diffuse and golden. The station steps had emptied and a molten calm crept down the hill from the back of Foys to Belmore Park. Above us the golfer on top of Sharpie's Golf House began, endlessly, to guide his bouncing neon chip shot along its illuminated path towards the nineteenth hole.

He was not as robust, I noticed with some surprise, as he had appeared inside the club. Once he paused at the window of a shoe store and dabbed with his handkerchief at a thick vein in his forehead. He walked slowly, and did not talk much. He hummed instead from time to time.

At last, off a lane at the far end of the city, we entered a chilly portico of sandstone and passed through a set of double doors into a restaurant. Leather club chairs gave way, beyond the bar, to two long alleyways of tables. I could smell the starch of the tablecloths, the sweet and desiccated scent of breadsticks. The mirrors were deep and edged with brass, the walls panelled with some dark unshining wood which still held the thrill of polish. The maitre d', an older man with thin red hair, greeted him by name.

'And how is Madame Holderigger?' he asked the waiter.

'She's very well, sir. Her grandson graduated this afternoon, an engineer, so she won't be coming in this evening.'

'That's splendid news. Please convey my congratulations.'

He sat, without glancing backward, in the heavy armchair as the waiter, in one smooth action, pushed it in and draped the napkin across his lap. My own descent was not so graceful. I hesitated when the waiter gestured; I perched on the chair's edge, then readjusted it myself. He asked if we would like a pre-dinner drink. Knowing of no other types I requested a gin and tonic. The poet ordered another for himself.

'I have known Madame Holderigger', he said, when the waiter left us, 'for almost forty years. She is a Swiss, originally. She must be nearly ninety. You will no doubt have seen her at some event or other. She wears her hair scraped up into a tiny lac-quered topknot like a cocktail onion. Many years ago she used to run some private clubs – when I was a young journalist she still had a reputation for sly-grogging.' He smiled faintly; the word pleased him. 'In the thirties she would go about looking for husbands with her daughter, an over-ripe spinster who tor-tured light opera. Gilda had the same broad décolletage and indelicate complexion as her mother – I used to think, when I spotted them in Martin Place, of two packet boats in full sail, rigged with lead crystal. Lindsay detested them, they always made him shudder. He used to say, each time they passed, "There goes the butcher's wife and daughter."'

Although I smiled I had begun to panic. I had imagined, when he first suggested it, that Holderigger's was another bar. I realised now that I had not enough money for this sober restaurant. I began to say that I should be on my way once we had shared our drinks, that I was not particularly hungry.

If I had another appointment, he said, he understood, although he had hoped that I might permit him to shout me dinner.

'May I show you something?' He reached into the inside pocket of his jacket, opened a leather bill-fold on the table, and produced an uncashed cheque for five pounds. It was a royalty, he said, for his last collection, published twenty years before, which had been recently reprinted. It was not much, he told me, for a lifetime's work, but it was the kind of thing I must get used to if I was to make poetry my life. One should regard writing as a pleasant hobby, he said, and never a career. In this way, any reward or word of praise would come as a surprise, rather than one's due. The trick, he said, was to enjoy each windfall when it came. It was his great pleasure, when those cheques turned up, to buy dinner for his friends.

Our meal arrived which he had 'taken the liberty' to order. I had never tasted oysters on the half-shell. Later I would also see for the first time a salad tossed at the table and a fillet steak girdled tightly by a piece of bacon. We drank a bottle of red wine. I did not say much. I remember that he spoke – as he forked and cut methodically with his dry white hands – of the managing board of the *Bulletin* and its effect on various journalists unknown to me, which I could only, dumbly, nod at; of other restaurants where I had not yet been; of his cadet days covering pet shows and sewing fairs and go-kart races where young boys with cunning faces lashed fox terriers and pugs like Mawson's huskies. He spoke fondly, too, of the architecture of the Harbour, although he did not mention his own great poems set there: of Beare's Stairs – he liked the rhyme – with their graveyard pillars made of sandstone above the stovepot roofs of Darlinghurst; of Miller's Point and its sailors' homes before it was levelled by the hefty stanchions of the Harbour Bridge.

As the food came he pointed out the rituals of the service, the way the waiters wheeled out another, smaller table and placed it by our own, the way they plated out the vegetables from a serving platter. In this way the labour of the kitchen remained invisible but the hospitality of the cook was performed before us, recreating what he referred to as the 'intimacy of the table'. He also made me observe the function of the furnishings and linen. The salmon-coloured tablecloths and napkins created, along with the brass and wood, the atmosphere of a cruising liner. The pale green menus which the waiters carried worked like a contrasting thread which relieved and lifted up the orange, he said, wound by their constant movements through the room.

Towards the end of the meal he ordered another bottle of the claret. I had been drinking cautiously but I still felt flushed. My eyes were vague and heavy. He sat upright in his chair. His spine did not touch the plush back, a posture I have come to think of since as the mark of a truly dedicated drinker, movement conserved, the body held in a state of relaxed anticipation. He seemed, if anything, to have become more pale and grave.

I do recall that a younger waiter about my own age arrived and dug ineptly with his corkscrew at the lead above the cork. The poet flinched and snatched the bottle from his hands. He opened it himself with a single turn and twist and poured out two full glasses. He spoke, more slowly now, about the flash Kings Cross landlords he had met as a cub reporter, about the best brains and tripe that he had eaten in greasy spoon cafés around the Rocks, about scandals involving politicians whom, again, I did not know. He disappeared for some time to the toilet while I waited. The wine stand and serviettes were whisked away.

When he returned he asked me who I liked to 'read'. I began to make my list. I had been reading the minor poets, from Clough to David Jones, for the last few months, I said, but I remained rather fond of Larkin. I found his adept use of half-rhyme and para-rhyme quite daring. It made me want to write.

'Wrong verb, wrong verb,' the poet said.

I stopped. There was the hint of a smile on his thin lips. Yet I sensed, in the way he looked about for the waiter and winced when he saw no one, the chill edge of some distilled, exquisite anger.

Poetry should be the least interesting of topics to a young man my age, he said. What about the great Germanic verb in our English language? Did I find myself at present in a domestic situation?

I looked down, and blushed. It was painfully clear from the length of time I hesitated that I had thought of making something up. No, I said, at last. Of course, I added quickly, there had been 'encounters'. I hoped the term was vague enough.

He gestured for the bill.

It was a deep blue night outside. The air of the laneway was still and damp. Five girls and three young men passed us, laughing, on the street which led up to the Gardens. He hunched over a cigarette and watched them. I noticed that he swayed a little as he lit it. He did not look at me. I had no conversation. I thought I could smell the tank stream which ran for blocks beneath our feet.

In the end, he said at last, as if he spoke to no one, he recommended women highly.

Women, with their tight little jackets and impossible perfumes, he continued, had always infuriated him more than they had pleased him. But they were indispensable for poets.

He turned and looked at me intently. 'They understand faith, you see. They are the great interceders. Between you and your reputation.'

I was not sure if he expected me to laugh.

He straightened and seemed suddenly quite sober. He began to walk, stiffly, ahead of me, in the direction of the Cross. I should not take him seriously, he told me. Seriousness was the affliction of old men. Here was a limerick I might enjoy, he said:

> *There was once a girl, called Priscilla*
> *Whose pubes were of perfect chincilla*
> *—Each day she would knot*
> *The hairs of her twat*
> *And use them each night as a pill-ah.*

He smiled tightly. His was a rather pedestrian para-rhyme, he feared, compared with Larkin's.

I followed because he seemed to like my company, or at least he did not mind it. Now and again, he would point out some place he remembered or pause to share a joke. He showed me the boarding house where Virgil the hunchbacked artist had invited pretty girls and sketched them for *Smith's Weekly*. And I seem to remember, although I have been unable to recognise the street again, that he took me through a breach in a wall behind a block of flats where there was a mossy grotto, its steps and niches carved into the cliff. It was all that remained of one of the colony's first gardens and the optimism of that time, he said.

We passed a revival cinema, a drycleaners, a corner shop with tables of pawpaws on the pavement, and took a narrow street towards the naval base at Garden Island. I found myself in the vestibule of his building. He stood back at the bottom of the stairs to let me walk ahead. It was a white mansion, divided into quarters. The carpets were grey. I had glimpsed a small chandelier behind one window. There were dwarf maples in the garden.

Inside I exclaimed at the view. There was a full moon and the Harbour filled the window of the lounge room. I had not yet learned that it was unacceptable to urbane modesty to draw attention to its follies. Nor, by expressing my approval quite so openly, that I had instantly disqualified it. The water had the febrile glow of cine-film, I added. He appeared with two glasses from the kitchen. He said he was glad I liked it.

I stood and looked about me while he searched a drawer for coasters. The flat was dustless. I could see a music room with books of libretto piled up on the floor, his study beyond it which also faced towards the Harbour. I noticed gradually the smell of thinning carpet and dark suits.

He poured two whiskeys and added water with a silver teaspoon from a jug. No ice, he said, not ever. And one teaspoon only. The water released the flavour of the scotch. He had also brought out a platter of stilton and some water crackers. 'Some of life's small compensations.' He placed them on the coffee table in front of the sofa where I sat. He settled in his armchair. He did not remove his jacket. His eyes closed each time he sipped the scotch.

There was a line of condiment bowls on the sideboard. He saw me looking at them. He liked to make curries, he told me, which took three days to cook.

I had placed my folio on the floor and it sat between us.

I decided at last to ask if he would look at them. I took a breath to speak.

'When I was a cadet journalist, about your age,' he began quite suddenly, 'I was approached to write a small pamphlet on Australian vineyards. I seized the opportunity eagerly. I had three weeks vacation owing to me, and I thought that this would supplement my wages, which at the time were not inspiring. I also imagined, quite correctly as it turned out, that I would enjoy the company of vintners.

'I caught a train to Melbourne and discovered at once that I despised everything about the countryside around it – the low skies filled with imperturbable grey clouds, the mournful cattle, the tattered yellow paddocks – but the wines were pleasantly surprising. On my last day there I met a German who made ice wines. The wine he brought out for me to try was miraculous; clear and sharp, and infinitely sad, as if cursed with an awareness of its own chill depths.

'He brought up three more bottles from the cellar and we walked across the overgrown yard towards his house. I had come to expect a cautious wife, a prolific flock of children, but the house was empty and quite bare, with the exception of a piano and a clock. He had devoted the main room entirely to his experiments with wine. There was a variety of corks lined up along the piano lid and there were grafted grapevines, their roots bound up in handkerchiefs, between us on the table.

'Each winter, he told me, he waited for the perfect temperature to pick his grapes. For a fortnight he would set thermometers among the vines and sit a vigil. He sang songs to the mice to keep himself awake. The grapes had to be picked, with the ice still on them, at precisely minus four degrees. By the second bottle he had become quite sentimental, and with the third he began to stop every few minutes and look about the room. I remember that he said he thought he was probably the greatest aristocrat upon this earth. For he could not bear, even for a second, the thought of an uncomplicated pleasure.'

A distant foghorn sounded on the Harbour. He looked at me and smiled, and I thought I felt a fleeting warmth.

'I have thought of him quite often since.'

I went to speak again but he seemed to have withdrawn himself from the room and into his armchair by some elusive alteration of his posture. When I put my empty glass down he did not offer me another. I reached for my folio. He jumped up to see me out.

At the door he shook my hand and said he hoped that we would meet again although I knew he did not mean it. He brushed aside my thanks for dinner. He said he hoped I had not found it boring. I said sincerely I had not.

'A young man who wanted to be a poet once asked for my advice,' he said. 'I told him. Invest in fine stationery. Be open to all social occasions. Always be shaved by a barber.'

I expected him to smile but his face appeared remote and blank again.

He closed the door behind me.

Outside, the night still held a gentle warmth. Random laughter drifted from the high white cupolas and minarets of the Del Rio apartments next door. A smell of gardenias mingled with the weed and mussel of the sea wall. I flattered myself, as I stood for a moment between the dwarf maples, that he would be standing at the darkened window, watching.

Then I began to walk towards my narrow rooms.

Author's note: The headquote is the last stanza of Kenneth Slessor's last published poem, which begins 'I wish I were at Orange . . .', written for class 5A at Orange in April 1962. It appears in Geoffrey Dutton's *Kenneth Slessor: A Biography*, Melbourne, Penguin, 1991, p. 11.

SOMETHING SPECIAL, SOMETHING RARE

REBEKAH CLARKSON

It was not the first time Graham and Liam Barlow had sat in matching chairs on the wrong side of a school principal's desk. Graham folded his arms across his chest and cocked his chin towards his son.

'Was it by accident, or on purpose, Liam?'

Liam shook his hair from his forehead. He began to open his mouth as the telephone rang shrill on the desk. The principal picked it up and raised an index finger midair.

Graham tried again to remember the principal's name. Using someone's name was a persuasion tool. Graham had learned that in the government program he'd done years ago, the New Enterprise Incentive Scheme. His enterprise hadn't worked out; landscaping was hopeless with a crook back, but excellence is a state of mind put into action, they say, and that's why Graham had called his new business Winners. The name was just right: relevant, memorable, a good ring to it. Winners would specialise in supplying medals and trophies to sporting clubs. Graham had a pitch ready for the Hahndorf Football Club, once the president returned his calls. He'd put Troy Campbell into his Contacts so as to be ready and while the principal talked he dragged his thumb across the bluetooth in his jeans front pocket. He wished he'd left the earpiece switched on and attached. He was a businessman, with work to do and people to see. He wouldn't even be here if Jenny hadn't refused to leave TAFE for the afternoon. She'd missed enough lessons looking after her mum and dealing with all Sophie's dramas, she said, and Liam's school didn't need them both to go in. Plus, she said, it was embarrassing.

The principal was making professional cooing sounds into the phone and nodding slowly.

Graham pulled his fingers into fists, resting them on top of his thighs, like kids do in the front row of class photos. Supplying the medals and trophies for Hahndorf Football Club alone would set Winners off and running. He tightened his fists till his knuckles turned white. Then there'd be word of mouth. Then you'd get your tennis, basketball, netball, hockey, all the carnivals. Other towns through the hills and the Fleurieu Peninsula would jump on board. Everyone would know that Winners had the best products and service, that online wasn't easier or cheaper, though how to make it cheaper and profitable really would depend on the bulk orders coming in. That was his biggest hurdle. It wasn't as if he didn't have a business plan.

'That's as stupid as a birth plan,' Jenny said when he showed it to her. 'You haven't factored in bad luck. Or bad timing. Or bad genes.'

The principal hung up the phone and pursed his lips. When he spoke, it was quiet and deliberate, just like the doctor after Jenny had been in labour for twenty hours.

'Well, that was Mrs Callow from the emergency department.

Josh has concussion. And he's been given six stitches across his left eyebrow.'

The principal paused, but Graham knew what was coming next. The kid could have gone blind. It was always about someone nearly going blind.

'You know, Liam, if your light saber had been just a couple of centimetres lower, just a fraction lower . . .' The principal lowered his chin, leaned over the desk.

Liam looked up and turned to Graham.

'Accident?'

The principal stretched back in his chair and put his hands behind his head.

'How do you think you'd be feeling now, Liam, if Josh was blind in his left eye?'

Liam's mouth flinched to one side. 'Not good?'

'No, that's right. I don't imagine you'd be feeling very good, would you?'

Graham wasn't feeling very good. He visualised his shop locked up again, the hopeful, hand-printed 'Back in 5 Minutes' sign stuck on the door with Blu Tack. He was going to have to close for half a day again tomorrow, in order to drive Jenny down to her mum's in Modbury North. Jenny was refusing to drive on the freeway. You're not going to die from driving on the freeway, Graham had told her, over and over. It's not the freeway per se, she told him, it's the trucks. She said she had a panic attack whenever she saw one coming up in her rear-vision mirror. She said she froze and when they passed, her whole car shivered and the first time it happened she had tears in her eyes and her life flashed before her like people say it does when you have a near-death experience. She wouldn't drive on the freeway, she said, because a man couldn't raise a girl without a woman around. This was so illogical, so off the point, that Graham hardly knew what to say back. And it miffed him; it wasn't as if Jenny had an all-star relationship with their daughter. Apparently, his was worse.

'Liam, what do you think you could do, to make this right with Josh?'

Graham wondered if he needed to spell it out to the principal himself: the kids were just mucking about; it could have been Liam's eyebrow with six stitches; and it wasn't a light saber, it was just a stupid stick. There seemed to be a fine line when you were in this position and Graham never really knew – was he meant to be on Liam's side or the principal's side? He knew which side he felt he was on. He felt it like a ball of fire in his gut.

'Say sorry?'

Graham's hands flipped over so that his palms were now facing up. He shuffled forward to the edge of his chair.

'Okay. Well, that's a start,' the principal said slowly. 'How do you think you could show Josh that you are sorry, Liam?'

Graham fell back into the chair. He'd seen the school's pamphlet on redemptive justice; this was going to take a while. At the previous school, they just suspended the kid. Straightforward. Except for the three-strikes rule, which meant that Liam had been expelled and none of that or anything else had been straightforward at all. They'd ended up moving house, moving everything; a fresh start. He rolled his neck anticlockwise. This was not the way to run a new business – not being there. He turned his attention to what Liam might do in the shop for the rest of the week if he got suspended. There wasn't much he could do. Rearrange the trophies? Paint more road signs to try and direct people to the old mechanics shop behind the disused servo on Hutchinson Street? He was under no illusions; Winners was in a rubbish location – you couldn't even see it from the road – but the rent was minimal. It was for now.

And then he thought: maybe Liam could man the shop while he drove Jenny down the freeway to her mum's? Kill two birds with one stone.

'Graham, what are your thoughts here? Liam's only been at our school for six months. Yet this is the third time he's been involved in an incident with another student where someone has been hurt by Liam's actions. What are your thoughts here, Graham?'

Graham felt himself heat up. He turned again to Liam. The way he sat slumped in the chair, with his legs splayed out in front made the roll of fat around his middle sit up like a sponge cake. The boy needed more exercise, or he'd be on the road to prediabetes like his mother. On the clean short carpet, his sneakers looked old and scuffed, the laces frayed and too long. He couldn't see his son's eyes through the hair flopped over his face. He'd thought he was the luckiest man alive to have a pigeon pair, a girl and a boy. He thought of Jenny again, probably home from TAFE by now. She was doing Certificate III in Aged Care and in less than eight months, she'd be qualified to get a job at Seven Oaks retirement village. They just needed to hold on until then, cash-flow wise. She was trying to lose weight too. Her biggest problem was using up all her points mid-morning with a Mars Bar or Snickers and then spending the rest of the day feeling cranky. None of this seemed an appropriate match to the principal's question. Had there even been a question? He shrugged.

'I understand that Liam was expelled from his previous school as a result of similar behaviours. Was there any kind of intervention done then, or since?'

Graham levered himself up to a straighter position. He cleared his throat; there was a cobweb in it, snagging over the word.

'Intervention?'

'Well, I'm not suggesting there's a specific problem, or what the problem might be, but I'm wondering if there's been any testing done? We've got some pretty aggressive behaviours here. Behaviours that, frankly, I'm not happy to have at my school. I think it would be good for Liam, for everyone, if we tried to get to the bottom of it.'

'Maybe Liam should spend some time at home, with me?' Graham offered. 'To cool off. Liam said it was an accident, and personally I believe him. He's a good kid.'

His eyes wandered again over his son. Sometimes looking at Liam was a bit like looking at himself, but a hidden, unknown part of himself, like an internal organ, his liver or his kidneys. It made Graham feel sentimental and protective and repulsed, all at once. He tried to focus his thoughts. Liam was a good kid. He just had a bit of growing up to do. Graham felt a sudden clarity and wash of affection.

'He always helps his mother around the house, puts out the rubbish, carries in shopping bags from the car. Rakes the leaves for his gran. He's not a bad kid. We have got his ears tested. No problems there. Excellent hearing, actually. He just gets a bit overexcited, is all. Loves his *Star Wars*. Wants to be Bear Grylls. You know what boys are like.'

Graham tried to laugh but couldn't get any traction beyond the first few syllables. It often went like this; he couldn't think of anything to say, but then suddenly he could. It was like finally seeing the face in one of those swirly optical illusion paintings, the way it all came together in his mind. It occurred to him to tell the principal that Liam's great-grandfather was a light horseman in the First World War.

When Liam looked up at him and smiled, Graham wasn't sure whether he wanted to cuff his son across the head or pull him into a hug.

*

The suspension wasn't allowed to be like a holiday, the principal told them. And Graham had to come back to the school in the morning to collect schoolwork from Mrs Murphy. He also had to be available to supervise Liam at least till the end of the week. Graham told the principal that, being self-employed, this wouldn't be a problem. He added that he had his own business. The principal just nodded, ushered them out, and said, 'Right, then. Good, then.'

They pulled open the door of the front office and felt the frigid late-afternoon air cut through their windcheaters.

'And Liam,' the principal called, 'I want you to really have a think about how Josh might be feeling; not just now, but tonight, and tomorrow, and for the rest of this week.'

Liam called back over his shoulder, 'Righto.' His voice sounded light and carefree, Graham thought – exactly as though he was about to go on a holiday.

*

'It's all the video games,' Jenny said later that night when they were lying awake, the wind knocking the broken awning against the side of their bedroom window. 'I saw it on *Today Tonight*, violent video games.'

'Nahsnot.' Graham rolled over to face her. He ran his hand across her hip and down her thigh. He picked up her hand and shifted her wedding band between his fingers. They'd hocked her diamond engagement ring eight months ago, right in between his job at the potato factory and a two-week stint at the abattoir. Remembering the boning room still made him twitch. He hadn't even got to the kill floor, but he'd seen it, and those two hours he'd spent locked in the coldroom had made their way into his dreams. He wondered if the engagement ring would fit Jenny again now, or not quite, even if he could get it back.

'Well, Soph doesn't play those games. She don't bash other kids up.'

Graham laughed quietly through his nose. 'Don't be ridiculous, love.' Sophie was small and stringy and kept to herself, like him. And she was a girl.

'You should shave off that moustache,' Jenny said. 'Makes you look shonky.' He smiled and rolled back onto his own pillow.

'Maybe we should do more things as a family,' she said. 'Maybe we should get a dog.'

Graham lay still, mulling over the bits of rope and lackey straps he'd kept from the shed at their previous place, something he could use to strap up the awning.

*

Liam sat at the front counter of Winners the next morning playing Solitaire on the old computer, his head resting sloppily in one hand. Graham had coached him for half an hour on answering the phone smartly but decided in the end it was best to switch the line through to his bluetooth. Putting in the landline didn't really make sense anyway; it just seemed more professional. But the boy's voice still hadn't broken and it didn't sound right, the way he squeaked, 'Good morning, Winners' – more like a question than a fact. It didn't really look right either, the boy in charge. Graham wondered when it would, how long it would take for him to fill out in the right places and lose the puppy fat and look like a man. Handing a thriving business over to your son must be an awesome feeling. Graham had thought about it a lot, had even wondered about calling the shop Barlow and Sons, Trophies SA. But he did have a daughter too. She hadn't shown any interest, but she wasn't interested in anything these days, and Graham wasn't sexist. She'd come round. He'd settled on Winners when he imagined Sophie and Liam telling their school friends, 'Our dad's the manager of Winners.' When Graham first came up with the business idea, he'd imagined himself becoming a sort of identity in sporting communities. He didn't know how it would happen exactly, but when he'd had this dream, he pictured the Graham Barlow Award. A trophy for something, maybe not even for a sporting achievement – maybe it would be for the display of a virtue, like never giving up.

'Who's number one?' he asked his son as he pulled open the heavy glass door to leave the shop.

'I am,' Liam smiled back.

As he looked back over his shoulder at the old petrol bowser, Graham saw that the set-up looked more like a garage sale than a proper business. He needed more stock, pure and simple. The opportunity to actually pick things up, handle them, feel their weight, was his point of difference with the major suppliers. He needed crystal trophies, fusion metal and acrylic, maybe some of those glass paperweights. Branching into corporate and giftware would make a lot of sense. It wasn't as if Graham lacked vision or ideas. What he lacked was capital, but his credit rating was rubbish. A loan for a Trotec laser engraver was what he needed most. At the moment, he'd have to send things away, not just for sand blasting but for any engraving at all. The truth was, Graham was just purchasing his stock from the online competitors.

*

Graham left the school and wound through the backstreets of town to Haydn Street where all the front lawns were overgrown and old couches grew mouldy on verandahs. As promised, Liam's teacher had left a stack of workbooks with a handwritten note.

In the pile was a thin soft book on Australian birds and, under that, a printed page from Wikipedia. Graham wondered if the teacher had assumed Liam didn't have internet at home. There'd been a couple of notes from both the kids' schools about that. If you didn't have internet access, the school would provide extra time at school. Things were tough, but he and Jenny weren't stupid. How would Sophie and Liam be able to do homework without proper internet?

He found Jenny waiting for him by their tin letterbox. She had a snarled expression on her face and a bag of oranges at her feet.

'Mum was expecting me an hour ago, Graham.'

She picked up the pile of books from the front passenger seat and climbed awkwardly into the car. She dropped the oranges to the floor, huffing and puffing, then settled the books onto her lap. She picked up the note and smoothed her hand across the small, thin book on top.

'Bird watching,' she said. 'I used to love bird watching.'

Graham snorted as he pulled out of the driveway and back onto the road. 'Since when have you been into bird watching?'

'I used to be into bird watching, Graham.'

They were quiet for a few minutes while Jenny read Mrs Murphy's note and flicked through Liam's books.

'I reckon she thinks we don't have internet.'

Graham indicated right and merged onto the freeway.

'I'm gonna give you driving lessons.'

'I don't need driving lessons. I know how to drive.'

'I can't take a day off to drive you down to your mum's every week, Jen. I've gotta be there, at the shop. And I gotta be net-working. No one knows me from a bloody bar of soap up here.'

'She needs me,' Jenny said. 'Imagine if I was all alone one day and our kids didn't come.'

A small part of Graham hoped they wouldn't. It didn't bother him that he and Jenny had never left Adelaide, there was nowhere particularly he wanted to go – Queensland, maybe – but he imagined his kids going places, doing things. For the past five years, since they were seven and nine, Graham had put their age in dollars into Bank SA student accounts. Every single fortnight. No matter how tough things were. He felt good whenever he thought about those accounts. He liked to see their names printed on the bank statements in that little window on the envelope. He wanted to believe that Winners might set them up.

*

Jenny's mum was sitting in her little cement porch on a fold-up chair.

'Well, I thought you were never coming,' she said as they got out of the car. She turned and hobbled back inside the unit and Graham saw that she was wearing the compression tights Jenny had bought her last week. She moved like Jenny: from the hips, awkwardly swaying sideways in order to propel forwards. She sat down on the floral lounge chair and sighed, rested her head on the backrest and stayed there while Jenny made cups of tea and worked through her washing.

Jenny passed Graham a load of her mother's clothes and said, 'Fold these. You're as useless as an ashtray on a motorbike, hon.'

*

On the way home, Jenny looked through Liam's homework again. Graham wondered how she managed to avoid getting carsick. She was competent, his wife, in so many ways and it bothered him that people wouldn't know it if they just saw her in the street. He thought of her TAFE studies and the high grades she was getting for the units.

'Look, he's supposed to fill this worksheet out,' she said and she held up one of the loose papers. 'Looks like the other kids are going bird watching, on an excursion. They're all going to the Laratinga wetlands. I never saw a form for that. Liam'll miss that.'

Graham glanced over the loose Wikipedia page Jenny was holding up. 'What's an Australasian bittern?'

'They say it's rare. Special. The icon bird of the Australian swamp. Might even be endangered.'

'And what, they reckon they've got them in the wetlands? I thought that place was just for dumping the town's shit.'

Jenny slapped the page across his arm. 'It's environmental, Graham. How's he supposed to get this worksheet done if he doesn't get to go on the excursion? They're just setting him up to fail, is what they're doing.'

'Well, he should bloody do it.' Graham remembered the principal's uninterested smile as he'd steered them out of his office, as though he'd given up on Liam already. He pushed his palm into the steering wheel. 'There's nothing to say he can't go to the wetlands, is there? It's a free bloody country. He can just do it, and then hand in that worksheet like everyone else. That's what he'll do.'

'Yep. He could walk there. Get some exercise. We could all go. We never do anything together anymore. Remember when we used to do things all together?'

Graham remembered the time he drove them to Willunga and they had fish and chips on the beach. How old was Sophie then? Six? Seven? With that wispy blonde hair. He used to call her his little princess, back then. That felt like a lifetime ago. He'd had no idea kids grew up so fast.

*

Graham rolled the Blu Tack around in his fingers and stuck the card back up on the front door of the shop. He switched the line to his bluetooth and clipped it over his ear. He still hadn't heard from Troy Campbell at the Hahndorf Football Club. As he locked the door, he decided he would call again himself that afternoon. Persistence was the key. Never giving up. He had to think like a winner.

Liam and Jenny waited for him in the car at the petrol bowsers. Jenny had claimed she didn't mind missing TAFE if it was for bird watching. When Graham had thrown his hands in the air, she'd made her eyes big and said, 'What?' They'd offered the morning off school to Sophie too, because bird watching was educational, but she said she didn't want to go anywhere that Liam was going. Then she'd walked off down the street with her schoolbag half-hanging off one shoulder, as if she might just drop it on the ground and leave it there.

*

Graham parked the car in the Homemaker Centre. Jenny had packed supplies: drink bottles and a collection of snacks.

'How long you planning on being here?' Graham asked.

'Well, you don't know. That's the thing about bird watching, Graham. You have to be patient.'

She and Liam were both puffing by the time they'd followed the asphalt walking trail to the first pond, flanked with native grasses that reached over their heads. There was no one much around on this Wednesday morning, just an older man on a bike who passed them and a couple of mums with prams. Jenny had packed the little digital camera they'd got for taking out a National Geographic subscription that no one ever read, but it wasn't charged so Graham put it in his jacket pocket and got out his phone for taking pictures. Liam had the worksheet in one hand

and a blue biro in the other and he dragged his feet as he walked, so that Graham saw how his sneakers had become so scuffed.

'There, mate. That's one of those ducks.' Jenny pointed an arm vigorously towards the pond. 'The blue-billed whatsaname duck. And look, there's a honeyeater. The New Holland honey-eater. Tick'em off, Liam. Here, give me that sheet.'

Liam handed the worksheet to Jenny as if it meant nothing to him, as if he didn't even know what it was. She took the biro from him too and rested the page on the book over her thigh to tick inside the boxes.

As they walked, Jenny read from the book and Mrs Murphy's printout. She told them how the effluent treatment worked, that Laratinga was a Peramangk word for the Mount Barker Creek. She said she had no idea there were so many different birds in the wetlands. That's the thing about bird watching, she said; until you actually watch, you don't see any birds. It's like you have to know that you're watching, you have to decide, in a way, otherwise you won't see anything. You won't hear them either, she said, unless you actually listen.

Graham listened and realised that she was right. It was amazing how many different birds you could hear when you listened. He had no idea what they all were. Trills, chirps, high-pitched squeaks, whistles, low throaty variations. A white cockatoo shrieked overhead. Graham thought again about how smart Jenny was, the way she had a knack for putting things.

They walked on, Jenny leading, then Liam, then Graham following behind. Every now and then, Jenny would stop still and turn this way and that and Liam would scuff his sneakers around at the gravelled edges. They passed the second body of water and then left the asphalt path for the unsealed trail. They wound further into the middle of the wetlands, a third pond and the boardwalk.

Liam spotted a group of blue fairy-wrens and Jenny held a hand on her heart as they watched the tiny birds flit about in the leaf litter. Jenny found the bit in the book about fairy-wrens and Graham took photos using his phone. They spotted more species of duck, a starling, lots of magpies, a group of corellas, a masked lapwing. Jenny ticked them all off. She continued reading as they walked. Sometimes, she'd stop and read something aloud. There are birds, she said, that breed in Japan and Siberia and then fly all the way here, to escape the northern winter.

Graham zipped up his jacket. He had no conception of a northern winter, hadn't ever seen snow. It was early spring and you could see signs of it, especially in the wetlands, but the air still had the bite of winter. There hadn't been a stretch of sunny days or blue skies yet. He'd never carried much body fat and the cold air nipped straight to his bones.

They didn't see any more birds for a while. Occasionally, they would think they had, but then they'd realise that one was already ticked off. Jenny said she wished they owned a pair of binoculars.

'These are all the common birds,' she said when they reached a bench and she looked over the worksheet. 'We still haven't really seen something special, something rare.'

Graham stood at the bench while Jenny and Liam sat at either end, pulling out the drinks and packs of flavoured crackers.

'Let's go back,' Liam said through a mouthful. 'This is boring.' He had flecks of orange seasoning around his lips. 'Just tick'em off, Mum. How would she know, anyway?' He kicked at the bolts holding the bench to the ground.

The kid had a point, thought Graham. It was tempting just to tick off all the boxes. But then he thought they should see it through, as a lesson in itself. When he'd closed up the shop yesterday, he'd seen that Liam had spent the whole morning looking at porn on the computer. If he wasn't at school, then he should bloody well be doing schoolwork. It was good to make him stay and do it, to finish the task.

Right at the bottom of the worksheet was a hand-drawn sketch of the Australasian bittern. Above it, Mrs Murphy had put three question marks and an exclamation mark. It had been sighted once or twice before by some serious bird watchers – it wasn't as if it was impossible to see one, but Jenny was right; it was rare. Graham turned from the bench and surveyed the vast expanse of inky water in front of them. He checked his watch. They'd been gone for almost an hour. He tried to imagine what it would be like if they saw a bittern, if he got a picture on his phone. He imagined how excited Jenny would be, ticking the box on the worksheet and, later, attaching a copy of the photo. He imagined Liam going back to school after his suspension with that. Mrs Murphy would send him to the principal's office, to show it off. No doubt they'd put Liam's worksheet up on the noticeboard at the front office and everyone would see it, all the parents and the other kids. Liam would get an A, for sure. Maybe sighting an Australasian bittern was so special that the principal would ring *The Courier*, and there'd be a story about it in the local rag.

The first drop of rain hit Graham's closed mouth. As he brought his hand up to wipe it away, another hit his wrist. He turned back to the bench and saw that Jenny was stuffing the drink bottles and empty wrappers back into Liam's schoolbag. She folded the worksheet in half and put that and the pen in there too. She passed Graham the bag and eased herself up, leaning on Liam's knee and wobbling as she stood. The raindrops became large and random and splattered generously. Liam stood up and covered his head with his hands. Another year and he'd be as tall as his mother. A breeze came up, shimmering through branches and leaves and turning them into wind chimes. A current swept across the large body of water.

Graham put both straps of the bag over his shoulders and led the way to the boardwalk.

'Shortcut to the main path,' he said and turned back to make sure his family were following.

The downpour came quickly and hard. The singular drops of rain turned suddenly into long vertical sheets of water. There was a crack of thunder over the valley.

Graham broke into a jog. He heard Jenny and Liam yell out and turned again to see them lumbering behind him, their mouths open, hair flat and dripping against their foreheads.

'Run!' he yelled, but even as the word left his mouth and was drowned in the wall of rain, he knew that neither of them could. Carrying so much extra weight and with that dodgy hip, Jenny was struggling to walk. All she could manage was a lopsided shuffle. Liam was slow too and his knees seemed to collapse into each other.

On every occasion that Graham had been called up to Liam's schools, he had privately wondered if his son was even capable of the injuries he'd allegedly inflicted. A twisted arm that had required an X-ray, a black eye, a chipped tooth, numerous blood noses. And now Josh someone, with concussion and six stitches across his left eyebrow. It didn't add up. He couldn't help wondering if they all just had it in for his boy, as if they wanted Liam in trouble, that they just didn't like him.

He stopped on the boardwalk and waited for them to catch up. The three of them stood still for a moment, soaked and helpless, unable to hear each other speak against the intensity of the rainstorm. Liam's face was pale, his teeth chattering, and Graham thought that Jenny might even be crying.

He realised then that he still had the bluetooth around his ear. As he pulled it off and shoved it into his pocket, he knew it was ruined. He might as well have had a shower fully clothed. He wiped his hands across his face to try and see more clearly. You couldn't bring cars into the wetlands; he would just have to guide them back to the Homemaker Centre at the pace they could manage. They moved slowly on, their arms wrapped around their own bodies, Graham in front, then Liam, then Jenny.

Finally, they reached the sealed path. The rain pulled back as quickly as it had started and then fell again in random, singular drops. It became strangely quiet, as if the heavens were recoiling from their own outburst. Everything around them softly ticked, like a resting engine when the ignition is cut. Graham slowed his step so the others could catch up again and he reached for Jenny's hand. With a gait so lopsided, it was hard to hold her hand while they walked and he rarely did. He reached over and put his other hand on Liam's shivering shoulder. His thumb nestled in the groove above Liam's collarbone, and with his other hand wrapped around Jenny's, he could feel the racing pulses of both his wife and his son. They are alive and real, he thought. His family is alive and real. They are flesh and bone, sinew and fat. And Graham understood then that being alive meant that one day they would die, like everything else, like all these living things here. He felt a tickle in his throat and behind his eyes, and a great burden of love for them in his chest. But Jenny was right. They should have made Sophie come too. Graham realised that he missed her. He really missed her. He'd been missing her for a couple of years. He squeezed Jenny's hand and firmed his grip on Liam's shoulder. He wished he could think of something to say, words to explain how he really felt about his family. He wanted to put this feeling into words.

What he did know was this: Liam's school could get stuffed. Troy Campbell could get stuffed. The whole world could go and get stuffed. Jenny was right. They needed to do more things as a family.

They continued walking the last stretch of the path, almost back to the Homemaker Centre. All Graham could hear now was the rasping breathlessness of his wife and son beside him, and the odd chirp of all those unknown birds as they ventured timidly back out into the open.

PUBLICATION DETAILS

REBEKAH CLARKSON's 'Something Special, Something Rare' appeared in *The Best Australian Stories 2014*.

TEGAN BENNETT DAYLIGHT's 'J'aime Rose' appeared in *The Best Australian Stories 2013* and *Review of Australian Fiction*, vol. 6, no. 1.

GILLIAN ESSEX's 'One of the Girls' appeared in *The Best Australian Stories 2010*.

DELIA FALCONER's 'The Intimacy of the Table' appeared in *Storykeepers* (Duffy & Snellgrove, 2001), *The Best Australian Stories 2002*, *The Lost Thoughts of Soldiers and Other Stories* (Picador, 2006) and *The Best Australian Stories: A Ten-Year Collection*.

KATE GRENVILLE's 'Bushfire' appeared in the *Bulletin*, vol. 118, no. 6255, and *The Best Australian Stories 2001*.

SONYA HARTNETT's 'Any Dog' appeared in *The Best Australian Stories 2003* and *The Best Australian Stories: A Ten-Year Collection*.

KAREN HITCHCOCK's 'Forging Friendship' appeared in *Overland*, no. 200, and *The Best Australian Stories 2011*.

CATE KENNEDY's 'White Spirit' appeared in the *Big Issue* and *The Best Australian Stories 2009*.

ANNA KRIEN's 'Flicking the Flint' appeared in *The Best Australian Stories 2014*.

ISABELLE LI's 'A Chinese Affair' appeared in *What You Do and Don't Want: UTS Writers' Anthology 2007* and *The Best Australian Stories 2007*.

JOAN LONDON's 'The New Dark Age' appeared in *The Best Australian Stories 2002*, *The New Dark Age* (Picador, 2004) and *The Best Australian Stories: A Ten-Year Collection*.

FIONA MCFARLANE's 'The Movie People' appeared in *The Best Australian Stories 2010*.

GILLIAN MEARS's 'La Moustiquaire' appeared in *The Best Australian Stories 2001* and *The Best Australian Stories: A Ten-Year Collection*. It became 'Le Moustiquaire' in her collection *A Map of the Gardens* (Picador, 2002).

FAVEL PARRETT's 'Lebanon' appeared in *Island*, no. 133, and *The Best Australian Stories 2013*.

ALICE PUNG's 'Letter to A' appeared in *The Best Australian Stories 2007*.

PENNI RUSSON's 'All That We Know of Dreaming' appeared in the *Big Issue* and *The Best Australian Stories 2009*.

MANDY SAYER's 'The Meaning of Life' appeared in *Heat 19: Trappers Way* (Giramondo, 2009), *The Best Australian Stories 2009* and *The Best Australian Stories: A Ten-Year Collection*.

BRENDA WALKER's 'That Vain Word No' appeared in *Meanjin*, vol. 66–7, no. 4–1, *New Australian Stories* (Scribe, 2009) and *The Best Australian Stories 2009*.

TARA JUNE WINCH's 'Cloud Busting' appeared in *The Best Australian Stories 2005* and *The Best Australian Stories: A Ten-Year Collection*.

CHARLOTTE WOOD's 'Honeymoon' appeared in *The Best Australian Stories 2005*.

CONTRIBUTORS

REBEKAH CLARKSON's short stories have been recognised in major awards, shortlists and independent publications in Australia and overseas. She was runner-up in the 2013 *ABR* Elizabeth Jolley Short Story Prize. She is currently completing a PhD at the University of Adelaide, where she also teaches.

TEGAN BENNETT DAYLIGHT is a fiction writer and critic. Her books include the novels *Bombara*, *What Falls Away* and *Safety*, and she is working on a collection of short stories. She lectures in creative writing in the Faculty of Arts and Social Sciences at the University of Technology, Sydney.

GILLIAN ESSEX has won several awards for her short stories. Her poetry has appeared in *21D* and the *Friendly Street Poets* anthology. Her non-fiction articles have featured in the *Age*, *Green Magazine*, the *Weekly Review* and on Radio National. She teaches creative writing and is also a singer-songwriter.

DELIA FALCONER is the author of two novels, *The Service of Clouds* and *The Lost Thoughts of Soldiers and Selected Stories* and the memoir *Sydney*. Her fiction and non-fiction have been widely anthologised, including in the *Macquarie PEN Anthology of Australian Literature*. She is a senior lecturer in creative writing at the University of Technology, Sydney.

KATE GRENVILLE is the author of many award-winning novels, including *The Secret River* (Christina Stead Prize), *The Idea of Perfection* (Orange Prize) and *Lilian's Story* (*Australian*/Vogel Literary Award). *The Secret River* was also shortlisted for the Miles Franklin Award and the Man Booker.

SONYA HARTNETT's award-winning novels include *Of a Boy* (Commonwealth Writers' Prize, *Age* Book of the Year), *Thursday's Child* (*Guardian* Children's Fiction Prize) and *Surrender* (Victorian Premier's Literary Award). In 2008 she became the first Australian recipient of the Astrid Lindgren Memorial Award.

KAREN HITCHCOCK is the author of the award-winning short-story collection *Little White Slips* and *Dear Life: On caring for the elderly* (Quarterly Essay 57) and a regular contributor to the *Monthly*. She is a staff physician in acute and general medicine at a large city public hospital, and has a PhD in English and creative writing.

CATE KENNEDY is the author of the short-story collections *Dark Roots* and *Like a House on Fire*, and the novel *The World Beneath*, as well as several poetry collections and a travel memoir. Her work has appeared in many publications and anthologies, including the *Harvard Review* and the *New Yorker*. She edited *The Best Australian Stories 2010* and *2011*, and *Australian Love Stories*.

ANNA KRIEN is the author of *Night Games: Sex, power and sport*, which won the William Hill Sports Book of the Year Award, *Into the Woods: The battle for Tasmania's forests* and *Us and Them: On the importance of animals* (Quarterly Essay 45). Anna's work has been published in the *Monthly*, the *Age*, the *Big Issue*, *The Best Australian Essays*, *Griffith REVIEW*, *Voiceworks*, *Going Down Swinging*, *Colors*, *Frankie* and *Dazed & Confused*.

ISABELLE LI's work has appeared in *Southerly*, *Sleepers Almanac*, *UTS Writers' Anthology*, *New Australian Stories*, *The Trouble with Flying* and *Cha*. Her script 'Mooncake and Crab' was made into a short film, which premiered at the Melbourne International Film Festival. Isabelle has translated a collection of poems, *Almost Everything I Know*, into Chinese. She is completing a Doctor of Creative Arts at the University of Western Sydney.

JOAN LONDON is the author of two prize-winning collections of stories, *Sister Ships* and *Letter to Constantine* (published together as *The New Dark Age*). Her first novel, *Gilgamesh*, was shortlisted for the Miles Franklin Award, won the *Age* Fiction Book of the Year, and was longlisted for the Orange Prize and the Dublin Impac Award. Her second, *The Good Parents*, won the Christina Stead Prize for Fiction. In 2014 she published *The Golden Age*.

FIONA McFARLANE has been published in *Zoetrope: All-Story*, *Southerly* and the *New Yorker*. *The Night Guest*, her debut novel, won the Voss Literary Prize and was shortlisted for the Miles Franklin Award in 2014.

GILLIAN MEARS's most recent novel, *Foal's Bread*, won the Prime Minister's Literary Award in 2012. Her fable *The Cat with the Coloured Tail* will be published by Walker Books in September 2015.

FAVEL PARRETT's first novel, *Past the Shallows*, was shortlisted for the Miles Franklin Award. She was awarded the Antarctic Arts Fellowship, allowing her to travel to Antarctica to complete research for her next novel, *When the Night Comes*.

ALICE PUNG is the author of *Unpolished Gem*, *Her Father's Daughter* and *Laurinda*, and the editor of the anthology *Growing Up Asian in Australia*. Alice's work has appeared in the *Monthly*, *Good Weekend*, the *Age* and *Meanjin*.

PENNI RUSSON writes, edits and teaches creative writing. She is the author of several novels for young adults, including the *Undine* trilogy and *Only Ever Always*, which won the Ethel Turner Prize, the Aurealis Award (Young Adult) and the WA Premier's Literary Award (Young Adult).

MANDY SAYER has published twelve books of non-fiction and fiction. Her awards include the *Australian*/Vogel Award (for *Mood Indigo*), the National Biography Award (*Dreamtime Alice*), the *Age* Non-fiction Book of the Year (*Velocity*) and the Davitt Award for Young Adult Fiction (*The Night has a Thousand Eyes*). 'The Meaning of Life' is excerpted from her forthcoming novel *Rules for Camping*.

BRENDA WALKER has written four novels, including *The Wing of the Night*, which was shortlisted for the Miles Franklin Award and won the Nita B. Kibble Award in 2006 and the Asher Award in 2007. She is Winthrop Professor in English and cultural studies at the University of Western Australia.

TARA JUNE WINCH is the author of award-winning novel *Swallow the Air*. Her short stories and essays have appeared in many publications, including *McSweeney's* and *Vogue*. Her body of work was awarded the Inernational Rolex Mentor and Protégé Award.

CHARLOTTE WOOD is the author of four acclaimed novels: *Animal People*, *The Children*, *The Submerged Cathedral* and *Pieces of a Girl*, and the non-fiction collection of writings on the meaning of cooking, *Love & Hunger*. Her fifth novel will be published in late 2015.